A PIRATE UNDER FALSE COLORS

In 1778 the pirate Charles Vane was the scourge and terror of the Bahamas. Governor-General Woodes Rogers of Nassau was in an especial dilemma. Charged with the capture of this audacious buccaneer, he thought it more likely that Vane would attack the island and capture him first.

But Rogers thought of a scheme for placing a man aboard Vane's black-flagged craft, and he sought his secret agent from a group of captured sea-wolves a-waiting the noose. The man he picked was the stalwart Philadelphian, George Rounsivel.

Rounsivel swore he was innocent, that he'd been a victim of his fellow criminals, not one of them. So Rogers gave him the choice—join Vane's band and learn what he was up to or join the gallows-bait and die by daybreak!

DONALD BARR CHIDSEY has made an enviable name for himself both as a writer of excellent historical novels, including such as *This Bright Sword, Captain Bashful,* and *Lord of the Isles,* and also as a writer of historical biographies, including those of Sir Walter Raleigh, Marlborough, and Bonnie Prince Charlie.

His own life has been as full of adventure as his writings. He has covered a good part of the earth in tramp steamers, pearl shell boats, and private yachts. He has lived in the South Seas, has been a newspaperman, actor, farmer, road gang foreman, mountaineer, boxer and fencer. During the war he served with the British, New Zealanders, Highlanders, the Free French, and the United States Army.

CAPTAIN CROSSBONES

by

DONALD BARR CHIDSEY

WILDSIDE PRESS

Captain Crossbones

Published by Wildside Press LLC
www.wildsidepress.com

THE LIGHT of a leprous moon swathed Fort Nassau, a pile that, while by no means old in this year 1718, had been so often and so savagely sacked by the Spaniards that it had about it the air of a ruin whose very ghosts have crept away. The ramparts were rubble, the gun platforms pocked with craters. Dismounted cannons were strewn like jackstraws across the bailey and along the base of the walls: spiked as they had been, their touchholes torn open, their muzzles plugged with lead, they were not worth their weight in junk, and nobody had even troubled to steal them.

Yet this fort was manned. A torch spluttered in its iron cresset. Sentries stood at the gate, from time to time apprehensively eyeing the town beyond, where many a rumshop still glowed, though it was near dawn. There were sentries, too, on the walls, which they paced with uncertainty, leaning forward like men wading waist-deep in water.

There was even a flag—the black flag of death.

The flag had not been raised above any part of the fort proper, but rather over a structure that stood at the base of the wall on the bay side. The last carpenter's hammer had sounded against this structure but a few hours ago, so that now it stood ready for its burden. It was strong. It could support all of the weight about to be suspended from it. A platform about four feet off the earth was supported by three large but empty hogsheads. Each of the hogsheads was encircled by at rope, and by means of a master-rope connecting them, these platform supports could be jerked away all at once. Other ropes dangled from a crossbeam, nine of them, and each one ended in a noose.

Silence hung heavy in that place. The sentries scarcely

grunted when they turned. No word of command came from the lighted chamber atop the guardhouse where the new governor, who had staked his career and quite possibly his life on this mass execution, could have been pictured counting the hours, even the minutes. Nor in the cell where the nine convicted men lay was there much conversation.

Moonlight seeped into this lugubrious place through a couple of gratings, and it was smeared hesitantly across the ceiling. The straw was clean, and so on the whole was the cell itself. The men were gyved, each by his right ankle, to a long and exceedingly strong steel chain. The ends of this chain were fastened to staples at the two ends of the cell. The prisoners could rise, stretch, and make their way in turns to and from the pail. They could hear the pacing of the guards, the challenges, even the slap of wavelets against the shore; but the gratings were high, and the men could see nothing that lay outside.

They were a motley crew.

The leader was John Augur, who had been serving under Jennings when the buccaneers first took over this island of New Providence. A middle-aged and flatulent man; he had hair that was greasy and gray. He stank. He belched. He scratched himself. Unspeakably the brute, he filled his last hours with expressions of outrage that he and his pals should have been tried at all, much less convicted.

"What kind of a cove *is* this? All the others always divvied with us. Does Rogers think he's better'n them?"

"Maybe we didn't offer enough?" suggested Will Cunningham, a small goat-faced man in his forties.

"We offered every dollar we had! Ain't *that* enough?"

These two were old and tough and fit to die. The others were young.

Two of the younger men were Irish.

Dennis Macarty didn't know the meaning of tears. Piracy had been just another lark for this light-hearted lad.

"I always said I'd die with my shoes off. D'ye suppose they'll let me kick them off when the time comes?"

"Shut up," said William Dowling.

Dowling was the other one from Ireland. Handsome in a dark way, he was morally a monster. He alone had put up no sort of defense. Far from showing remorse, he had boasted in court that the reason he'd left Ireland was that he murdered his own mother: he had beaten her to death, the brave boy.

Tom Morris, George Bendell, William Ling, all were under twenty. They said nothing, but their eyes were open and sometimes their lips moved as though in prayer. They were badly frightened.

"The only one I feel sorry for is Rounsivel here," said William Lewis, cocking his head and squinting at the contents of the bottle he held, to measure the amount left.

A giant, Lewis was amiable when drunk but at no other time. Once, in London, he had been a promising pugilist, but now his hand wobbled and his step was not steady.

"*He* never was on the account, yet they're going to stretch his neck the same as us."

"That's because he's a lawyer, and they hate lawyers," Augur put in. "He told 'em, didn't he? He said that Rogers' commission don't authorize him to make up no court of vice admiralty. We should've been sent home. Our trial was illegal."

"Which will help us," chuckled Macarty, "when they knock those planks out from under our feet."

"Shut up," said William Dowling.

"Illegal," said John Augur, "that's what it is."

The ninth man, the one to whom reference had been made, was in his lower twenties. Long, lean, hard, but not coarse, sartorially, perhaps because he'd had the furthest to fall, he showed the poorest of the lot. His salmon-colored drugget coat was smudged. The buckles were gone from his shoes—

stolen. He had succeeded in keeping his holland shirt and colebatteen ruffles tolerably clean, but he had no manner of cravat left. He'd been obliged to throw away his periwig, so infested with lice had it become. Now, like the others, he wore his own hair: but his, cropped, made his head shine baldishly in the eerie light of the moon. It was a long, slightly equine head, and the absence of hair made his face show even more saturnine than would normally have been the case.

George Rounsivel, not because he meant to be aloof but only out of weariness, spoke no word. He had done as well as he could for the others, shifting at each chain-change, waiving his turn at the pail, even from time to time trying to cheer them with a story. But now he uttered no sound, for he was sick of them and their kind. It was not the least bitter of his reflections that he, who a month ago wouldn't have known one of their sort, soon would hang with them in the last great ghastly companionship of death, unidentifiable from the others save perhaps by the quality of his shirt.

Arms around his legs, chin on knees, he sat and stared at nothing, brooding. Oddly—for in every other way no two men less like one another could have been conceived—he resembled John Augur in that it was not grief that consumed him in this his last hour, but indignation. Damn it, that trial *had* been irregular! All of George Rounsivel's professional training was outraged, all his sense of decency as well.

Time was what he had fought for. If these prisoners had been sent back to England for trial, as they should have been, George Rounsivel would have been able, if only by post, to establish his bona fides. He could have proven that he was a gentleman, a member of the Pennsylvania colonial bar, and that he had been dispatched to the Bahama Islands by financiers who had commissioned him to study the possibilities of cotton planting there He could not prove this now; the pirates had destroyed his papers. But in England he could have proven it. He might have spent some months in a noisome jail, and it was unlikely that he would ever have gotten his belongings back, but at least he would live.

In a way, George Rousivel could not blame the governor, who was obliged to take strong measures—or else knuckle under to these knaves. Bearing a royal proclamation of pardon for past offenses, he had come to a place where piracy was not so much an adventure as a way of life. Bahamans ate and drank piracy, and slept and dreamed and danced it. It was their *raison d'etre*. They had listened to royal proclamations in the past. They would renounce the wickenedness of stealing on the high seas—provided they were not called upon to give up their loot—and then, when the next opportunity came along, they would once again, in their own words, "go on the account." It was the accepted practice. If you weren't a working pirate it was only because you couldn't get a berth, or else because you were in cahoots with the active ones and as a buyer of stolen goods made more money ashore than you would have made at sea. Nothing else was imaginable, here.

And then . . . along had come this man Woodes Rogers.

Hundreds had given themselves up; but when it was suggested that they work—repair the fort, for instance, against expected attacks from the French or Spaniards—they had held up their hands in horror. They were pirates at heart, every one of them.

It was ironical too. If, as the authorities feared, the residents of the town of Nassau rose in arms and rushed the fort to free the prisoners, it would not be for him, George Rounsivel, the only honest one, but for the other eight.

Those others, to give them credit, had stoutly stood up in court and sworn that Rounsivel was no pirate by choice but had in fact been forced. Nevertheless this plea was thrown out. It was, after all, too common. Three out of four pirates, caught red-handed, protested that they'd been forced. Many refused to sign articles of brotherhood-and-association for that very reason—fear of putting themselves on record as members of a conspiracy. Instead they were satisfied with a lesser share of the loot. Others, when they joined a pirate crew, first pleaded with their companions to give them a paper testifying that they had been coerced. This was a regular practice. Indeed, it was precisely because they craved somebody who could frame a document with long legal words and phrases that these outlaws had seized the young attorney, George Rounsivel, from a vessel they'd sacked at sea. Illiterate, they had immense respect for the written word. If it was on paper, they thought, it couldn't be wrong.

And so George Rounsivel too had been convicted—by a court that had no jurisdiction in such a case.

To be hanged as a pirate would be bad enough. To be hanged as a pirate *illegally* was insufferable.

The ruffians to right and left of him had fallen silent. His thoughts were not with his Maker, as they should have been, but rather with the possibility of a final speech, a speech from the very gallows. He had never heard of such a speech being effective. They were for the most part given out of vanity, he supposed. But the instinct to live is very strong. George Rounsivel's law degree could not protect him here, nor yet his taut, trained athlete's body. Would he become like the others, or even lower, and scream and plead for mercy? Could he find the power to make a last-minute speech of the sort traditionally permitted of the felon who was about to be "turned off"? Would words come?

"I tell you I was forced! I was a prisoner, not a pirate, and I could prove it if they hadn't thrown my papers overboard!"

He could picture in his mind's eye the hangman stolidly waiting for him to finish, the officer of the day with drawn sword, the governor fingering a timepiece, and the nervous guards, who would watch the crowd.

*"Send to Philadelphia, if you don't believe me! Ask any-
one in Philadelphia who George Rounsivel is!"*

Would he rant on, repeating himself, hysterical, sobbing?
It was a thought to turn a man's stomach. But you never
knew. You never could know until you were there what you'd
do.

If on the other hand he did speak with some eloquence
and did stir the spectators—it was certain that everybody on
the island would be there—he would stir them only to anger
against the new governor, not to pity. George Rounsivel
might precipitate a riot; he was hardly likely to survive one.

He was pondering this point when there came the sound of
a scuffle, and a woman screamed.

They called her the Angel; in truth in that scorched
pestiferous frontier of civilization she loomed angelic, a
vision.

Previously the women of the Bahamas had been divided
into two classes—the bad and the worse. This difference was
but one of price. There was no large plantation, and properly
speaking no household. There were no slaves. The colony did
not boast any commercial firm, or naval station, and until
the arrival of the new governor with one hundred aging
soldiers it had no military establishment. The population
might have been ninety per cent seafaring, and almost all
English. If any of these men had wives they didn't bring
them out to the islands, where until lately a lady never had
been seen.

This made the jolt harder when Woodes Rogers sailed
into Nassau Bay attended, not only by those shakey soldiers,
but, also by a bevy of secretaries, a wife, two small children,
and a niece.

The latter, Delicia, daughter of the governor's beloved
younger brother John, who had been killed by the Spaniards,
was the Angel.

Small, dainty, in her hoop petticoats, and her bonnets, she looked a marionette—and proved a whirlwind. There was a great deal to be done; unhesitatingly she set about doing it.

As though it had been another passenger aboard the governor's vessel the plague came. The attack was abrupt, but the ache was long, the pain debilitating. At lurk in these waters, raiding any vessel they met, regardless of flag, and perhaps preparing to pounce upon Nassau itself, were Charles Vane and ninety-odd unreconciled rascals who had broken out of the bay the very night Rogers arrived.

Bigots averred that this plague had been brought about as a punishment for the colony's many sins. The governor pointed out that Vane's men, before they made their hasty departure, had skinned out all the cattle, leaving corpses widely scattered, polluting the air, so that for almost a week the island was encased in an unholy stink, a miasmatic infection. *There* was your sickness, Woodes Rogers had said.

Whatever the reason, the Angel, asking no questions, had sallied forth to nurse the ailing. She was what they chiefly remembered of that bad time, when the vomiting and fever had faded from mind—Mistress Delicia with her serious smile and that unfailing bottle of brandy.

It was the same when the Augur gang was rounded up. Delicia was not as affable with them as she'd been with the victims of the plague, but she was fully as efficient. All on her own authority she had ordered their cell scrubbed and fresh straw strewn there; she brought them fruits, food and wine . . . rum too, for Lewis. She even brought flowers. "Why shouldn't they have flowers?" she had snapped at a scandalized jailor.

She had been solemn as she went about these ministrations, greeting the prisoners and departing from them without a smile. A determined woman, dedicated to her duty, but not graciousness personified, as she had been with the victims of the plague.

The men answered her when she spoke, and were respectful, but they did not have the courage to engage her in talk. Only once had George Rounsivel ventured to speak to her.

This was the previous day, just after the conviction had been announced, the sentence passed.

"You must know, ma'am, that my case is different from the others. If I could speak to your uncle in private . . ."

She had looked up in that swift birdlike way of hers, and her eyes, the color of Parma violets, for an instant swam with moisture, but she had looked down again.

"My uncle makes it a point of policy never to interfere with the findings of the court."

"Yes, ma'am."

That was all that had passed between them.

Yet it was this same girl who had given the scream outside of the cell door—the scream that turned nine heads as though they were worked by a single wire.

It was not all her blame. Corporal Pugh, admittedly, had sprung out of the shadows with an abruptness that might have jogged anybody. For Pugh himself was scared.

He was characteristic of the company Woodes Rogers had brought. Rickety, cough-racked, and like so many of his companions he was a pensioner taken from hospital. Here were men that the army no longer wanted and even the navy wouldn't have. There was not much about their appearance to point at a military past. They weren't alert, they lounged, and they snoozed on sentry-go. If ever these miserable totterers were called upon to defend the enfeebled walls of Fort Nassau the result would be sure. The buccaneers were a rabble, granted; they were unorganized, stupid, and in many ways unskilled men, besides being prodigiously lazy and very often drunk; but when stirred to action they could be furies, and they knew every dirty trick in the game.

Corporal Pugh was aware of this. When he had been assigned to stand sentinel at the cell door, on this night of all nights, he knew that if the rumshops suddenly were emptied and the pirates came storming into the fort, here was the spot they'd head for. He had no dream of making an heroic stand. He had, therefore, marked out in his mind a route of retreat, and instead of standing smack before the door he had hunkered down in the shadows thrown by a charcoal bin twenty feet away. There, alas, he had all but fallen asleep. At the sound of Delicia Rogers' step he had sprung to his feet with an abruptness that brought from her that involuntary scream.

They grinned sheepishly.

"Ma'am, you shouldn't ought to be out on a night like this. You should be at Government House, where you got a guard."

"And what a guard! All of them hiding their heads like ostrichs—like you here, for that matter!"

"Now, ma'am—"

"No matter. I've been talking to my uncle, and I think I have at last persuaded him to reconsider the case against Rounsivel."

"Good. That lad's innocent. He just got into the wrong company, that's all. You have a let-pass?"

"Here—"

The light was poor. Pugh could not read anyway, but he did know the governor's signature, and he made a show of spelling out the words.

"Yes, that's right. But I'm not going in there alone, ma'am."

"The men are all chained!"

"Aye, but they're desperate. I'll call out the guard."

He did this, and he summoned the armorer as well, and for a few minutes he made a deal of bustle. He even went into the cell—with the armorer and two others.

"To what am I indebted for this service?" asked George Rounsivel as they knocked the chain off his ankle-ring.

"Show you when we get outside," muttered Corporal Pugh.

There was no need to extend this information. Rounsivel saw the girl the instant he stepped through the doorway.

"Oh," he said softly. He went to her, and made a small stiff bow. "You pleaded for me after all? Thanks. You've been kind."

"Sir, not kind, only human. I saw you in court, and heard you."

"I shall remember it, whether or not your uncle relents. I'll know at least that somebody spoke up."

She hung her head—not at all in shame but shaking it a bit, as though irked to find herself at a loss for words.

"Master Rounsivel, my . . . my uncle is an extraordinary man."

Here was an understatement. Woodes Rogers stood alone. A mariner in Rounsivel's position might have said: "I am about to meet the finest seaman alive." A merchant: "Here's the fellow who on an investment of less than £14,000 came home with loot of more than £800,000, the most profitable privateering trip in history." A patriot: "The Spaniards fear him more than anybody since Drake." He of literary tastes could be awed by the prospect of meeting the author of that classic: *A Cruising Voyage Round the World.*

George Rounsivel's reaction was different. He wasn't thinking of past glories. He was about to meet, not an author, a navigator, a maker of money, but the captain-general of the royal plantations of the Bahamas. He was not asking himself· *What kind of man is this?* He was asking· *Will this man let me off?*

"I don't know what he'll say to you, Master Rounsivel. I think he might ask you something."

"Ask . . . me?"

She nodded, mute for the moment.

Surely there was nothing sleek about this young woman, Tonight, with the worriment that was upon her, and her earnestness, she showed rather tousled. But her small smooth head was adorably shaped for caresses, so that, seeing it, you were tempted to try to pick it up, like a separate thing, a warm, pulsating thing, and fondle it, the way the aged Chinese fondle their jade fingering-pieces.

Standing there a few feet from her in the fitful light, George Rounsivel had all he could do to keep from reaching out. with tender fingers, for the sides of that head. Pugh and the other soldiers, of course, had their hangers out, and they would have cut him down if he took a step toward her.

She, on her part, could hardly be harboring a wish to fondle *him*, he reflected grimly. Smudged, ashen, hollow-eyed, his wigless pate covered by no more than a fuzz, while the stench of the cell was upon him, he was no figure of romance.

"You must realize that the governor is in . . . well. in a position of great peril, Master Rounsivel."

"For that matter, so am I."

"Yes, but in your case it is but your own life—"

"The only one I happen to have."

"—while in the case of my uncle it's his career. It might mean his life as well . . . and the lives of all who are dear to him."

"Meaning yourself? You shouldn't be abroad on a night like this."

They had been whispering, as though in church, but he said this last aloud, Corporal Pugh nodded a meaningful agreement.

George stared down at a small shapely head, and he was all one marvel inside. A short while ago she had seemed so crisp and sure of herself, and now, though her shoulders didn't sag, she had about her an air of helplessness. She was extremely feminine.

"Ask *me?*" he repeated, dropping his voice again. "Ma'am, forgive me, but until now I had supposed that the purpose of this interview was to get *me* a chance to ask *him* for something?"

He did not, properly, mean a pardon. Only the king could grant that. What he really meant—as he the lawyer knew— was a commutation of sentence pending royal decision on an *application for pardon.* In other words, Woodes Rogers might have recommended that this one prisoner be freed, keeping him from the gallows until word came back from London. Such recommendations almost always were acted upon favorably. But this would have been difficult to explain to the small beauty who stood before him.

Now she raised her head. There were tears in her eyes.

"Master Rounsivel, my uncle is not made of putty. I know that he loves me, but even for me he wouldn't have consented to receive you if he did not have something else in mind."

"What else?"

"I don't know. I'm not sure that I'd tell you if I did, but I don't anyway. But whatever it is, I hope you'll consider it. And as you consider it I hope you'll think of his position."

"I am not likely to forget it, ma'am. Now . . . where do I go?"

"This way, sir," said a soldier.

Delicia Rogers for the first time put out a hand.

"Good luck."

He did not touch the hand, only bowed over it.

"Thanks," he said again, and he turned and went upstairs, a soldier before him, a soldier behind.

One floor above the level of the court they paused. There was a door, but no light slid from around it. A light did glow, faintly, indirectly—for the stair curved—above.

"Yours," said one of the soldiers, and they clumped away.

George Rounsivel fetched a deep breath.

He went upstairs.

There was a narrow door, light beneath it. He knocked.

"Come in," said a voice.

He opened the door and went in.

CHAPTER II

THE ROOM was large, the ceiling high. The windows to right and left were real windows, not musket-slits. Floor and walls were bare. On a table was a branch of candles, and by the side of this an unpowdered wig and a sword-and-sword-belt.

Behind the table, asprawl in an X-chair, was Woodes Rogers.

The governor was alone. Since he received a felon this implied either high courage, not to say foolhardiness, or else a naiveté not likely to be found in the man who had held Guayaquil for ransom and captured the Acapulco treasure galleon. He lounged. His coat was open, the waistcoat un-buttoned, and it was patent that he carried no pistol. The sword he had tossed upon the table was not even near his hand. It was no seaman's cutlass but long and thin, a "court" sword.

Bristling with defensiveness, George gave a bow.

"*Ave, Caesar! Moriturus saluto!*"

"There's no call to be caustic," said Woodes Rogers. "Sit down."

A large man, he had a high, curiously effeminate voice. He seemed indeed to speak with difficulty, as though the words hurt his mouth. George remembered that this man had had a good part of his upper jaw carried away by a Spanish ball.

George glanced at the indicated stool, and shook his head. In the first place, he was nervous. In the second place, the thing had the look of a penitent's chair in some puritan church, or the sort of stool you'd find in the prisoner's dock in court, and George wished to avoid all hint of guilt.

"I'll not crawl before you," he declared.

"I didn't ask you to crawl. I asked you to sit down."

Still George stood. He was angry.

"I can't tell your Excellency more than I told the court, for that was the truth," he blurted. "I was a passenger in the brig *Barkus* out of Philadelphia bound for Jamaica, but I was to be put off here. Somewhere south of Hatteras we were beset by as mangy a pack of rats as ever prowled around a garbage dump—my so-called 'associates' downstairs. They stripped us of everything, as they stripped the brig itself. But when they learned that I was a lawyer they insisted that I go with them. And when I say they insisted I mean they pointed pistols at me. So of course I went."

"Of course."

George looked sharply at him. Was this meant to be ironic? The captain-general, however, waved for him to go on.

"The Barkus had no extra canvas or line left then, so she put back for Philadelphia. They took everything, those scavengers. *Everything!* Deck fastenings, belaying pins, lanterns, even the skipper's small square of rug from his cabin.

"The skipper wouldn't risk coming down here in that condition, right in the middle of the hurricane season. And those damned pirates, your excellency, treated me like a pig in a sty—"

Here Governor Rogers held up a hand. Though amazed and seemingly somewhat amused by George's presumption in breaking into speech before he'd been granted leave, Rogers had listened to the first part with a wry smile; now he called a halt.

"That will do. A vice admiralty court has heard you and has found you guilty, and there's enough for me."

"Then why in the name of the Devil are you having me up here?"

"I am not doing it in the name of the Devil, my impious friend. I'm doing it in the name of self-defense. I need help."

"Eh?"

"Your sentence stands. There is nothing I can do about it. But there are a few facts that I'd have you know—"

"Damn any facts you'd have me know! You're cat-and-mousing, and I won't stand it!"

Then he did a very foolish thing. Augur, Cunningham, Lewis, and the others had thought of George Rounsivel as a man without emotion. They were mistaken. He had seethed inside. And tonight, the unexpected summons after those hours of waiting, the talk with Delicia Rogers, the abrupt dismissal of the plea he had forced himself to start —these were too much for him. Something snapped. He sprang.

To snatch the sword and lug it out was the work of an instant.

Had the governor tried to cover himself it might have been his last living movement. But the governor only smiled.

"Captain Robinson," he called.

The door was flung open. George whirled around.

Thomas Robinson was no ordinary member of that tatterdemalion company of foot the governor had brought from Bristol. He may have come along for adventure or simply to escape his creditors. Whatever the reason, he was young and elegant. His shirt was silk, his manner silken. His wig hung almost to his waist, a notably narrow one. He wore blue velvet garters just below the knees, caught up at the side with gold buckles. The heels of his shoes were scarlet. Yet though he was a dandy it was evident at once that he was no coward. He smiled. He drew.

"Stand aside," cried George, shifting toward him, meaning to spring past him to the door.

For answer Robinson swept into a long exquisite lunge. George's parry, a left counter, was instinctive; it was barely in time.

Robinson, who had recovered with the speed of a cobra, attacked again.

Again George, though he did manage to parry, by reason of the other's phenomenal speed could not get in a riposte. Choking with humiliation, he crouched low and began to move forward, his point going in small tight circles.

Robinson still was smiling, though not so much.

"That will do," called the governor. He had not stirred, but his voice cut the air like a whip. "Captain Robinson, retire, please. Rounsivel, put my blade back where you found it."

He was obeyed. Eyeing one another warily, the swordsmen stepped back, each lowering his guard. Then Robinson gave a creditable bow, and sheathed, and departed.

"He's no fool," panted George Rounsivel.

"That's more than I can say of you. Don't you realize, man, that with one shout I could have had this place thronging with guards?"

Miserably, "Yes."

Rogers made for the window on the shore side, moving with a limp, for his left heel had been shot away in another Pacific encounter. Despite this, he was lithe, and though thin certainly strong. George, a runner, a swimmer, a fencer, could appreciate this. Woodes Rogers had been well assembled, and was all of one piece, brain and organs, muscles and nerve-ends working exquisitely together. Though mild in his manner, he was possessed of a tremendous impatience, a power that it cost him all his strength to control. When he crossed a room he resented the strides necessary, the pieces of furniture to be circumvented; he wished to be there, instantaneously.

"Lookee, Rounsivel. You can see it from here."

Fascinated, George went to the window.

His first sight of the tropics will stun any man. The magic is quick to strike. The polychromatic unreality of the scene refuses to vanish when the eyes are blinked. The breath is caught up, never to be wholly released again, no matter how long the onlooker lives in those parts.

George Rounsivel was seven weeks out of Philadelphia, but much of this time had been spent at sea. The pounce of the pirates under Augur had come almost as a relief after that monotony. They had, however, cooped George in a bilge-fragrant hold, where they kept him while they tried to decide what it was they wanted him to write—they never did make up their minds.

Then they were surprised at Exuma by an armed sloop from New Providence, and captured, every one. George's surge of hope was soon squashed. The leader of this patrol, the redoubtable Ben Hornigold, was not one to trust a pirate or anything even remotely resembling a pirate, possibly because he himself had for so long been on the account. Dazzled by the unaccustomed sunlight, hardly able to see anything—not that there was much to see at Exuma anyway —George had been hustled from one vessel to another, from one hell to a second, equally portholeless, and if possible even more vile. Nor had he been granted more than a glimpse of Nassau. Fearing that the sight of pirates being led through the streets in chains might raise a riot, the canny Hornigold had sneaked back under cover of darkness. Still protesting his innocence, George in the dead of night had been dumped ashore and hauled up to the fort without being given a chance to make note of his surroundings. Since then, except for a few hours in the court room, where the windows were blocked by morbid spectators, he had lain in a cell whose only outside opening was a grill far above his reach.

Thus it was that after a month in these fabled isles he was being vouchsafed his first look at them.

And he gasped.

The moon was scounched low against an horizon outlined with cabbage palms and Spanish bayonet, and its light lay bland upon the bay. Wavelets were susurrant along the beach, which gleamed like molten gold, while arched above it, now gawky, now incredibly graceful, the coconut trees bobbed and flirted, their fronds atwinkle in the moonlight—pink, deep blue, orange, red, yellow, and most of all a giddy bright green. The boats at anchor did not rock, so tranquil was the water.

"No, not out that way," cried Woodes Rogers. *"There!"*

George dropped his gaze—and saw the gallows. It looked incalculably strong, and it was tall. Nine ropes hung from it.

"Those men deserve to hang, Rounsivel, and hang they shall. But how long d'ye think the townsmen back there are going to stay honest? They'll watch this execution a few hours from now, and they'll be impressed—for a little while. Then they'll begin to mutter that I only got some small fry. And they'll be right! It isn't the John Augurs and Will Cunninghams I want. It's the leaders. But . . . what can I get them with? You've seen the soldiers I brought. I'm organizing several companies of militia, but they'd desert to a man if some popular pirate sent in word that he wanted recruits."

"The Navy?"

"I yield to no man in my admiration of the British Navy, sir. But I tell you the Navy don't *want* to stamp out piracy in these waters. Lookee, here's a map—"

He hobbled to the table, George following him.

"Here's Panama. Hispaniola. Jamaica. And here *we* are. Any seaman will tell you how the trade winds blow in this part of the world. Vessels sailing home from Jamaica have to come near us here. They might use the Mona Passage to the east or hug Florida to the west, but either way they come close to this island. Right?"

"I see."

"Now if the pirates have this place to themselves, the way they did before, then the merchants in Jamaica have to ship their stuff by convoy—with a warship."

"But I don't understand why the Navy—"

"Do you see any frigates out there in the bay, Rounsivel? No. The Navy keeps one stationed back in your Philadelphia, and they keep three at Kingston. But they never even drop in here to say hello. Why? Why, because the R.N. captains are being paid by the Jamaica merchants to guard their vessels in convoy. That's the truth! They get as high as twenty per cent of the value of the combined cargoes. They're waxing rich!"

"Why hasn't London been notified of this?"

"London has been. But by the time somebody in White-hall gets around doing anything about it we might be all dead here. Why, I can't even get an *answer* from London!"

"I see," said George Rounsivel. "But what I don't see," he added, "is why you are telling me all this?"

Woodes Rogers appeared not to have heard.

"It's the leaders I must lay hands on. Not the rank and file. Barrow's loose, and so is Martel. Teach and Bonnet are in the Carolinas, but they'll be back here if they hear that the place is wide-open. England's gone to Madagascar, good riddance. Hornigold has stayed on, and Cockran, but I think they'll hold fast; they made their pile before I came. But . . . Vane? I've got to find him. I've got to get a man to go after Charles Vane and learn everything about him—

where he is, where he careens, where he gets his supplies, everything."

"And how can your excellency find such a man?"

"I believe that I have found him."

"Eh?"

"I regarded you in court. My niece has spoken for you, and I have faith in her judgment. Just now I saw you fight—"

"He was very fast," George muttered.

"To my knowledge he has killed four men on the so-called field of honor. He's rated as one of the finest swordsmen in Christiandom."

"I see. But . . . what's all this to do with me?"

"Only that, as I said, perhaps I have found my man."

"I'm honored," George remarked dryly. "But I am also puzzled." He pointed to the gallows. "Has your Excellency forgotten that within an hour or so I shall be dangling? A dead man can't catch Charles Vane."

"You could escape, couldn't you? Come here—" He limped to the other side of the room, the other window—"Suppose I went below—to the jakes, say? Couldn't such a man as yourself, left alone here, climb down the side of this tower? A lot of cement's been knocked out from between the stones. That makes toeholds and handholds. An active body should be able to reach the wall, and run along it a little way to where it's been knocked down. After that he'd only have to slide on his bum through a heap of rubble. Oh, some sentry might shoot! But the sentries ain't very observant just before dawn, and they're damnably bad shots anyway."

"But still—how could I learn all about Charles Vane?"

"By becoming a pirate. You were caught up in a pirate band when you *didn't* want to be, you say, so why should it be hard when you *do?* Truth is, you'd be a hero to them . . . now."

"These are strange words from a royal governor."

"This is a strange place."

George stared again at Nassau Bay, so serene, assured. He saw sand, palm trees. The magic prevailed, but there was an uneasiness about it now.

"And if I was to bring you a good report—"

"Then I'd recommend your pardon."

"You'd trust me?"

Woodes Rogers looked at him for a long while.

"Yes," he said at last, "I would."

"And if I refuse?"

"If you refuse," said Woodes Rogers, "I'll hang you."

"Even though you believe my story, as I think you do?"

"I would infallibly hang you."

Bemused, George leaned out of the window and looked down the side of the tower. He saw the cracks. He believed that the thing was possible, though speed would be needed, for already the east was pale.

"That's against the law, of course."

"It is," the governor agreed. "So many things are against the law, out here. But there would be nobody to punish for having permitted such an escape—nobody but the governor himself, which is unthinkable."

"Yes." George grinned a little. "All right," he said.

"Good!"

They shook hands.

"You'll need money. Here's a purse. And now, if you'll excuse me, I think I shall go down to the necessary-room."

"Yes, your Excellency. But . . . one thing more. What if I should fail? What if I should be caught and hailed before your court?"

The governor nodded toward the gallows.

"That," he replied.

"I see," said George Rounsivel. "Thank you, sir."

CHAPTER III

MOONLIGHT can be deceptive. Those cracks proved not nearly as deep as they had seemed, and the wall of the pineapple-shaped tower turned out to be much steeper than it had showed from above.

Given time, George was sure he'd make it, but already the wall whitened, and soon he would be visible for miles.

He moved as quickly as he dared, making every split-second count. Dreading dizziness, he would not let himself look down. If he fell he would land upon the ramparts, which this tower abutted. That was his immediate aim anyway. If then he toppled over to the ground—which was rock-strewn—he might crack his skull. Even if he managed to stay on the wall he could fear a turned ankle. They'd hang him all the same. *One leg less to kick with,* was his thought.

A sentry passed below, stumbling as though in weariness. George froze. The sentry did not look up.

Precious though the moments were, George made himself stay motionless a little longer against the fear that the sentry would return. The way he had gone, to George's right, was a place on the wall where Spanish cannons had opened a breach. This breach was backed from the inside by spike-topped logs, a palisade intended only to be temporary, a stopgap. It was here that, as Governor Rogers had said, an agile man need only to slide to the safety of the ground outside, for the rubble had not yet been cleared away. A few planks had been thrown across this gap. George, breathless above, had not heard the sentry cross those planks; he paused. After a while, however, he started down again.

His hands were wet with sweat, making his grip unsure. He had taken off his shoes and left them in the governor's chamber, just below the window, for he believed that he could climb down better in his stockinged feet. But the stone was spikey and cut his toes, which began to bleed. The pain was not great, but he was in an agony of suspense lest a foot slip.

He calculated that he was about two-thirds of the way down to the ramparts when the alarm was sounded.

It came from an unexpected quarter. George's fear had been centered *below*. It was from *above* that he was challenged.

He heard the door of the governor's room opened, and heard a step. It was not the walk of Woodes Rogers, for there was no limp in it.

The window was agape, and George's shoes just below the sill could be seen by anybody in that room.

George looked up just as Thomas Robinson leaned out.

Robinson's face was shadowed, but there could be no mistaking that periwig or the magnificent spread of rose-point at the throat.

The two faces were twelve or thirteen feet apart, George's being bathed in moonlight.

"Stab me, the dog's . . . *The guard! Ho, the guard!*"

Robinson's head and shoulders vanished.

George drew a deep breath . . . and let go.

It was not far. He landed lightly, never in danger of tumbling backward over the rampart. He turned to the right and sped away.

Almost immediately he came upon the board bridge. At the far end stood a sentry, a matchlock in his hands. Startled, this man stared at George. The match lighted his face a little from underneath.

George dived for the space below the planks.

It was dark there. He took the word of Woodes Rogers that rubble was heaped high. For all he could see, he might have been pitching head-first into a chasm.

But here was rubble. It buffeted him. It caused him to

cough. But it didn't do much about breaking his fall. He felt that he was plummeting. His chest got tight.

Choking, gasping, spitting, he started to run.

He heard a gun, then another, and a little later he heard a third.

That a prisoner who had escaped from the persecutor of pirates would find welcome anywhere in Nassau went without saying. But George's presence at a time like this might start a riot. The cry would go up: "Let's take out the rest!" No more than a spark was needed.

He surmised that this fear of an explosion was the reason for the failure to chase him. Woodes Rogers would not risk sending search parties into Nassau. Indeed, he probably couldn't have made them go there.

If the fort was taken Delicia Rogers would be taken too, and it did not call for much imagination to know what would happen to her. She was there instead of at Government House, he remembered, because of him.

So he altered his course, and made for the hills.

Doors were being opened, heads thrust forth, questions shouted. Nassau was no teeming metropolis. Many of the houses were mere shacks of thatch and braziletto. Others were tents. The only ones with floors and proper roofs were the rumshops, of which however there were many. The rumshops had been operating all night. Hundreds, womanless anyway, had stayed up to get in shape for the ceremony down by the beach. It isn't every morning that you can see nine men strangled.

Figures loomed in the doorways, blurred by dawn. Men shouted at George, who shook his head and ran on. The truth is, he was at the end of his tether. At any moment he'd collapse. It was his wish to be far from everything—alone.

Soon he was behind the town, climbing, and nobody paid attention to him, their eyes being drawn, naturally, toward the fort.

George came to the corner of a sugar field. A less inviting spot for a nap it would have been hard to conceive, for the ground was bumpy and damp, the canes close together. George didn't care. He plunged in, fought his way for a few yards, then fell, sobbing; a great empty roaring blackness, like that of the outer spaces, engulfed him.

The sound that George heard was not a keening, though it was high, as it was thin. A sea gull? He sat up, his head throbbing.

No, it was not a sea gull. It was not that . . . that . . querulous.

On hands and knees, groggy, George inched toward the sound.

The cane was thick. It was almost like poking his head out through a doorway when at last he came within sight of the man seated on the stone. This man was short, dumpy, a pudding. His lips protruded. His jowls waddled. His eyes were gooseberries. Across his lap lay a piece of canvas, and on this rested a cutlass. His left hand held the hilt, and with a stone in his right hand rhythmically he honed the edge. His movements were exact—yet he gazed toward the bay.

"Trouble?" asked George.

The man didn't jump, he only turned his head; he put his hone away very carefully. The cutlass he simply held in his right hand.

"There's trouble down there, yes," he said, pointing.

Pain skittering through him like small bolts of lightning, George got to his feet, and straightened, and looked back toward Nassau.

He knew instantly that several hours had passed. The sun was well above the horizon, shining full and fierce.

The show was over. People already were leaving. He could

see them drifting away, small and buglike from this distance.

The water was a blue not known elsewhere in this world. No catspaws ruffled it. The fronds of the palms were limp, like the black flag. There was not a wisp of breeze. The bodies of the men, too, hung motionless; they did not seem real.

"He can't do that to us." The pursy man, with a grunt, got to his feet. "I said he wouldn't dare to, but he did. So I'm going away. What about you, stranger?"

"I . . . I'm going away too."

The short fat man came around before George, and stood there looking up at him. He rubbered out his lips, twirking a mouth that, incongruously, was a Cupid's bow. But the eyes were ice.

"Well, he *did* do it!"

"Yes," said George.

He was enthralled by the sight of the crowd moving away. Gulls wheeled low over those bodies.

"But he *did* do it. And so I guess I'll go and look for some goods that maybe are assigned to me."

George chafed his temples.

"You mean," he asked, "that you're going on the account?"

"There's other ways of putting it."

"Whom?"

"Eh? Well, damn me, stranger, I don't know you from Adam."

"Vane?"

"Um-m. Charlie Vane has always been square in his dealing. Leastways as far as I've had anything to do with him."

"And where do you find him now? How do you get there?"

The little fat man was glaring at him, but George still looked at the bodies.

It had happened. There had been no riot, no assault.

Woodes Rogers ruled here, and his niece, that girl with the small dark head, still lived.

A great victory had been won, without huzzas.

Yet the threat remained. Nassau was a powder keg to which anybody might apply a match. Those ragged men down there, who, having looked their fill, were slowly moving away from the fort; they were sullen, unconvinced, quiet but not yet cowed.

"I'm not sure I like your face, stranger. But I've got a periagua over on the far shore that's not big but it's strong."

"Vane?"

"Yes. Charles Vane. I know him well."

George sighed, and sat down for a while.

"You know about this business?" the man asked suddenly.

"Enough."

"Well, come along then. Look—" He gestured imperiously. "That's what we'll get if we wait, mister."

"Yes."

The cutlass glistered in the sunlight. Past it, the way it pointed, those bodies never would move again. John Augur . . . Will Cunningham . . . laughing Dennis Macarty . . .

"So're you coming?"

"Yes," said George Rounsivel. "Yes, I'm coming."

CHAPTER IV

CAYO JOROBADO—or, as the English had Englished it, Hunchback Key—might have been built by sea robbers. It stood alone. All of its beaches had a gentle slope, ideal for careening. In addition, on the north side there was a small bay, the pass to which was narrow, and probably, George Rounsivel reflected as he paddled through it, too shoal for a warship yet deep enough to permit the passage of a sloop. Pirates, understandably, favored shallow-draft vessels.

The island, lush, would have wood and water, probably also plantains and coconuts, and the bay would furnish fish. Upthrust at the center, it even provided its own lookout tower in the form of the knob of shards that had given it its name. On this mound, or hump, starfished in all directions, had been mounted half a dozen brass cannons. In the midst of these, on a wooden platform, a glass across his knees, sat a sentinel who could see for many miles south in the direction of Cuba, west toward Andros Island, east toward Eleuthera, and to the north the channels that led on one side to the open Atlantic, on the other to the Florida Passage.

In a failing light the cannons gleamed like bosses on some great shield. Blue-purple shadows slipped out across the bay. Beyond a half-circle of sand the dark banana fronds, nasturtiumed at the edges where sunset smeared them, moved with a lazy languor like great tired birds that fuss themselves to rest. Despite the human beings, here was a scene calculated to stir the soul of any artist.

George Rounsivel was not an artist, and he was so tired that he could hardly hold up his head. He didn't care how lovely the place was. All he cared about was sleep.

The plump man was named Monk Evans. For all his flabby flesh he was hard. For all the red round mouth and gooseberry eyes he was mean, suspicious. He seemed to have taken an actual dislike to George, whom he placed in the bow of the periagua, a tippy narrow craft. Evans himself did little paddling, but he did guide the boat with an uncanny skill, having no sort of navigating instrument. He must have been one of those men who could find their way among the islands unstumblingly, moving not by instinct so much as by sure familiarity, as a man might walk about among the articles of furniture in his own pitch-dark bedroom. Evans was a dirty-mouthed little man, who cursed George each

time George paused to rest on his paddle, and threatened
him with that cutlass; but George was so tired that he
couldn't care, and ignored the fat man now and then to
slump forward on the thwarts for a short stunned sleep.

These cat naps, if they could be called that, might have
done more harm than good. For the sun was terrible through
all that long day, and it seemed to hit him the hardest when
he did not stir. The blistered hands, and the ache of shoulder and back muscles, together with the agony of cramped
legs—for he scarcely dared to stir for fear of upsetting their
small frail craft—these he might have endured. But he
feared that he was about to succumb to the sun. He giggled,
light-headed. What remained of his shirt helped somewhat to
protect his shoulders and even a part of his neck, but his
head, having no hat or wig, at first began to itch, and then
to sting, as though literally on fire. The dizziness was as bad
as the pain itself, so that George swayed where he sat.

It was Evans who saved him by passing forward a flimsy
raffia hat not unlike the one he himself wore, albeit even
dirtier. Much of the damage had been done before Evans
produced this garment, but George, under it, was able to
survive.

George was never to forget that trip, a paddle through hell,
his first prolonged exposure to the sun of the Caribbees.

They were not challenged when they beached the canoe.
At this spot George would have collapsed, but Monk Evans
seized him by the arm and marched him to the center of
the camp.

"Got to report. They'd only wake you up anyway."

"Yes."

It made sense. Even in such a sloppy place it was unthinkable that two strangers could be accepted at sunset without
being called upon to give an account of themselves. Only
half awake, George lurched along.

The camp churned. There showed no sort of plan to it.

Fires were being lighted, but these were as irregularly spaced as the men who tended them. Most of those men were drunk; it seemed to be an accustomed condition. There were no fights, true, and there was a certain amount of singing; but for the most part the camp at Jorobado, if raucous, was not gay. Neither was it solid. There was not about it even the air of semipermanence that Nassau could show. Even the cooking arrangements were primitive, temporary. Indeed the one splash of human ingenuity in this out-of-the-way place was provided by the sloop that they'd hauled up on the beach for careening. She was a slim craft named Agnes. Her masts had been drawn, her deck and hold stripped of everything movable. In this condition, and by means of a series of windlasses anchored deep in the sand, she had been tipped to her side, where she looked singularly helpless, like a fish out of water, one that has ceased to flop and simply lies there with gaping mouth and pop-out eyes. The exposed side of her, the larboard side, already had been scraped, and men even now were stuffing the seams with a mixture of sulphur, tallow, and tar, the tangy smell of which mingled with the more humdrum odors in the air of Jorobado—rum, rotting fish heads, molasses, urine, sweat.

> "I'd climb, I'd fight,
> "To pray all night,
> "To be my manhood back-o!"

In the middle of this, seated on a stump, in his fist a mug of bumboo, was Charles Vane, a course giant, drably dressed, without jewels. The features of his face were bulbous, bloated, except for the small sunken vulterine eyes, bloodshot now.

"Where's Rackham?" he asked, and belched.

"Out looking for Anne. He wants to be sure she's in her own hammock when it gets dark."

Vane belched again, then sampled the bumboo and made a face.

"I hope he don't find her with her breeches down," he said, "or we'll have another murder in this camp."

"Wouldn't she take 'em down for you, skipper?"

"Shut up." He had noticed Monk Evans. "They hang?" he asked.

"Aye."

"All of 'em?"

"All except this man here. He's a lawyer."

"You mean a real lawyer? Not just a sea lawyer?"

"Aye, that he is, captain."

Charles Vane put down his mug, making a little hole in the sand with it, and then, the heels of his hairy red hands pressing his knees, he regarded George Rounsivel.

These pirate captains or chiefs were known as "kings." There was nothing regal about Vane, and surely nothing that suggested a court about the place in which he sat. Yet the man's very massiveness could impress. A brute, a beast, he was not without cunning, and it was clear that he was used to being obeyed.

Now he hiccupped thoughtfully. He started to pick his nose.

"All right," he said at last. "We'll take you. Now you sit right down and draw me up some articles of comradeship. And don't forget to put in there that the captain's supreme —even over the quartermaster, and in fact *especially* over the quartermaster."

"No," said George Rounsivel.

That word jolted Vane forward like a blow between the shoulder blades. He gawped, temples throbbing, while his face became so dark as to be almost purple. Somebody sniggered. Vane heaved himself to his feet, fists clenched.

Fatigue lent insolence to George Rounsivel, who knew anyway that boldness would be the best policy here.

"I'll write your God damn' paper for you," he added, "but not now. Why, I'm whipped for sleep! I couldn't hold a pen in my hand!"

"Oh," said Vane.

"Besides that," George went on, "I haven't had anything to eat all day."

Vane sat down again. He waved his hand.

"Feed him," he commanded.

The men of Jorobado might be fussy about their personal possessions, such as trinkets, bits of treasured loot, but it was clear that their food was communal. They ate any time, anywhere, and as much as they pleased.

George was handed two calabashes, one for food, one for blackstrap, and these were kept full despite his protests. The blackstrap was rum and chowder beer spiced with nutmeg. The food was better. There was a salmagundi of uncooked herbs mixed with oil, leeks, garlic, and hard-boiled green-turtle eggs; there were, as he'd expected, bananas; there were chunks of cane for chewing, chunks of coconut too, and there was a great deal of tender white meat which George at first mistook for some notably tasty fowl. By the time he learned that he had been eating iguana he was too tired to care.

His early supposition that he had scarcely been noticed proved wrong. Two minutes after his interview with Vane every man in camp knew that George had been captured and sentenced to hang but had escaped, and that he was a lawyer, a real one. These facts enormously interested them, and they plied George with questions.

Silent, sagging, George shook his head. He was filled with loathing of these greasy uncouth scoundrels who jabbered for details about the killing of their own kind, and with the same breath made suggestions for the articles he was to draw up. But he knew that he could not let this contempt show. Pirates, as he had already learned, are a touchy people, ludicrously easy to insult. Outcasts, they were forever in a position of furious defense. So he kept his head averted, wolfing the salad and meat.

At last he got away and made for the hill. This was wooded and might afford some protection in case of a shower, but his real reason for going there was to be alone.

It had been his first thought to flop down anywhere just outside the camp. He soon saw that this wouldn't be wise. There was no latrine; while some of the pirates performed right where they were, causing the fires to spit and splutter, others, more fastidious, would retire to the edge of the camp at a call of nature. A man sleeping in the darkness there might be wakened most rudely.

So George climbed, dragging his feet.

When he stepped among the trees it was almost as though somebody had whuffed out a lamp. He paused, waiting for his eyes to get used to the darkness. Overhead the tree branches were javelined by the sun's last rays, but immediately around him it was hard to see anything.

"Looking for a blanket?"

The speaker was seated, almost at George's feet, as he saw with a start, and was indeed on a blanket. He was a slim slight lad, pale. Smiling, he moved aside.

"Thank you," said George.

The blanket looked thick, the boy clean, and they were deep enough in the wood to be safe from prowlers George fell full-length.

Sleep did not seize him instantly, as he'd expected Probably the pain accounted for this. His limbs shrieked, the joints too, as though he were being stretched on a rack; his head was all flame.

"You're the one that came back with Monk Evans,' the

lad said, his treble voice reaching George as though from far away.

George made an effort to be polite.

"I suppose *you're* going to ask for some special article too?"

"Yes. I think you ought to write in a provision against prostitutes. You see, I don't want any competition."

George's face was turned away, and he grimaced. *"Good God, one of those!"* was his thought. But he was too tired to move.

"You don't know who I am?" the lad pursued. "I'm Anne Bonney."

Oh, fine! He was so far depraved that he let them call him Anne!

"Why 'Anne'?" George asked coldly. "That's a woman's name."

The other giggled. George heard a string drawn, a button popped. Then his hand was lifted from his side and placed over something soft and warm.

"And what do you think this is, mister—a mosquito bite?"

He sat up, gasping, snatching his hand away. His eyes told him now what that hand already had reported. Despite the dim light, despite the male clothes, beyond all doubt this was a woman who sat by his side. She laughed softly, and exposed her other breast.

"There are two of them," she whispered.

"There usually are."

She reached for the belt that held up her trousers.

"Would you like to see more?"

George groaned, falling back on the blanket.

"Save it, sister," he advised. "I'm too tired. Besides, I haven't any money with me."

He had in his pocket the purse the governor had given him, but it was his experience that the quickest way to get rid of a trollop is to tell her you are cashless. He expected this one to relapse in a huff. Instead she slapped him, hard.

The slaps stung, one on each cheek. Startled, he opened his eyes.

Anne Bonney, girlish, slender, blonde, might have been easy to look at in any light, in any mood too. Now, furious, her eyes flashing, she was lovely. As she leaned over him her mouth worked in rage.

"By God, I'll teach you to call me a whore!"

"What else was I to think?" he asked bluntly.

With one hand she covered her breasts, buttoning the shirt back into place. With the other she drew a small sheath knife, and she held this before George Rounsivel's face.

"I'll slice you so's no woman will ever look at you again! I'll—"

Fascinated, George did not hear the step of the man who approached. But the girl did—and she was off like a frightened deer.

The man came quickly, from the direction of the beach, the camp. His mouth was a little open, his eyes darted here and there, and when he saw George Rounsivel he stopped short.

George didn't stir, pretending to be asleep.

This man was young, strong, well set up, and handsome in a brash, coarse way. For a pirate he was uncommonly trig. A stiff black enameled hat was perched on his head, held there by red ribbons that went under the chin. His trousers and shirt were made of fine calico, striped vertically in red and dark blue. Around his waist was a white silk sash, and into this had been thrust two silver-hilted pistols. A sheath knife hung at his right hip. In his hand he carried a cudgel.

This man should have swaggered. Instead he paused, irresolute, even a mite frightened. It was plain to George, who watched him through slitted eyes, that he was thinking of a challenge. He decided against this, visibly shaking his head, and ran on.

George waited a little while, though he didn't stir. He half expected Anne Bonney back, and he was prepared now to resist her. But not even the thought of those flashing blue eyes—and that knife so near to his own eyes—could hold him back from the brink of sleep, which engulfed him with a great soft roar.

CHAPTER V

CHARGED to report on the system of piracy as practiced in Caribbean waters, George Rounsivel was lucky to be given, thus early, a lesson.

His visitor of the previous night, he now learned, was none other than John Rackham, "Calico Jack." George had heard of this desperado whilst lying in a cell at Fort Nassau.

Calico Jack was Charles Vane's quartermaster. A quartermaster in a pirate gang was no mere assistant! Vane had a mate, one Robert Deal, a dour middle-aged man. The quartermaster was an officer of almost as much importance as the captain himself. He raised supplies, settled personal squabbles, and oversaw the distribution of the loot. As such he was close to the men and a natural center for any dissidence. A wise pirate king kept his quartermaster on short rein.

In the morning Rackham appeared as he should have done when George first saw him—and would have done, had he not been tortured by jealousy. He had thought himself alone then, and was suffering. Now, his hat gleamed in the sun. The long thin black cudgel hung from his right wrist by means of a leather thong, and now and then he would fan the air with it.

"We don't want you, is that clear?" (*Swish!*) "We're sick and tired of your timidness! We should have gone after that Frencher, but you called us off because you were afraid. You heard what I said—" (*Swish!*)—"I said 'afraid'!"

Vane rose, trembling with rage, yet already he was in retreat; he knew he was beaten.

"You can't call me that!"

"I have, haven't I?"

"By God then, Jack Rackham, you'll fight me!"

The quartermaster deliberately turned his back.

"I don't fight graybeards," he drawled.

Swaggering, he winked at his doxy. Anne looked much as she had last night, though indisputably a woman now, for her hair fell down over her shoulders: it was wavy, dark gold or light brown in color, depending on the light. Her lips were fixed in a permanent pout. Her eyes were sultry.

This woman had been born to get into trouble, George reflected, and so far from bemoaning her destiny she gloried in it. When she saw George, for instance, though she did not actually smile her eyes lit up noticeably, and she gave him a lingering significant look.

If Calico Jack had chanced to see that look there would have been bloody doings on Cayo Jorobado.

Rackham, pleased with himself, cocky, his thumbs hooked into the top of his sash, the cudgel swinging authoritatively before him like the sporran of a Scottish Highlander, strode back and forth.

"You can have the *Agnes* and whoever'll go with you," he tossed off. "She's almost fit. You can clear out today."

"We've got to take a vote," Vane shouted.

"We *have* taken a vote, Grandpa." (*Swish!*) "But if it'll make you feel any better we'll do it again. Here—" He drew a line in the sand. "Now, all those that want to refit the *John and Elizabeth* and go out and get some goods that might be consigned to us . . . let them step over here

And any that want to crawl along after Charles Chickenliver Vane, let them stay where they are."

Twelve men, including Monk Evans and the mate Deal, took the Vane side of the mark. The others, about sixty in number, ranged themselves alongside of Calico Jack, who beamed.

George paused. Anne Bonney touched his elbow.

"Aren't you coming with us?"

"I don't rightly know. Haven't any notion what the spat's about. I wasn't here then."

Whether Rackham overheard him or suddenly remembered him, he looked up sharply, pointing the cudgel, a sceptre now.

"You, lawyer, you'll stay here anyway. You're going to draw us up the best God damn' set of articles in the whole Brotherhood of the Coast. So start looking for ink and paper, right now."

Until that moment George had been uncertain. His assignment was to track down Charles Vane, who was now about to leave the island. Should he go with Vane? In a larger sense, though, his assignment was to study piratical methods and conditions in this part of the world, thus helping to remove the immediate threat to New Providence. Rackham, then, would be the best leader. Calico Jack not only had youth on his side, he also had the men.

Rackham, however, had given George no choice.

"So that," he muttered, "is that."

"I . . . I'm sorry I waved a knife at you last night," the girl whispered. "But I wouldn't have slashed you, really."

"I'll know better next time."

They saw that Rackham was eyeing them, and prudently they drifted apart. George turned back once. Rackham still was staring after him.

This camp abounded in shocks. Seeing them as he first

had, all besotted—and many were still drunk this morning —George Rounsivel would have assumed that these men would take at least a week to right, refit, and refloat the sloop *Agnes*. Yet they had it done by sunset. It was patent that there were no privileges where work was concerned. They all joined in. And they knew their ships, as they knew their guns. They might have been ignorant in many other respects, but these things they did know.

The farewell was curt, even savage.

"You're lucky we let you take the *Agnes*," Calico Jack said.

It was an opinion in which Charles Vane undoubtedly concurred.

"Well, I was never personal about these matters," Rackham went on. "You're a cowhearted rascal, that's sure, but you didn't try to use anything that belonged to me. So you can go. That's what I wouldn't ever want to happen," he continued, speaking very slowly, while his eyes went back and forth in search of the woman he worshipped. "I wouldn't want anybody to touch something that belongs to me—not ever."

The reason he had not been able to see Anne Bonney was that she was standing behind George on the outskirts of the crowd. George knew this when he felt her hand slip into his.

"Not ever," Rackham said again, swishing his cudgel.

Anne leaned close, so that George could feel her breath on his neck.

"They'll all get drunk tonight. Why don't we go to that same place again, as soon as the sun sets?"

The sloop *Agnes* was making for the pass, her rail lined with men who jeered and were jeered at. Obscenities flew Some of the pirates fired their muskets.

"Now d'ye know, that's a good idea," George whispered over his shoulder. "I'd admire very much to meet you there."

For he had, at last, a plan.

If these men were for the most part simple, easily moved to excesses of rage or grief, and as easily mollified, Calico Jack was an exception. He was complex. Not only could he read and write, he could even reason. He was a man to be watched.

George learned about Rackham from two sources: indirectly, Anne Bonney; directly, the king himself. And what he learned was disquieting.

Rackham had planned this action with care, biding his time, in constant conference with disaffected members of the gang. The details of the event that had brought about the overturn George Rounsivel did not know—something about a French ship that they had started to chase. In pursuit and in actual combat traditionally the captain of a pirate crew was supreme. In this particular case, though most of the men were eager to go for what looked like a rich prize, no vote was taken. Vane simply had decided against it. It was then that Jack Rackham struck, coming out into the open, insisting upon the general council that was held a few days after their arrival at Jorobado. And Rackham had won, as he knew he would. Charles Vane was vain indeed; he was harsh, grasping, unpleasant, and when it seemed that he was a coward as well, howsoever fleetingly, his doom was sealed.

His successor would not make that same mistake. Jack Rackham believed that he should expect no obedience from a man he couldn't whip. With pistol, knife, cutlass, or cudgel, even with his fists, Rackham was willing to fight at the drop of a sombrero. Not that he was a truculent character! Quick with a quip, a shoulder-slapper, he loved to sing, was willing to do his share of the work, and—though he was cautious here—he never *seemed* to refuse a drink. But he was the master. He wanted the men to know that, and know it they did.

Jack Rackham had one weakness, as George had surmised

even before the overthrow. In truth it was no secret. Subtle in many respects, in love he was a fool. He would become a different man when he spoke to Anne Bonney or even mentioned her name. Sometimes as the chief was conferring with George about the articles his voice would trail off and a faraway look would come upon his face. That meant that he had glimpsed Anne, who might have been strolling down the beach or brushing her hair. Then it was another Rackham, a man caught up in a dream, fatuous.

She, taking advantage of this, in time had done herself out of friends; for with a cat's fondness for torture, she strove to flirt with every man she saw—and was snubbed for the reason that they were all afraid of Calico Jack. Thus she was lonesome. She had swung her hips too often, and smiled provocatively too many times.

Jealousy must have hurt Calico Jack like a band of steel squeezing his ribs, making his eyes pop, closing his throat Maddened by the pain, he might do anything.

"Like to kill Andy Thompson, that afternoon on deck," a pirate told George. "Took four of us to peel him off."

"Don't you have enactments against felonious assault?"

"Huh?"

"Well, mayhem. Physiological attack. *Smashing somebody.*"

"Oh, that? Sure. But it's not a very strong article, and everybody's afraid to bring it up against Jack. They might get killed theirselves. Because the next one he *did* kill "

"Yes?"

"That was up at the Turks, where we was taking on wood. The party was in Jack's charge, and she went along with us."

"To stretch her legs, I suppose?"

"To wriggle her arse," the pirate snorted, though he lowered his voice when he did so. "And at poor Joey Bailt She got him behind a bush, somehow. I don't know what happened there. Nothing, most likely. *She* don't want to be hopped, really, she just wants to be fought over."

"And . . . was she?"

"Wasn't much of a fight, mister. We heard Rackham yell like an Injun, and by the time we got there he had Joey on the ground and was clouting him with that black stick of his. We didn't dare grab him that time. If you'd seen his face you'd know why. Maybe Joey was already dead by the time we got there. I hope so. Makes me feel less to blame. But he was sure dead right afterward anyway."

This amazed George, who had heard that pirates were sticklers for law, so long as they had made it themselves. Dueling was allowed, as it was among their betters; but this case sounded to Lawyer Rounsivel like one of unprovoked aggression.

"And Rackham wasn't tried?"

"We was afraid of him. Even Vane. Rackham claimed Joey had hit him first. We wasn't there when it started and we couldn't rightly say—to swear to it, that is."

"What about her?"

"Oh, she backed up Rackham, naturally." The pirate sank his voice still lower, leaning close. "*She's* the one ought to've got her head bashed in, you ask me."

And in less than an hour George would be meeting this woman again, for the fourth successive night, in the glade where first he'd seen her. How could he have known that Anne Bonney would prove such a perilous prize, that in their snatched moments together he would learn from her little about a lover who was available and accessible anyway?

Yet there was an undeniable thrill about those meetings in the glade. He did not delude himself about Anne Bonney. She was a bitch born. But she was a delectable bitch, a flame to quench.

It couldn't go on. Rackham, newly elected king, had made a practice of mixing jovially with his subjects at the end of each day of work. He was punctilious about this. But it couldn't last. Even though with his keen edge of suspicion he himself had not yet noticed anything out-of-the-way, somebody else was sure to do so, some bootlicker who would go to Rackham with the news. The wonder was that this hadn't happened already. George Rounsivel, spy, was in peril here anyway, among these outcasts. But now for certain he was walking the lip of a fiery crater. One slip—just one little slip—

"So she's a *femme fatale*, eh?"

"What was that?"

"French."

"Oh, no. She's Irish. Comes from Ireland."

At this time George, who was supposed to be recasting the articles of comradeship, instead was gazing down the beach at Anne Bonney. She came slowly toward them.

In butt-tight man's breeches, a breast-tight man's shirt, her feet bare, her hair down around her shoulders, she no longer played the brazen hussy. She had passed beyond that. She did not now carry her hands on her hips, her head high. Those hips needed no outlining. Her chin was low, her hands demurely folded, but as she walked, she was as feminine as ever. She had tasted human blood, and like a tigress she would not rest until she had tasted it again . . . and again . . . The circumspect manner, the puritan-clasped hands, deluded nobody, not even herself. Though she walked with eyes downcast she was aware that every man in the camp was watching her—and squirming.

"She's coming here," the pirate whispered. "Well, I got to see a dog about a man. I've noticed you eyeing her, mister. I'd keep out of her way, I was you."

"I sure will!"

George did not look up as she passed, though she walked within a few feet of where he sat writing.

"Don't forget—tonight," she whispered.

Still he did not look up. He gave an almost imperceptible nod.

A few minutes later there was a tap on his left elbow.

"Begging your pardon, sir?"

The pirates were mostly young men. Vane and Deal had been exceptions. Even Monk Evans, for all his fat, could not have been more than thirty. Calico Jack might have reached twenty-two. But the lad who accosted George was only that—a lad, perhaps fourteen. Such were not often permitted aboard of pirate vessels. Ashore, when havens like Port Royal and Trinidad and Samana were operating, the pirates could get all the women they wanted. But at sea there were long, hot, steamy stretches when the presence of a handsome cabin boy might wreck discipline. Many gangs stipulated against boys. A boy couldn't fight or work as well as a man, though he'd eat as much. The notion of a body servant was repellent to pirates, a determinedly democratic lot.

Peter Knight would not have caused a quarrel on the longest of voyages. He was lumpy, all knobs, his face awash with freckles. One eye squinted—it would have been better if both had. His hair, the color of damp hay, didn't look real. He was exceedingly short. He giggled a great deal, being half-witted. Perhaps that was why he had been taken into the band? A lunatic is supposed to bring good luck.

It occurred to George as he looked up from his writing —and a cold hand seemed to hold his throat at the thought— that such a boy would be used only to run errands for the captain or the quartermaster. One man held both those posts just now.

"You come from . . . Rackham?"

Peter had been gawping at the words on paper, which he found marvelous. Now, awkward, he essayed a sort of salute.

"Yes, sir From Captain Rackham. He wants to see you."

"Right away?"
"Right away."

The king wore his calico trousers and shirt, in blue and buff today, but he wore as well a salmon-colored silk drugget coat, and on his head was a huge tricorne. There were knives at his sash, and from each pocket the butt of a huge horse- or holster-pistol protruded. His hair was black, his eyes ice-green. His chin was blue.

He tossed George a negligent nod, greatly to George's relief. The monarch, then, was not in a rage. Rather he showed worried, an appearance he did nothing to hide.

"I thought we might go over those articles again."

Rackham's interest in the articles at first had baffled, then amused George Rounsivel, as he came to understand it. Even a man who had not read for the courts might marvel that ruffians who had deliberately placed themselves outside accepted conventions should insist upon having, nevertheless, a law of their own. They were *declared* thieves, avowed enemies of mankind. Having said to the rest of the world "Go to Hell!" they could not and did not expect any sort of sympathy. Yet law they must have, and the fancier the better. Each little group of cutthroats laboriously framed a constitution.

John Rackham was no fool. He knew that the men he led attached a disproportionate importance to the so-called articles of comradeship or fellowship. He himself could have drawn up such an agreement, being familiar with the custom. He might have done a better job of it than George. "But I want a lot of 'whereas's and 'hence's," he had pointed out.

George had reminded his master that any such constitution would have no standing, would be backed in world opinion by no precedent, emperor, king, parliament.

"It'll be backed by us. Now, you write it."

Whereupon George had scribbled a set of articles. But he'd done this so readily that Rackham, leery, scrutinized it with disapproval.

This was simple and perfectly clear. George always did strive to eschew polysyllables and anfractuosities of legal jargon, though obliged, on occasion, to signify to a client that some of those top-heavy phrases were put there for the purpose of protection and that it wasn't all the lawyer's fault.

Jack Rackham however had said that it wouldn't do at all.

"First-off, I don't like the way it says 'one' and 'two' and 'three' and so on, with just figures. It ought to be 'Firstly' and 'Secondly' and 'Thirdly'. You change that."

So George had changed it.

He changed too the word "booty" to "share-out," which a shocked chieftain told him was the proper expression.

Then Rackham objected to the use of "band," a word he considered crude. He would substitute "association."

"And while you're at it, why can't you make it 'aforementioned association'?"

"Well, for one thing we haven't mentioned it before."

"Well, mention it then!"

Rackham squawked also at "lashed." Too harsh.

"Flogged?"

"That has a nasty sound too. Why can't you say 'Such a miscreant shall receive Moses' Law'?"

"What's that?"

"Forty stripes lacking one, on the bare back."

"Why do they call it Moses' Law?"

"I don't know. But never mind that. Put it in."

Thus it went, a collaboration rather than an editing of this precious paper. George must have made a dozen drafts, and still Calico Jack had faults to find, complexities to insert.

For four days, whenever Jack Rackham had a little time to spare he summoned George for consultation about the articles. And George soon came to see that this was not all a propensity for the pompous. The talks were held on the open beach, within sight of the work being done on the sloop *John and Elizabeth,* now careened. These pirates, despite their high-sounding phrases about the Brotherhood of the Coast and everlasting friendship, did not like to let their fellow pirates out of sight.

The editorial discussions, then, being public, polished the king's prestige. Rackham knew that, and took advantage of it. His literacy had struck with awe the hearts of his subjects, but to be properly appreciated it had to be seen in action. Here on the beach the great Calico Jack not only reviewed the work done by a Philadelphia lawyer, a member of the bar, but even learnedly—and audibly—pointed out mistakes and commanded their correction. This all helped Rackham in his position.

Again, the longer the pirates waited for the list, and the more fuss they saw made, the likelier they were to abide by the compact when at last they had sworn to it.

That was the rite George Rounsivel dreaded. He gathered from overheard talks that they made much of it, that each participant took the oath solemnly and separately. George knew that in the eyes of the law all pirates were *Hostis humani generis*—that is, outlaws, by definition enemies of the human race—so that no contract entered into with them would have standing, no agreement, verbal or otherwise, would be valid. But this did little to ease his conscience. The law after all was not everything.

He sought to postpone the event of signing. This was one reason why he submitted so meekly to all of Jack Rackham's editorial meddling. The matter couldn't be drawn out too long for George.

He did not reproach himself for his decision at the fort.

Not only his neck had been at stake, but also his honor. Unless he did Woodes Rogers' bidding he would be branded a pirate.

George's common sense, then, told him that he was doing the right thing. But how would he feel after swearing eternal obedience to these ridiculous laws he himself had concocted and eternal fidelity to scoundrels he despised?

It was for this reason that his heart quopped softly when Rackham, after a long look at the latest draft, nodded affably.

"I think that's about right now. Make me up a fair copy, and we'll have the swearing-in tomorrow morning."

George swallowed hard, looking down.

"I . . . I suppose you'll want me to read the thing aloud? And I'll write down the names and show 'em where to make their marks?"

"You won't be here," Jack Rackham said.

George looked up quickly. The king was gazing at his sweetheart, and in his eyes was that light of tenderness that shone so strangely there—but only in these circumstances.

"What do you mean?" George asked.

Anne Bonney had passed from sight, and her lover, relieved, spat into the sand, a man again.

"Rounsivel, you're not known in Nassau, are you?"

George shrugged.

"A few turnkeys, the governor, and," more softly, "the governor's niece. That's about all—excepting the sailors who took up from Hornigold's sloop to the fort."

"D'ye know Ben Hornigold himself?"

"He asked us some questions, but I wouldn't say anything. I wanted to see the governor and explain that I wasn't a pirate."

Rackham nodded absently, not even troubling to sneer. It had been plain from the beginning that he did not believe George's story of having been kidnapped. Nobody seemed to believe it.

"Why do you ask this?"

"Rounsivel, we've got to get a base. We can't *eat* bales of silk, can we? Where's the fun in going to bed with bullion? This gang will go mad if they don't get some women soon. It ain't a natural life, Rounsivel, a life like this. We have to be established somewhere."

George nodded.

"And you're thinking of taking Nassau?"

"Thinking of it. But it'll have to be soon. This man Rogers means business. He's proved that already. Now . . . tell me about that fort."

George told what he could, not much, though such as it was, it was good hearing for Jack Rackham.

"There's nobody I have that ain't known in every rumshop there," Rackham remarked, "excepting you. If you was to stay away from the fort, where they might recognize you—"

"Great God! You mean you're asking me to go back to a place where they were going to hang me only last week?"

"The more reason why nobody would look for you there. And I could give you the name of a man who can be trusted. John Hay could ferry you over in that periagua Monk Evans left. We've stepped a mast into it. John wouldn't go ashore, of course. He'd just arrange a rendezvous with you, to bring you back. And you'd both get an extra quarter-share in the next prize, by order of the captain."

"I see. And, uh, when had you planned to launch this little expedition?"

"Well, if you was to start right now John could get you there before daybreak. He's a smart sailor."

George looked away, to keep Rackham from seeing the joy that must have leapt into his face. He would escape the ceremony! He could make his way quietly to Governor Rogers and give a report on the pirates' strength and plans It was almost too good to be true. He rose, hands clasped before him so that their trembling would not show.

"It'll be damn' dangerous, you understand?" Captain Rackham said.

"I don't doubt that."

John Hay was uncommunicative. A wasp, small, mean, he made only one thing clear: that he had no thought of stepping ashore on New Providence, where, George deduced, there were those who did not like him.

"I'll stand off," he said. "I'll be a fisherman."

George wondered how anybody could hope to be mistaken for a fisherman in so frail a craft as this periagua, but he said nothing. Instead he watched Hay handle the boat.

Hay had raised New Providence, a mere blur, and made for it like a bee for the hive. What caused George to marvel was the ease and certainty with which the little man selected the very part of the south shore he wanted, picking it from that murky jungle as readily as he might have picked a peach from a basket.

This was the same spot from which Monk Evans and George had pushed off a week ago—a shallow cove grandiosely called Boar's Bay.

There was no sand, only tidal muck. More important, there were no houses nearby. Nobody would see George scramble ashore.

Using a paddle, Hay made for the screened entrance of the "bay," and the only word he threw George, over a reluctant shoulder, was: "Right here any time after sundown."

"What'll I do if I can't find you?"

"Whistle. But you'll find me."

"But see here, suppose that—"

But Hay had gone. And George Rounsivel was alone.

He felt in fact most *emphatically* alone. He shivered, and set forth.

When he had crossed this island on foot in the company of Monk Evans a week ago, he had carefully remarked the way. Of course he couldn't recall every step; but as he emerged from the morass-like thicket that bordered Boar's Bay, and looked around at a landscape lit by the earliest rays of the sun and straked with columns of smoke, he had no doubt that he could find his way to Nassau.

There were no roads, not even drift-lanes. There were not many houses, and those were widely spaced and like everything else on this island of a *temporary* aspect, jerry-built, each being no more than a rickle of sticks with a palmetto-thatched roof.

George made a point of avoiding even such houses as did present themselves. He kept walking but never ran, and though he refrained from turning and twisting his head his eyes were always busy. He would not show furtive, even from afar. He must look as if he knew what he was doing.

It was his intention to go directly to Government House and to present himself to Woodes Rogers as unobtrusively as possible. He believed that he had already fulfilled the pardon requirements, but he had no wish for complications on the way. After all, he could be shot on sight.

If he was alert, if he was wary, he was at the same time in a state of amazement. It occurred to him yet again on that long rough walk that his associates and clients at home, could they see him now, would not believe it.

What had happened to that tall grave young man from Philadelphia who dressed so carefully? Where had he gone? The fugitive who slinked across New Providence this morning in no way resembled him. George's face was so scorched by the sun, and his light brown eyebrows so bleached, that his mouth must have shown like a knife-slash, while his dark blue eyes gleamed bright. The backs of his hands were a furious red. His head itched, again from the sun. That duck-fuzz, his hair, was growing in, but gingerly; the raffish raffia hat tickled his scalp. That hat, the one

Monk Evans had passed him, was the most incongruous touch of all.

Here then was Mr. Lawyer Rounsivel, he of the impeccable manners, the irreproachable past—an overgrown ragamuffin now, a stuffed Guy Fawkes, a scarecrow, a buffoon.

He did not carry a sword. There were ten or a dozen court swords on Hunchback Key, and George might have had his pick of them for this mission, but he refrained . . . for two reasons. He had tested them all and didn't like any, for he was fussy about swords. More important, the carrying of such a weapon, as distinguished from cutlass or ordinary hanger, indicated a gentleman. There were precious few gentlemen, or even men who tried to look like gentlemen, at Nassau in the Bahamas. George would not call attention to himself.

He had in truth no weapon at all, save his wits.

Thus it was that in the middle of that morning, the promising young barrister, scarlet-faced, covered with dust, strode into Nassau and made straight for Government House.

This pretentiously named structure was the only two-story building in the Bahamas, excepting the captain's tower at the fort. It was also the only one that had ever been painted. Square, stolid, in color a liverish brown, it stood in the very center of the town, surrounded by a small and not notably private garden. It was also surrounded, unexpectedly, by a trim white picket fence.

The governor would be either there or at the fort. Government House was the nearer of these two places. It was also, for George, the less perilous. At Fort Nassau he might be recognized by guards.

To the left of the gate stood a bulletin board, a somewhat ambitious thing, since there were no publications in the Bahamas, where seldom any ship put in with mail, and most of the residents were unlettered anyway.

Two militiamen guarded the gate, one on each side. George

glanced at them but once, and decided that he had nothing
to fear. In the first place they were in a fluster of self-con-
sciousness and not likely to pick individual faces out of the
crowd, and in the second place they were new recruits,
such oafs as would not have been permitted even to do guard
duty at Fort Nassau.

George walked past them to the bulletin board.

It contained but a single item, and that limp and torn,
having been washed by rains, baked in the sun, a pathetic
thing. It was a copy of the King's proclamation "for Sup-
pressing of Pyrates" dated 15 September, 1717, applicable
until 5 January, 1719. It had almost expired—this was but
two days before Christmas—and no doubt the intention was to
keep it in full and fair sight until that time.

"Whereas we have received Information, that several persons, Subjects of GREAT BRITAIN, have, since the 24th
Day of June, in the Year of our Lord, 1715, committed
divers Pyracies and Robberies upon the High Sea, in the
West Indies or adjoining our Plantations, which hath and
may Occasion great Damage to the Merchants of GREAT
BRITAIN and others trading in those Parts . . . we do
hereby promise and declare, that in Case any of the said
Pyrates surrender him or themselves, to one of our Planta-
tions beyond the Seas, every such Pyrate or Pyrates. . . .
And we do hereby strictly charge and command all our
Admirals, Captains, and other Officers at Sea, and all our
Governors and Commanders of any Forts, Castles, or other
Places in our Plantations, and all our Officers, Civil and
Military, to seize and take such of the Pyrates, who shall
refuse or neglect to surrender themselves accordingly. . . .
God save the King!"

George shrugged. A man beside him also shrugged.

"Not good much longer, eh?" the other observed.

"No."

It was then that George noticed that the proclamation

wasn't alone on that bulletin board after all. Lower down, and much less conspicuous, was a small written notice to the effect that a reward of £50 would be given for the person (dead or alive) of the escaped pirate GEORGE ROUNSIVEL. No questions, it was added, would be asked.

"They hold me cheap," George muttered.

"What's that?"

"Nothing." George glanced up at the house, the front door of which was being opened from the inside. "You wouldn't happen to know whether Governor Rogers is here now or is he at the fort?"

"The governor? The captain-general? Oh, he's not here at all."

"Oh?"

"He sailed a couple of hours ago for a visit to some of the other islands. Won't be back for four-five days."

"I see."

"The man that's acting governor—why, here he is now, coming out through that door, coming toward us Captain Robinson his name is. Thomas Robinson. And if you was to ask me—"

The man turned, having become aware that he was alone, and he scowled indignantly after a fast-retreating back.

"Now that was bloody rude of him," he said.

CHAPTER VI

A PASSENGER on the *Barkus* brig, a man who on a previous voyage had sailed into Nassau Bay, once described this town as resembling "five or six acres of unmade bed." The description had amused George, who however at the time put it down to a desire to *be* amusing. Now George granted its accuracy.

The settlement that sprawled near Fort Nassau was sloppy; it was disheveled, and it was, truly, like a just-left bed, permeated by the flat stale odor of sweat and skin many times magnified.

Though startled, George was not unduly dismayed to learn that Woodes Rogers was away. True, it was a possibility that had not occurred to him, for he did not think that the governor of so explosive a colony would stir from his home base, at least at first. But George had another string to his bow. He wasn't cornered, yet.

Jack Rackham had given him the name of a person, one Ellison, who was to be trusted. If anything went wrong, if George needed advice or assistance, or for that matter a hiding-place, he should seek out Peter Ellison. That was all. There was no estate name, no street name even. But everybody knew Pete Ellison. Just ask for him.

George did.

The first man did not answer at all, but scurried away like an almost-stepped-on crab. The second rubbered out his lips, lowered his head, seized the loose of his chin between thumb and forefinger before he spoke.

"What d'ye want of him?"

Smiling, George refused this information. The man nodded sadly, as though he had expected such a refusal. At last he jerked a thumb toward the south edge of the town, up a slope.

"Next to the last hut on the right," he said, and hurried away.

Chez Ellison was no mansion. Its uprights were coconut trunks stuck into the sandy earth, its roof thatch, its walls in part dark rough splintery porous shingles of the sort that in Pennsylvania would have been called "shakes," and in part plain tarpaulin, which was not in good condition. A stiff breeze would have blown it down. There was about it an air of desolation and decay. The fireplace in front was cold.

When George rapped on the jamb—there was no door—he was answered by a grunt of annoyance. Then:

"Who is it?"

George called: "Peter Ellison live here?"

The grunt this time was one of astonishment. Something that might have been a bottle clacked upon something that might have been a table, and a chair squeaked.

The curtain was pushed aside, revealing a man in the uniform of the governor's guard. George had often seen this soldier at the fort.

"Now look here—"

He was very large, slovenly, and not a little drunk. He surveyed George with small, red-rimmed, piggish eyes.

"What do you want of Ellison?" he grumbled.

"No, no, not Ellison. I said Jameson. Peter Jameson."

The soldier wiped his mouth with a hairy hand, but all the while he kept staring at George. He seemed to be puzzled by something far back in his fussy memory, something muffled in rum fumes.

Rackham had been right. Nobody would think of meeting an escaped felon so near to the scene of his escape. All the same, this man was beginning to believe, if groggily, that he had seen George somewhere before. His mouth slacked open, but the deep-set eyes were gimlets.

Jack Rackham had been right too about his friend Ellison, and probably *too* right. It occurred to George, thinking fast, that Ellison had got into trouble with the colonial authorities. Something must have happened recently, to explain the way the mention of his name had been received. No doubt the guardsman had been posted here to arrest anybody who came looking for Peter Ellison, and he had whiled away his time with Ellison's rum. But his head was clearing. He took hold of George's sleeve.

"Ellison'll be back pretty soon. Come in and have a drink."

George Rounsivel's politeness was instinctive, not simply acquired, and he knew that though it was bad manners to refuse a drink anywhere it was especially serious in some blistered outpost like Nassau. All the same he snatched himself free, laughing an apology. He was mortally sure that the guardsman sought to detain him only so that he could study George's face, fumbling in his memory for a clue.

"Sorry," he cried. "I've got to get this man Jameson. It's important. Captain Robinson's orders."

And he started down the slope toward the bay.

He walked rapidly, resisting an impulse to run. He was tense, expecting at any instant to hear footsteps behind him.

The soldier did call "Hey, you! Hey, come back here!" but George kept walking, pretending that he had not heard.

At the waterfront he turned into the nearest rumshop. He was hungry. Also, he thought it might be well to keep cover for a while.

The place was called Mahogany Charley's, and clearly it was one of the fancier establishments, for there were four tables, a counter for standing-drinking, and no fewer than five women. There had even been a certain attempt at decoration—twisted strips of red and green paper hanging from the ceiling and bunched into rosettes here and there around the walls. The rum—there was nothing else to drink—was so-so; but the house specialty, boiled turtle eggs with pimento sauce served on biscuit soaked in goat's milk, was excellent. George sat in a corner, having brushed the bawds away.

It was nearing noon and he'd accomplished nothing, yet he was not discouraged. He believed that, given reasonable luck, and if he kept away from the fort, he would be safe enough. True, the situation had its somber side. The news that Robinson was in command had been a blow. Except for Robinson, George might have surrendered himself anyway, trusting to the deputies to hold him until Woodes Rogers' return. But Robinson, given this particular prisoner, would hang him out of hand.

George was sure of this. He had seen Thomas Robinson for not more than two minutes, but they say that there is no better way to get acquainted with a man's essential nature than by crossing steel with him.

This was a time of crisis. The Bahamas were under martial law. The commanding officer on New Providence could do away instantly with a convicted pirate, an escapee, and he would. He'd even have as excuse, when the governor came back, that he had acted in an emergency—that it would have been poor military policy to permit such a dangerous prisoner to remain alive when the news of his incarceration was all over town and might raise a mob.

As George saw it, the best thing for him to do was wait until nightfall, remaining as unobtrusive as possible. Then he would set forth for Boar's Bay and the periagua. The distance was about seven miles, but the way was not rocky or steep, and after the sun had gone down it might even be rather pleasant. He would whistle for John Hay and return to Jorobado.

He had gone voluntarily to the pirates' camp in the first instance, and voluntarily he would return. If he had not been present at the oath-taking this morning it was only because of the command of the king. He could tell Calico Jack that a single day at Nassau was not enough. He could readily explain his immediate return. John Hay, not notified, might have loitered too long in or just off Boar's Bay, and been captured. The governor's absence had caused a shift in the routine, making it awkward for George to get military intelligence. The arrest or near-arrest of Ellison (here he would be guessing, but it would be an informed guess, a shrewd one) had caused a stir among possible pirates, resulting immediately in a tendency to look hard at every stranger. And there were other excuses. George was sure he could talk Rackham into giving him the same assignment again, a week hence, when Woodes Rogers would have come back.

Meanwhile he would drift from rumshop to rumshop, drinking as little and overhearing as much as ever he could.

Mahogany Charley's was too popular a place for George's purposes. George paid his chit and left.

As he'd guessed, there were few secrets in this town. Everybody knew that the governor had gone away for a few days, but they did not curse him as vehemently as they did the captain of his guard. Most of them were angered or frightened by the execution of eight members of the Augur gang, whose bodies, George was gratified to note, had been cut down. Nobody even mentioned George himself. Charles Vane often was spoken of. News of the change-over of power had not yet reached Nassau, where indeed George gathered that nobody dreamed of the pirates being as close as Jorobado.

On one subject sure to be of interest to Jack Rackham, the fortifications, George was fairly flooded with data. It appeared that Woodes Rogers, desperate, all his arts of persuasion having failed, had used his extraordinary power to call up laborers. Indignation over this was noisy, yet, many of the complainants nevertheless had gone to work. From their wailing George learned a great deal about this work.

Thus it was that when the shadows were long and the sun low George Rounsivel felt that he had not wasted his afternoon. There were any number of small rumshops that he had been able to enter and leave without fuss, working his way gradually from the water front up to the southern edge of town, the edge nearest the shore to which he meant to go. He planned to leave this place just as quietly. He called for his total.

It was then that he became conscious of somebody looking at him, looking hard. It was a curious feeling. It shook him. He *had* to lift his head from the total. He *had* to lift his eyes.

Directly before him, not ten feet away, sat Monk Evans. The instant he saw George's face he sprang to his feet.

"That's him! That's Rounsivel! Grab him!"

George was granted no time in which to piece this together. Men were leaping up, their mouths open, as they reached for knives or cutlasses. Monk Evans, cheeks purpling, dewlaps atremble, stabbed with an accusatory arm.

"It's Rounsivel, I tell you! There's fifty pounds reward for him!"

This was madness, a scene of insanity. George as he rose swept the stool from under him and hurled this at Monk Evans, and then he ran for the door.

Luck, not forethought, had placed him near that door. He was in the open before anybody could put a hand on him.

There his luck ran out.

The cooking pits of Nassau were as helter-skelter as any other feature of the town. Invariably they were outside of the habitations, some before, some behind. At a given time there were always fires, for regularity of eating was not the custom. Just now, just after the click of sunset, there was a prodigious number of them. Charcoal spat softly, wood snipped, and as sparks went toward heaven smoke swirled lazily. The street in which George found himself was lighter than it had been twenty minutes before, when he quitted it.

To his left, south, the direction in which he had intended to turn, he saw four large gawky sailors. They might have been drunk. Certainly they were startled, and like one man they snicked out their knives.

He did not dare to try to plunge through them. Instead he whirled about and ran down the slope toward the bay.

"They hold me cheap," George had said before the bulletin board. He was mistaken. Fifty pounds was a lot of money in a Nassau whose inhabitants had been deprived of an easy if illegal way of living, and forced to work instead. *Fifty pound!* He heard it right and left, back and forth, as he ran. *Fifty quid!* The news went faster than he could, spreading out in all directions. *Catch him! He's worth money!*

Behind George they massed, and increased; the roar grew louder. On either side as he sped down toward the bay he saw in the jumpy light of fires men who leapt to their feet or popped out of tents and huts. Their teeth gleamed, their eyes glittered as they joined the chase.

Ahead too the mob-sound rose. The waterfront hells were emptying, and men swarmed up the slope.

He might plead. He might throw himself to his knee, babbling for mercy, crying out that he knew Rackham, that he'd all but been hanged with John Augur. It was not likely that they'd heed, or even hear. They were ravening, and reason was not in them.

For a split-second he was alone. He stopped, his heart beating furiously, body all soggy with sweat. A hare, not merely *pursued* by yammering hounds but actually *surrounded* by them, he knew panic.

He swung sharply to the left, and began again to run.

He came upon a low white picket fence. Government House! This must be a side of it, the side toward the fort. With no hesitation he vaulted the fence and dropped to the ground behind an oleander bush.

Logic, if it had been absent, gratefully returned. This, he told himself, was the same lion's-mouth tactic that he had planned, though in reverse. The garden of Government House would be the last place a mob would seek an escaped prisoner.

The building behind him was touched by a dab of light only here and there, and it was quiet. He saw no sentries.

The earth smelled damp and clean, a good smell. He pressed his cheek against it, panting.

His ears told him that the two main groups had met halfway down the slope. Doubtless they were comparing notes, learning that the quarry had somehow slipped away from between them. They would fan out, then, to curry the whole settlement.

It had been George's hope to get behind one of those irregular groups and to slip unnoticed into their midst, later to lose himself when the excitement subsided. It was not probable that anybody save Monk Evans really knew George on sight; and Monk—George could hear his strident voice over there, urging the search ahead—could not be everywhere at once. On the surface George Rounsivel was not remarkably different from many another who rampaged here tonight except for one thing: He had no weapon.

In the daytime this hadn't mattered, for others would suppose that he carried a knife or pistol beneath his coat. Now it would make him stand out. Tonight any man who ventured abroad in Nassau was taking his life into his hands if he didn't have a weapon there.

George looked around. Even a club might do. A picket from the fence? But they had felt sturdy when he vaulted that fence, and to rip one off would make a noise—an *immediate* noise, a *near* one, as distinguished from the mumble of the mob—that might bring soldiers.

The garden was not large, the space between fence and house at this point being no more than twenty feet. George indeed was lying almost directly beneath a projecting part of the house, a sort of small low Spanish balcony, the railing of which was overgrown by a stout vine. The French windows to this balcony stood wide-open, and the space beyond seemed dark.

The cries, the jumble of voices, the thud of running feet, grew nearer . . . and nearer . . .

George climbed the vine to the balcony.

The window, it developed, was covered by two sets of blinds overlapping where they touched. The slats were tilted upward on the outside. This was why he had not been able to see the light from the ground. He could see it now from the top of the railing, and it disconcerted him. Also, he heard voices. He tried to crawl back. A heel caught in the vine. He fell.

He landed on his feet, but he was windmilling his arms to catch his balance, and in this way he burst like a hurricane between the two sets of blinds and into the room beyond.

The blinds clacked back into place behind him, but he didn't hear this, for he stood transfixed by what he saw.

"Well, I'll be God damned," he muttered.

The room was high-ceilinged, as are so many rooms in the lands where architects know the need to catch each vagrant breeze. It was square, its floor smooth and well waxed, the ceiling white, the walls cream. Government House, George had been told, was in part an administrative building, and in part the residence of the captain-general. What George had burst into must have belonged to this latter section. Some attempt had been made to make it resemble a chamber in Woodes Rogers' own Bristol. Only at one end was there an exotic touch—a teakwood chair that had a Spanish colonial look about it, and above that, on the wall, a panoply consisting of a wierdly tinted leather target that must have come from some cannibal island, with two long crossed cavalry sabers above it, and below it a cluster of small curved daggers, all, obviously, souvenirs of the governor's celebrated trip around the world. The rest of the furniture was domestic, inexorably plain, homey.

It was the two persons in the room who had caused George

Rounsivel to gasp. They were face to face, near a table with candles, and they had been quarreling.

Delicia Rogers stood very straight. There was nothing on her head, nothing to decorate that tight-fitting dark hair, which indeed needed no decoration. There was a small diamond in each earlobe, but no ornament around her neck. Her arms were bare, the shoulders too, and George, looking at them, wondered why he had never suspected their existence when the rather prissily clad governor's niece brought flowers to the felons at the fort. They made up a breath-taking ensemble. Below them swept a gown of pink silk with variegated leaflike figures over a blue silk hooped petticoat. The skirt was open, and pinked at the edges. He could not, of course, see her slippers.

It was her attitude that told the most. She was a bowstring just touched, as taut as that, quivering. The two spots of crimson high on her cheeks were caused not by rouge, and her eyes hurled poniards at her companion.

Thomas Robinson a little while ago had been much at his ease, as was attested by his plumed hat and cloak, together with his sword and swordbelt, which were folded on a chair at his side. He was not at his ease now. He had stepped back in rage and mortification. On his left jaw, the one toward George, shone a bright red imprint about the size and shape of a woman's hand.

George's urge was to laugh. He stifled this. Yet the setting was undeniably ludicrous, and what had happened was as plain as a pikestaff. The elegant captain of the guard had tried to take advantage of his chief's absence to seduce the said chief's relative—and had been most ignominiously repulsed.

"Forgiveness," George murmured as he swept into a bow, making a leg, holding that absurd straw hat over his heart as he looked upon the floor, for he knew that Delicia would not care to be grinned at.

George could not pose as a gallant rescuer. The girl was not in the slightest trouble, and surely would have known what to do in those circumstances even if she had not been able to summon with one scream a dozen servants. But she was embarrassed.

It was George Rounsivel who stood in peril. He could hardly hope to get back between those jalousies, nor yet past Robinson, without being skewered.

"Forgiveness," he said again. "*Any* intrusion would have been unmannerly, but this one is positively gauche."

Robinson whooped. He slapped his hip.

"*Gut me, he's fallen right into my lap!*"

"Not so, captain," cried George, and ran to the other end of the room.

He jumped on the teakwood chair, reached into the panoply, wrenched out one of the sabers, and hopped back to the floor again.

Robinson had drawn. His point was firm, his guard high.

Delicia, not from prudence but in astonishment, had stepped back a little. Her hands went to her breast.

"*Defend yourself, sir!*"

George attacked.

It was ridiculous, preposterous. The blade he wielded was very long and heavy—it was meant to be swung from the back of a horse—and against even a poor fencer he could not have prevailed. But what did he have to lose? He slashed the air wildly, advancing.

It is said that the best swordsman in the world would not fear to meet the second-best swordsman, but he might well be afraid to meet the *twentieth*-best. He wouldn't know what that fellow might do. Thomas Robinson assuredly was not afraid, but he required a chance to think. So he sprang back, his guard still high. His left foot jarred the table on which the candle-branch rested. The branch wobbled, the lighted candle in it swaying. Delicia screamed. Robinson broke his guard position to put out his left hand and steady the table. And George Rounsivel, laughing, ran out of the room.

"Another time, captain," he called.

From the doorway he threw a kiss to Delicia.

He slammed the door behind him.

He found himself in a large and well-lighted entry hall. On his right was a big door that might have been the main outside one. Before him was a smaller door that could have led to offices, while on his left was a flight of stairs. There was nobody in sight.

The stairs were the way they would least expect him to take. He went up, three at a time.

He found a window, opened it, put the saber between his teeth, wriggled over the sill, clung by his fingertips for a breath, praying that he wouldn't twist an ankle—and dropped.

A minute later he was making himself part of one of the wild little groups that cluttered the town, while he swung the saber fiercely.

"Where is that rat?" he screamed. "I'll kill him!"

Ten minutes later he was leaving town.

CHAPTER VII

IT IS A MATTER to marvel at, what the human body can endure. Noon was near, the next morning, before George Rounsivel let himself collapse to the bottom of the boat, willing at last to die.

He had found Boar's Bay easily enough—but not Hay. There still had been some moonlight then, though it was wishy-washy stuff, and he could see that no periagua floated there. He had been about to whistle when he heard a footstep. A man had passed, not twelve feet away, sidling wraithlike through a column of moonlight. This man had been roughly dressed, and in his hand he held a huge horse pistol. The pistol had been cocked.

A moment later George had heard a sibilant whisper somewhere near at hand, and then a click, a small sharp metallic sound that might have been the cocking of another firearm.

He believed, though he could not be sure, that the man he had glimpsed was the same who had been seated beside Monk Evans in the rumshop early that evening. From this he could deduce what had happened. Evans had given up the hunt in Nassau, guessing that George had somehow slipped out of town and would make for Boar's Bay. So he had summoned a few companions and made for the south shore. Knowing the way better than George did, and not being obliged to avoid farmhouses, they had reached the place first.

George had made his way out of the thicket for a mile or so along the shore in an easterly direction. He had come upon nobody, nor any sort of habitation, when he stumbled over the dugout.

It was very small and looked rotten. It contained only half a calabash, presumably for bailing purposes, and a barrel stave. An uninviting vehicle, but George had not hesitated. Monk Evans and his friends at any moment might be pushing east and west along the shore, if they had not already started. So he had shoved off. It had not even occurred to him to cast about for fresh water.

At first he had been too eager to get out of gunshot to feel dismay at the sight of the fading stars. Indeed he had even been pleased when the moon, completely smogged by clouds, at last had gone out: this would make it harder to see him from the beach.

The stave was a clumsy paddle, and the blisters on his

palms, scarcely healed in the week since he had made this trip with the irascible Evans, swelled again, and broke, stinging him.

Coming across with John Hay the previous night, he had studied the stars, and he believed that he could find his way back alone. After all, Cayo Jorobado was scarcely more than over the horizon from the eastern tip of New Providence.

What he had not taken into account was an absence of stars. The ones he had marked in memory, the ones high in the sky, had been missing from the beginning, and those near the horizon soon blinked out as well, leaving nothing but a low ugly dirt-gray, once the moon was gone. George could not even see any light behind him, on New Providence.

He was lost.

Nevertheless, and even at the risk of moving in a circle, he had kept the dugout in motion. It had been his hope that by taking one stroke on the right side, then one on the left, putting the same force into each, he would keep moving in the same general direction.

At that, he had done well enough until the rain started.

It could not be said simply to have rained, as it might have done in any proper place, such as Philadelphia. Rather the surface of the sea was lashed, now this way, now that, as an ambidextrous bosun's mate who is laying lashes on some poor devil's back crosses his cuts by switching the cat from one hand to the other. There was the same satanic deliberation about these rains. They were jumpy, jerky, and remorseless. Sometimes they'd stop altogether. Sometimes George could hear a storm coming, whether from right or left, from before or behind, announcing itself by a tinny clatter; but other showers appeared to come from directly above, and were upon him, engulfing him, before he could catch up his breath.

He had started to shiver, and kept up the paddling only in a half-hearted way to keep warm.

The dugout did not leak, but a few minutes of such rain half-filled the small round-bottomed boat. It wouldn't have sunk, of course, being wooden; but unless he kept it empty he'd have a hard time propelling it. As far as his own person was concerned, he was as wet as he could be. He was more concerned about his thirst, which was furious, scratching him (and it was a measure of his light-headedness that he never realized, at the time, that he was bailing out quarts and gallons of good rain water). He would hold his face up, his mouth open, and catch a drop now and then, though it had seemed as though the air was solid with water. He held out the calabash too, and caught a little in this, but it was brackish stuff from the bailing, and made him retch.

He did not know when the dawn came. His ears rang with the clang of rain that had some time ago ceased, when groggily he became aware that it was day.

There wasn't a thing in sight, not so much as a sea gull.

He bailed again, clearing the boat. He paddled for a while.

The sun came up. From the beginning it was hot, savage. It seared him. His clothes started to steam. He did not dare to take any of those clothes off. Fortunately he still had his raffia hat.

It was then that he began to have the fainting spells. There was nothing dramatic about them. He simply found himself, from time to time, with his head between his knees, or sprawled halfway across the thwarts. The spells sapped his strength; he was babbling like a man in delirium; his thirst was horrid.

It was when he had pulled himself out of one such swoon and couldn't find the paddle that he gave up. The thing must have fallen overside. He might have been unconscious for half an hour, an hour. With eyes that throbbed from the reflection of the sun on the sea, he scanned the water all around his boat. There was no sign of the paddle.

He quit. He slumped over backward, not caring about anything any more. He tilted the raffia hat over his face.

Not until that hat was removed did he know that anybody had been near at hand. If there had been any shout he hadn't heard it.

"Oh . . ." he said, blinking.

He was gazing into the small sardonic face of John Hay.

"Trying to kill yourself?"

"I . . . I guess I was."

Hay, no stranger to these parts, had a flask of water, and he passed this to George before George could ask for it. Later he helped George to get into the periagua. But the saber flabbergasted him.

"What's this?"

"It belongs to the governor," George mumbled. "I . . . I borrowed it."

Hay seemed unsure of himself, which was not like him. He studied George, his brow corrugated with perplexity, and twice he looked back toward New Providence, as if he couldn't believe what he saw. George was too dazed to pay him much heed.

George took another long drink of water, and then he curled up on the bottom of the periagua, in the shade of the sail.

The distance between the two islands must have been greater than he had calculated, or else he had gotten far off his course. At any rate, it was at the very edge of sunset when at last they nosed into the small bay on the north side of Cayo Jorobado.

The camp was strangely quiet. Few were preparing dinner, as ordinarily would be the case at this hour.

They stared at John Hay and his charge. Hay seemed uneasy.

"Where's Jack?"

"Here he comes now. He's been talking to Anne Bonney."

"With a razor strop," somebody added.

Calico Jack Rackham did not have his usual swagger as he approached. His eyes were fire, his mouth a steel-toothed trap.

"I think I have an interesting report, captain," George said.

Rackham ignored this, glaring at Hay.

"I told you to leave this man on Providence!"

"I did, Jack. But he found some foreigner's tub and started back this way on his lonesome. I spotted him this morning. I couldn't let him stay that way. So . . . I brought him back."

Rackham nodded abruptly.

"I'm glad you did," he said.

He turned to George Rounsivel.

"I told Hay to leave you there because I didn't like the way you was looking at Anne."

George wetted his lips, but said nothing.

Rackham drew a breath that might have been flame, scorching his lungs. When he moved at all it was with the stiffness of a marionette.

"But I'm glad they brought you back anyway, because I've been talking to Anne, just now, and she tells me that you and her—"

His voice was rising, a screech. His face was so dark a red as to be almost black, and huge blue-purple veins pounded at his temples.

"That you and her—that the two of you—"

Then he sprang.

He was swinging a cudgel as he came, and George jumped back, raising his arms.

Somebody seized Jack Rackham, as somebody at the same time seized George, from behind.

Rackham raved, gibbering. He struggled. George even thought that he saw a fleck of foam at each corner of the man's mouth.

"*Trice him up! Tie him to the muzzle of that cannon over there!*"

Men began to jostle and hustle George toward the cannon, a brass twelve-pounder, one of those taken from the sloop when she was about to be careened. Others got rope.

"What're you going to do with him, Jack?"

"I'm going to blow him in half, that's what I'm going to do! I'm going to blow the middle right out of him!"

They were afraid of Rackham. Even while he struggled in their arms, as he cursed George, they were afraid of him.

What startled George, was the realization that they were also afraid of *him*.

Yet they went about their preparations.

With a long brass conical-ended ladle they slid a pile of powder into the cannon, and, turning the ladle, left it there. They tamped this home with ram and rag. But they didn't shot it. They stood George so that the cold metal mouth was pressed against his back. They tied his ankles separately to the wheels, and his arms they extended behind him, fastening the wrists to lines that they passed through the trunnions, afterward making them fast beneath the barrel. But all the while they seemed frightened. It was as though they feared that George, rather than the cannon, might explode.

They even—under their breaths—begged his pardon.

He offered no response. The sensational nature of the act made it hard, just at first, to take it seriously; but once he was fastened, and saw that they meant it—or that Rackham did anyway—his mouth went dry, his throat got tight, and he decided against speaking until he was sure that his voice would be firm.

In addition, he was puzzled. If they wished to kill him, why didn't they hack him to pieces? He had heard of this business of blowing a man to bits. The Spaniards had introduced it into the Little Indies, though they used it sparingly, and largely against escaped slaves and deserters, or else captured spies, seldom against one of their own kind. Not a ball—there was no ball—but the outburst of burning gases, smashing against a man's soft middle parts, would, quite literally, tear him in half. There was no torture connected with it. Death itself would be instantaneous. Yet so spectacular was the setting, so loud the deed itself, and so gruesome the results, that the device was esteemed by certain governors as one to be used for its effect not upon the prisoner but upon the onlookers.

Why should Jack Rackham go to such lengths? At first, clearly, he had chanced to see the cannon, which shone bright in a westering sun, and with a wild rage upon him had screamed for the most violent death immediately imaginable. It was different now. His fury had turned cold; the lips no longer were working; the face which had been thunder-black became the color of old ashes. He was blind no longer, but had a purpose. What was it? George, not seeming to be interested in what went on around him, as they bound him to the twelve-pounder, yet from the corners of his eyes watched Calico Jack.

The king recovered his cudgel, and the feel of it, the swish of it through the air, seemed to settle his resolve. Whether or not he consciously knew this, there was something symbolic about that whippy black stick. It represented power. It epitomized *him*, the dark, the brooding, unpredictable chief.

"All right," he said. "Now where's your passing-box?"

The gunner was a bulky moon-faced man named Walker, a man who never smiled. George knew him. They had played draughts together one night after George's return from the fatal glade, and had sat up late, drinking.

Tom Walker was the only man—unless Woodes Rogers did —who believed that George had been forced aboard a pirate vessel. Walker however did not appear to find this any cause for spleen. He took it that everything was for the worst in this worst of all possible worlds, and he had long since passed, if ever he had passed *through,* the need for tears. A lumbrous fellow, Tom yet was curiously good company—when you could get him to talk. There was something about his very largeness, and his imperturbability, that comforted a soul. He had been a blacksmith, unmarried, the support of an invalid father in a small town north of Portsmouth. On a visit to that seaport one day he had made the mistake of falling into talk, over a few drinks, with some seamen. When a press gang accosted them, grabbing the seamen, Tom had made another mistake: after protesting in vain that he had never set foot on any ship and wouldn't know a stays'l from a whipstaff, when they started to drag him away he had fought. He remembered little of what happened for two or three days after that and he never saw the seamen again—or the members of the press gang.

He had spent three years aboard of a third-rate named *Charon*. He was never permitted to go ashore, and never paid, it being feared that with silver in his fist he might bribe his way to freedom.

The Navy had not used Tom Walker as a blacksmith. There were forges on the first- and second-rates, but not on the third- and fourth-rates. The naval blacksmiths ashore were mainly civilians, and it would never do to allow Tom to go ashore. So he became a gunner's mate, and later a gunner.

He was a very good gunner—thorough, precise, if a trifle slow. It was in his nature to do whatever he did well. For example, he played an excellent game of draughts.

No swimmer, Tom Walker had not found a chance to desert until the *Charon* was hauled up for scraping at Port Royal, Jamica. After that, piracy was the only thing open to him—unless he wished to skulk in the hills, starting at every sound, living a beast's life. He couldn't get back home (he never did learn what had happened to his father) on a merchantman. They were all escorted by Navy vessels, and inevitably, with a war coming on, checked in the Channel for deserters. Tom couldn't afford that. Mere hanging he might have risked; but he had seen what the Navy did with yanked-back deserters; he had no wish to expire slowly, after hours, perhaps even days, of savage slashing. No. There were lower forms of life than piracy, he had decided, and so he joined up with Vane.

The twelve-pounder was Tom's gun, and he would not permit another man to fire it. But he did not like what he had been ordered to do, so he took an inconscionable while doing it.

There was no laying or aiming. The target was right there, unmissable. Nor did the situation call for special precautions against a flare-back: George's body, plus the wadding, would offer even less resistance than an iron ball.

"Gunner, do your duty!"

Tom Walker fetched out his linstock and strung a new wick through it, paring it with his knife. He struck the sharp end into the sand, changing the spot several times. He took a brand from one of the fires, dropped it as though he had burned his fingers, and took up another, and dropped that. At last he got the match, a piece of tow, lighted. He blew on it—and blew it out, and had to light it again.

All of this George Rounsivel couldn't see, but he could guess it from the sounds he heard, also from the expressions of such men as remained within the line of his vision on right and left—for an obvious reason nobody was standing directly before him. There was something strained about those faces. The men knew and largely liked Tom Walker, and it could be that now they sensed a spark of revolt in him

Rackham at least showed in no way alarmed. George looked squarely at him, meaning to demand a fight. But George forebore. For Rackham was smiling.

It was not a pleasant smile. It was small and tight, and had thorns in it.

Swaggering again, fists on hips, the cudgel swinging from

its thong, Jack Rackham came over to the mouth of the cannon.

Everything was still. Even Walker must have ceased whatever it was he had been doing. Nobody moved his feet or cleared his throat. It seemed as though nobody breathed.

"You were asking for mercy?" Rackham drawled.

The sun some time since had plummeted into the sea. The stars were tumbling out. The moon had not yet risen. The camp was lit only by the jumpy red flames of cooking-fires.

George shook his head.

"Not mercy, only justice," he answered. "But what's the use of asking that of a man who is afraid to fight?"

"*Pimp!*"

Despite the poor light, George saw the cudgel start up, and he moved his head. The blow might have been meant for the side of his jaw, which it could have broken; but it flicked past his face, no more than grazing his lips, which started to bleed.

There was a quick snatched-away hiss from the crowd, an angry hornetlike sound. Rackham, knowing that he had gone too far, stepped back. But the smile still was fixed upon his face.

"Maybe you would like to stay here a while? Until sunrise?" Then, without moving his head: "*Anne!*"

It was here that George surmised Jack Rackham's intent. The chief would expose his, George's, humiliation. Gloating, he would let his doxy look upon it. He would even force her to do so. At the moment triumphant, Rackham still was not sure of himself with Anne Bonney. She might harbor a fond thought or two for the memory of George Rounsivel. He wished her to see George—for the last time—as a suppliant. That would be the ideal end. If George would but break down, whimper, weep, plead for mercy, it would be wonderful, a sight Anne could never forget. And if not now, then perhaps later. The night would be long. Many a man who puts up a brave show in the face of death at first, will weaken after a few dark uncomfortable hours alone.

She came. Stooping to get through the door of the tar-paulin-and-thatch hut that was known in camp as the Palace, she looked as though she would have been hunched over anyway: she hardly straightened, outside. Her head was bowed, chin on chest. Her hair, silken, tawny in the firelight, fell all around her head. Her shoulders sagged.

"Come here," called Calico Jack Rackham.

She moved toward him like a somnambulist. Gone was the slut of yesterday, the flirt. When at last, trembling, she stood before Jack Rackham, she suggested nothing so much as a dog that expects to be kicked—and hasn't the spunk to run away.

He scarcely looked at her, though the others, all the others, gawping, saw the tip-ends of welts at the back of her neck, and the great ungainly bruises that blackened her wrists.

"Bring me a drink of rum!"

She turned, and all but scurried away.

George licked the blood at his lips. It tasted salty.

Anne returned, nobody meanwhile having moved, and handed up a shell of rum to her master. Then Anne gratefully crept back into her Palace.

"Put the match out, but keep it handy," Rackham said. "And pull a cover over that priming, in case of rain."

"Ain't you going to let him loose even for a little while, Jack?"

"No."

He drained the shell, but he did not swallow the rum, instead swirling it in his mouth for a moment, as he made a grimace. Then he spat it all out into George Rounsivel's face.

It stung George's eyes and burned like fire on his cut lips.

"Keep him here," commanded Calico Jack. "And call me whenever he changes his mind."

And he turned and went back into the Palace.

With a shrug of weary graciousness, as though doing the world a favor, slowly the moon rose. The bay was strewn with sequins.

George Rounsivel remembered the saw about a drowning man having his life flash through his mind in an instant. Who invented that? *He* at least was having trouble in recollecting events of his boyhood and youth in Philadelphia; of his mother and father, newly landed from the west of England, Devonshire folk, whom he had scarcely known; of Uncle Paterson, dead now, who had brought him up; and London, where he'd studied. Since he was so soon to die he took it to be his duty to remember those persons and places; but he couldn't. Two much more vivid sensual memories crowded all the others out—one of sight, one of smell.

They were not really of his past at all, being too recent.

He remembered the way the earth smelled behind that oleander bush—damp, clean, deep, as he lay panting, pressing a grateful cheek against it. This might have been silly, or addled, but he couldn't help that. The smell was sharper in his nostrils right now than the acrid smell of smoke, frying fish and rum.

Also he remembered how Delicia Rogers had looked, in pink silk over a blue hooped petticoat, as she stood, furious, in the light of that single candle. This was romantic, knightly, an attitude suited to Galahad or Bayard, but not to George Rounsivel. *He* hadn't the time for chivalry and such, but should be devoting himself to thoughts of how to live a little longer.

Nonetheless those were the things he thought of—the damp earth around the oleander at night and the superb proud figure that the governor's niece had made—for all of an hour, perhaps longer.

Then he began to speak.

For some time, despite his reverie, he had been conscious of faintly stirring figures all around him. No pirates roistered, as they ordinarily would have done; they huddled in small groups, whispering. Now and then one would pass, on his way between fires, but giving George a wide berth. Yet one did proffer him a half-calabash of rum, which he refused, asking for water; the man got water. Another, furtively, hastily, clucking his tongue, with a wetted handkerchief wiped the blood and spittle from George's face. Most amazing of all, a man George did not remember ever having seen before came directly to him and asked outright if he couldn't help George to relieve himself. George thanked him gravely, accepting the offer. The man untrussed George's breeches and stood by patiently during the process, afterward carefully trussing the breeches up again. Then he left without another word.

This incident touched George Rounsivel. He wondered: *Do you always find a friend, somehow, where you least expect one?*

These things for some time, however, did not coax his thoughts far from the memory of Delicia and the earth around the oleander.

He shook his head, reminding himself again that he had an obligation to struggle.

Not struggle in the ordinary sense. That would have been wasted. Even if he could break loose—he wasn't tightly fastened—how could he get away from Cayo Jorobado?

He sensed that the pirates were troubled. The ethics of the action bothered them. The code was being violated, the very articles George himself had framed. Two brethren of the coast who had a private quarrel customarily settled it in a private manner, like gentlemen. Jack Rackham was not doing that. He was ordering a cold-blooded execution for an offense that had nothing to do with the band as a whole.

It was only in part a sense of fair play in these depraved men: it was also a realization that any such act could form a precedent they might live to regret.

George had heard the gasp that went up when Rackham struck him with the cudgel, and the even louder gasp when Rackham spat into his face. Each of those events, he believed, had helped him.

Now it was time for him to help himself. If he waited until dawn it might be too late.

"Where's Tom Walker?" he asked suddenly.

Utter silence greeted the question.

They squatted, most of them, each in the middle of his own shadow, for the moon by this time was almost directly above, and they might have been men smitten by some magical spell, paralyzed. Food was stopped half way to mouths; jaws hung open; George even saw one man who had been about to toss a piece of wood onto a fire stiffen to a statue, his hand not more than a few inches from the flame.

But there was no *verbal* answer.

"Bring him here, please," George went on.

After a long while while somebody quavered: "Mister, we can't do that."

The "mister" might have been significant, for the breathren of the coast hated all manner of title.

George nodded sadly.

"No, I suppose you can't," he replied with a mildness that struck them. "But . . . will you do this: Will you tell Tom that I don't blame him for what he's going to do, so long as he has to do it? I don't hold it against him. Will you tell him that, please?"

There was a mumble of acquiesence. George had scored.

"And tell him if things had been different I might yet have got to where I could beat him in a game of draughts now and then."

After that he was silent, hanging his head as though in thought.

Somebody coughed, apologetically. Somebody else cleared his throat. And from the middle of the bay came a resounding splash as a fish jumped.

"A pity," George muttered at last, as though to himself. "Anywhere else, anywhere in the world, I'd be given a right to fight . . ."

He waited a long while, but nobody spoke.

But they edged closer to him, sidling like sand crabs, fascinated. And after a while he started again to speak, in a low voice, bitter, as though to a single friend, a confidant.

He had defended felons in court. He had never thought to be defending himself before such a court as this, a jury of ragged outlaws.

He pointed out that he had committed no crime according to the articles of comradeship, the only ones they acknowledged. He asked if they were prepared to do murder on a man simply in order to balm another man's vanity. He reminded them that power corrupts, and warned them that if they allowed their leader to ride high like this their own lives —their loot as well—would no longer be safe.

"Look at me," he commanded. "Did I do a damned thing that any one of you wouldn't have done if he got the chance? Jack Rackham says I diddled his whore. And what if I did? Was I the first? Or the tenth? D'ye suppose I *raped* her? Hell, I didn't even have to say please!"

They liked it, shuffling closer. He had most of the camp within his hearing now. And still there issued no sign from the Palace.

Grimly, looking down, George called upon the shades of Demosthenes and Cicero to stand by him. It is an eerie thing to plead for your own life.

"If Rackham thinks he's been affronted, why doesn't he stand up and fight, like anybody else? Are you going to allow him to go on leading you, if all he wants you for is to do his dirty work? What kind of men do you call yourselves?"

He used no tricks, didn't look up, didn't raise his voice, and could not have made a gesture had he wished to do so, being fastened. But he was telling them what each had told himself, if secretly; and that was the strongest talk of all. He was their concentered conscience, speaking like an oracle.

"Now there's something more I want to say—"

He was about to picture their future under a tyrant like Rackham, to tell them how they would be crushed, each right, so dearly won, snatched from them; he was about to assert—when the flap of the Palace was thrown back.

"That will do!"

Jack Rackham should have spoken sooner. Perhaps he knew this as he strode toward the center of the camp.

"We've had enough," he cried brusquely. "Stand back, everybody. We'll get this thing over with right now. Walker, fire that gun."

There was a pause, during which nobody stirred. Then Tom Walker's voice came out of the shadows, clear and harsh:

"No."

"What!"

"He's right, Jack," somebody said.

It was as though a dam had broken.

"You've got to fight, Jack. Just like anybody else."

"We're going to let him loose."

"You and him can have it out, face to face."

The pirate king whirled his cudgel above his head, but it appeared to have lost some of its power.

"What's this—a *mutiny?*"

But they were in command, all of them, none hanging back, and they went about the business of untying George

Rounsivel, who stood impassive, knowing when to keep his mouth shut.

Calico Jack swallowed, trembling with the intensity of his effort to hold his temper. But he was no fool. He nodded.

"Good," he said. "I'll be delighted to kill him personally. Don't know why I didn't think of that in the first place. Fetch out the cutlasses."

"Not now, Jack. This man's got to get some sleep first."

An arm beneath him, Tom Walker started to help George toward his tent.

"You better get some yourself," he called over a shoulder. "Because this is going to be a real fight, this fight."

CHAPTER VIII

ONE OF THE prime purposes of Caribbean piracy, George had learned, was the avoidance of a fight. Personally pugnacious, when they worked together these outlaws preferred to gain all without any struggle. You tried to overwhelm an enemy by sheer force of fear, as you closed with him. A boarding party was a risk, a last resort; you never knew how much resistance desperate men might put up.

It was for this reason that the pirates remodelled their sloops—"sloop" being a generic name for all smallish fast shallow-draft vessels, regardless of rig or the number of masts—with very high gunwales, especially forward, or, sometimes they erected false gunwales by means of stanchions between which sheets of canvas the color of the ship's sides were spread. At the last moment, when the prey was near, and the demand to put about had been shouted, when the red flag had been run up, then the pirates themselves would be dramatically exposed, whether by springing to their feet or by the dropping of the false gunwales, and they'd scream and jump about, brandishing their weapons, a fearful sight. This, George was told, usually did the trick.

It was the same with the firing-pieces. The giant to which George had been tied, the twelve-pounder, was too big for the *John and Elizabeth*, from which it could only be fired as a chaser, not in broadside. Iron six-pounders, three to a side, were the real work-horses of the pirate artillery. These were on the beach now, while the sloop was careened, and each was draped in a tarpaulin, to be from time to time uncovered and wiped, the tompion changed. Finally there were the six brass guns, two-pounders. These were not much more than salutes; they might have been discharged while closing, but they could hardly have done much damage, even at point-blank range. Yet they were shiny, and made a brave show. Being light, they had easily been hauled to the hump that formed the center of Jorobado, and there, while the sloop was being scraped, they served much the same purpose— that of show, menace. The top of the key was a natural platform made of soft coral rubble, roughly round, and about forty feet across. The brass guns were mounted at the lip of this little plateau, facing several ways; but in truth they could not be depressed so that they'd fire down the slope. But from the sea, especially on a sunny day, they set up a great glister.

These, together with a breastwork made of brush, might have led any person a slight distance away to think that Jorobado was protected by a sort of fort. *Up there* the aspect of the place was quite different. There was no magazine, nor had the guns been shotted. The "breastwork," as flimsy as paper, was purely for the purpose of deception. Not only were there no bastions, no scarp or counter-scarp, there were no horn-works either. In fact, the only thing up there, besides the brass guns, was the wooden platform upon which all through the daylight hours a lookout was posted.

This platform, placed upon palmetto piles driven into the

rubble, was square, about ten feet to a side, and about ten feet high. It was reached by rude steps cut into one of the palmettos. Ordinarily all it contained was a chair fashioned out of a barrel and canopied by a clumsy rawhide umbrella.

No lookout sat in that chair, under that sunshade, this morning. For the watch tower was to be the site of the fight.

"Two cutlasses, same heft, same length," intoned Tom Walker. "Two daggers, same length blades. Two dags, with powder and cut ball and rammers on the side. Same length barrel, same weight butt."

"Ain't we going to leave 'em loaded, Tom?"

"No. Whichever gets up here first, if he thinks he has time to load one of 'em, that's his affair."

"Or they might get up here at the same time and each take one and pace off the distance and shoot it out proper."

"They might," Walker conceded, "but that's up to them."

This delicacy, the business of turning the top of the hill over to the contestants, was an unexpected feature of the arrangements, and one that touched George Rounsivel, who had not relished the prospect of performing in public like a trained bear or a pugilist. There were no seconds. Everybody in a sense was to be a participant, seeing to it that a fair start had been provided; but nobody was to be a witness.

A duel to the death, these ruffians reckoned, ought to be a private affair. Whatever happened up here under the broiling sun would be known only to Calico Jack Rackham, George Rounsivel, and their God. The others were to stay below, on the beach, to await the issue.

Two men would go up, but only one was expected to come down again.

"You want to jiggle the blades, Rounsivel? Or the guns?"

George shook his head.

"I trust you," he said simply.

"You, Jack?"

Rackham just at first did not answer, for he was wrapped

in his own black thoughts. What were these of? Probably not George Rounsivel. Probably they were of Anne. At last he snarled a negative, and turned abruptly and went down to the camp.

"He's anxious to get started," Walker deduced. "How 'bout you, Rounsivel?"

"Why, yes," said George. "By all means, let's get started."

There were two paths or trails up to the top, one opening upon each end of the horseshoe-shaped beach that bordered the bay. The slope was the same with each, the distance the same, this since the lookout structure was situated in the exact center of the space up there no preference could be descried. Nevertheless, and with a scrupulosity not always observable in them, the pirates insisted that straws be drawn.

Contemptuous, refusing to answer, Jack Rackham turned his back. It was a symptom of nervousness, George believed. He himself drew unhesitatingly, and even managed a smile as he did so. He drew the path to the west.

"Now go to your places. If either one starts to run before I fire off this musket he'll be shot dead on the spot. I don't care which one it is. Is that clear?"

They nodded, or George did, and, each escorted by a clump of pirates who were less like supporters than referees, walked to the two ends of the beach. Actually, so sharp was the curve of the horseshoe, so narrow the pass, that only a couple of hundred feet of water separated them; they were nearer to one another than either was to Tom Walker.

It was a glorious morning, scraps of the opalescence of dawn still clinging to things. The bay was a mirror, the jungle, unstirring, a coat of dark green paint upon the side of the hill.

George tightened his belt, took off his hat. He had already removed coat and waistcoat, and now he rolled up the sleeves of his shirt. He took off his shoes and his stockings.

His trail, the west one, led right up through the glade where he had dallied with Anne. A coincidence? It could have been.

Most of the pirates stayed in the center. A little behind Walker, further from the water, the Palace stood alone, without sign of life, the flap down. Nor had Anne Bonney joined the crowd.

George looked around for a place to pray.

"Excuse me, gentlemen."

"All right," they mumbled, turning away.

George was brief. An Anglican, he did not believe in supplicatory prayer, only formal prayer. He soon rose

"Thank you," gravely. "Now—is Captain Rackham ready?"

"They just gave their signal. You want we should give yours?"

George was brushing off his knees.

"Why, yes," he said. "Go ahead."

Somebody raised an arm full-length. Almost instantly, as if that gesture in itself had pulled the trigger, the musket was fired.

It made a loud hollow "boom" and from its muzzle a gray blob of smoke rose.

George put his head down and started to run.

It was dark under the trees, after the blazing reflection of sun upon white sand. There was a certain nightmarishness about it. George did not really feel afraid, but he knew a choked, baffled sense of outrage. It was as though he sped on a treadmill. Even when he jumped over the place on the ground where he had lain with Anne Bonney it felt as though he was getting nowhere.

It had not rained the previous night. Jorobado was a generally dry key. Yet his feet seemed to slip and slide. This added to the illusion of nightmare, the leaden-limbed feeling.

As he got near the top he wondered whether, if he stopped a moment, he would hear Jack Rackham thrashing through the thicket at his right; for the trails all but converged at the summit, emptying into the open only about twenty feet from one another. But he did not stop.

At last he could perceive a blur of light ahead. This broadened, brightening.

Then he was in the open, running evenly up the last slope, bare of undergrowth, that led to the breastwork. The breastwork itself he crashed through rather than tumbled over, losing no time.

He landed on the stones that, loosely scattered, formed the floor of this "fort."

At that instant, as neatly as though they had rehearsed it, Calico Jack tore through the breastwork facing him, and like George started to run for the tower, and the weapons.

It was a matter of yards, but it seemed miles. George thought that a man who falls a great distance, keeping consciousness, knowing that the crash will soon come, and death, praying for it, must feel like this.

For all his show of nonchalance he had been laying plans. He was tall, but Rackham was slightly taller, somewhat longer in the limbs too. Rackham was thicker of build, with large wrists, large ankles, broad hips, and almost certainly he weighed more. George moreover was a practiced runner, one who had often taken part in holiday sport events along the bank of the Deleware. It was for this reason that he believed he would win the race to the tower. He might not get there in time to ascend the rude steps to the platform where the weapons were, but surely he would get there in time to prevent Rackham from doing this.

If Rackham got to those weapons, then he, George, was dead.

The pistols could never be loaded in time. A pistol was a desperate resort at best, there never being any assurance that it would go off.

George knew nothing about the management of a knife.

In London he had studied fencing, and he had continued the practice in Philadelphia. Physically he was well equipped as a swordsman, being fast and in fine condition. But his weapons were a gentleman's—the small or court sword (the despised "bird spit") and the Spanish rapier. He had toyed with back sword and shearing sword, also with the German Düsacks and Schlaegers; but as for falchion, saber, cutlass, he had never so much as swung one.

Rackham, on the other hand, might be assumed to be as much at home with a cutlass as he was with his beloved cudgel.

So—George must get there first.

Yet he saw that he was no more than a stride ahead, if that.

And suddenly Jack Rackham did an unexpected thing, and did it very adroitly indeed. Without the slightest break in his run, it would seem without any effort, he stooped, scooped up a fist-size piece of coral, and hurled this at George.

It struck George on a shoulder, causing him to swerve.

Rackham threw another, and another.

The second missed, but the third clacked against George's left ear, cutting the skin. Dazed, he ducked. And Rackham ran on.

The toe holds cut into the palmetto would have made precarious footing at best. The pirate king was not halfway up, and had just grabbed the rim of the platform with outstretched hands, when a recovered George Rounsivel reached him.

George grabbed the ankles, and pulled.

Even as he fell Rackham was kicking—kicking viciously like a mule. He had not taken off his shoes, as George had done, and the kicks, when they hit, hurt.

Striking the ground, both men rolled. It happened that they rolled away from one another.

They rose. George was the nearer to the tower now, but

he did not dare to jump for it. Instead, without waiting to catch his breath, he raised his arms, the fists with knuckles out and palms in, and started toward Jack Rackham.

Here, to his own surprise, he found himself at something of an advantage. Weaponless, Rackham was maladroit, perhaps even a mite frightened. Apparently he had never before fought with his fists.

George had only slightly more experience, but he strove to make the best of this superiority. He had taken a few lessons from an itinerant pugilist at the fencing academy in London, soon to give it up as a disgusting sport, if it could be called sport at all; but he had at least, in that time, learned to block. His very posture, as he approached, appeared to unsettle the pirate. George had spread his feet far apart, and he kept them that way as he moved forward with tiny cat-steps. His knees were bent, his heels were firm on the ground. His elbows were high, about on a level with his chin, his fists higher still.

Rackham came in swinging wildly. George hit straight, choppy down-punches that hurt his hands—but hurt Rackham's face even more.

Rackham roared, a wounded bull, and stepped back. George immediately attacked. Not for George were the finer points of the prize ring—the roundhouse, the flying mare, the cross-buttocks, the uppercut—but his rudiments at least stood him in good stead.

Rackham's face was red now, and wet. The blood, George supposed, must have been smeared on his own fists, but he could not feel it there, and in fact, what with the punching and the blocking, he could feel little of anything in fists and forearms.

Rackham switched back to earlier tactics when he stooped to pick up a stone. But he had been stunned and was not so swift this time. George's right fist caught him high on the nose, and he went over backward.

At this point George might have won the fight, if he had been fast enough. He could have run for the watch tower and climbed into it and got a cutlass. Or he could have jumped with both feet and all his weight on the belly of the prone Jack Rackham, knocking the wind out of the man. This latter assault was accepted practice in the prize ring; but George's instruction had not gone that far.

He paused, an error. Rackham kicked up with both feet, and one of these caught George's left kneecap, spinning him around.

Before George could right himself Rackham was up again and coming in with arms widespread like the arms of a catch-as-catch-can wrestler, his head wholly unguarded.

Backing away, George smashed that head again and again. It was like striking a stone wall. Once or twice Rackham gave an involuntary squeal, but he never ceased to bore in.

George sobbed, and stepped back. His foot met a round stone, and slipped, so that he teetered, his guard too high.

Jack Rackham closed.

They fell, Rackham on top, his chest pressing George's chest. Black specks swam before George's eyes. There was a great roaring in his ears. He was being suffocated. But somehow he rolled.

Indeed they rolled a great deal after that, blindly, back and forth, each striving to get on top; but while George's effort was directed toward breaking the bear-hug that was crushing his very ribs, Rackham, more active, tried to bring a knee up into George's crotch.

This was the way they were when they struck the "breastwork." They went right through this and crashed down the slope toward the jungle.

As they did so there flashed into George's mind, incongruously, the thought that today was Christmas. "Happy Christmas," he mumbled to himself, slamming this way, slamming that. "Oh, merry Christmas!"

The slope was steep. There were no trees on it, but there had lately been many bushes, some of them exceedingly tough, which had been cut off in order to clear this space for defending musket fire and also in order to provide material for the sham breastwork. These stumps, struck hard, could be cruel. One stabbed George in the left side with a force that surely broke the skin; it drove out of him what little breath he had left, so that when they were stopped at the tree line by a bole he was for a moment unable to stir.

He heard Rackham jump up. He even saw Rackham start a kick at the place his knees had previously been trying to reach; but George could not do anything about that.

The pain seared him. Sweat sprang out on his face, and he believed that he screamed. His eyeballs were triphammers. All of his middle was afire.

When he rose he had to get to his knees first, and stay that way a moment, like a small child.

Jack Rackham was not in sight.

Lurching, sobbing, George ran up the slope, pushed again through the violated breastwork, ran to the tower.

Calico Jack was gloating. As he hefted a cutlass in one hand, a dagger in the other, he did not think to face the ladder, so sure was he that the fight was finished. George had one foot on the edge of the platform before Rackham whirled around.

George dived for his knees.

The platform was not large, and they almost went over the edge. George hipped and shoulder-bumped away, snatching the other cutlass as he went, and somehow he got to his feet.

There was not much room between them as they faced one another. There would be no retreating. They stood straight, each with his guard high, depending on the basket-hilt to protect his hand, the blade itself to cover his head. They slashed right and left.

This was madness.

It was Rackham who tried a thrust—for George's throat. George took a step back, extending his arm full-length as he brought the saber directly down.

Rackham looked startled, like a man who has heard a clap of thunder on a clear day. Blood began to gush out of his hair and run down each side of his face. His sword-arm dropped. His legs buckled. He still had that look of astonishment on his face while he swayed, and then toppled sideways.

George picked up a dagger. He kelt beside his mortal enemy. The head was back, the throat bare. The eyes flashed hatred at the approaching face of George Rounsivel. Rackham said something, a guttural sound. Then the eyes got glassy.

There were no cheers on the beach when they saw George. Scratched, slashed, shirtless, panting, he must have presented a frightful appearance.

A few advanced toward him, as though to tender congratulations. He brushed past these. He went to the Palace.

"Anne," he called. "Come here!"

She crawled out, literally crawled. She must have known whom to expect when she heard that voice.

"Now, God damn it," he said, "bring *me* a drink of rum!"

CHAPTER IX

GEORGE was to learn that waving a sceptre was not the all-in-all of kingship. He did have a sceptre of sorts, as a symbol of his authority. He spurned the whippy black cudgel that was associated with the personality of Jack Rackham, and used instead the long heavy Spanish cavalry saber he had snatched from the wall of Woodes Rogers' drawing room. Its very size, though it made it clumsy, also made this weapon impressive.

He believed in the use of symbols, visible tokens of power, especially when dealing with a simple people, as was the case here.

Yet he did not belittle these criminals. That a man had the mind of a child would make no difference to you if he stabbed you to the heart. A musket in the hands of an idiot would kill as quickly as one in the hands of an intellectual giant. Again and again George Rounsivel had to remind himself that his educational superiority counted for little, and that too much confidence might cause him to crash. Because he could outtalk these pirates did not mean that in the event of a slip they wouldn't turn on him.

It was not so much that the men of Jorobado were *stupid*, it was that they were *over-emotional*. They were forever flying into a passion of one sort or another, for they wept as readily as they screamed with rage. They were intensely suspicious of everybody, attributing a base motive to the most innocent of deeds, yet in the same breath, and fervently, they would protest everlasting devotion to the gang, to their comrades. The settlement of squabbles, some of them over ludicrously small matters, but all of them dangerous, made up the greatest part of George Rounsivel's work. His decision in each case was final, and was accepted as such. Ever since the council a few hours after the fight with Rackham had elected him king—at the same time electing Tom Walker quartermaster, at George's own request—that his wisdom was superlative was taken for granted.

But how long would this last? Could a man, any man, keep on being infallible? Enthusiasm for the Philadelphia lawyer, the conqueror of Calico Jack, sooner or later was sure to fade. These outcasts never would follow any leader for a long time. Could George hold them together well enough to lay plans for his own escape?

He never knew what the pirates might do or say. They were more than merely volatile; they must have been at least a little mad. Ruling them was like juggling a large number of loaded, cocked pistols. It left a man little time in which to relax.

Still, there were compensations. Though his title was captain, and most of the men referred to him as the "skipper," a word they had picked up from Dutch sailors, he was not called upon to display any sort of seamanship. Despite the rum, work on the *John and Elizabeth* went briskly along, with George doing no more than now and then calling a word of encouragement. The carpenter, known as Chips, was in charge of scraping and caulking, while the maintenance and replacement of the cannons was in the hands of Tom Walker, who when he became quartermaster had not ceased to be chief gunner. The canvas and all standing rigging was the province of the sailing-master, who once the vessel was floated again would also navigate. All the king was expected to do was keep the others from killing one another and when the time came lead them into battle.

This left him leisure, and he spent it, generally, in the Palace, which he had appropriated. Though subject to call at any hour of the night or day, he did enjoy a certain amount of privacy in the Palace. At least it had been stipulated that nobody was to approach that shack without first crying out a request. It was the only spot in all Jorobado that was held proof against marauders. To a man of George Rounsivel's temperament this was a boon beyond rubies, rarer than gold.

Besides the Spanish saber, he had that other, that equally efficacious symbol, Anne Bonney. She cooked for him and at night he commanded her to stay indoors, but in the daytime more often than not he sent her away, for he liked to be alone, pondering upon the position in which he found himself.

Time after time he came back to the same thought,

which occasionally made him sigh but more often, regretably, caused him to chuckle: *If they saw me now what would my friends in Philadelphia say?*

Man loses dignity, at least in his own eyes, when he is always being jostled. To the others privacy was unthinkable, unnatural. To George Rounsivel it was precious. He could only really laugh when he was alone.

Anne was a mixed blessing, if she was one. She could be good company; she'd lost none of her skill, and her flesh was as soft and sweet as ever. But the edge had gone from her ardor. She was the only woman on this island, the personal possession of the king, which was as it should have been; yet Anne was a perverse little devil. She was morbid. If she flirted with men it was less because she was a minx than because she flirted in fact with death, which she liked. What she had done with George a little while ago, up in that glade, had held all the delight of peril. Caught, they would have been slashed to ribbons, both of them. Now George was legitimate. It was as though, from her point of view, she and George had been formally married. To some women marriage might prove the beginning of romance, but Anne Bonney was not one of those.

She was discontented, a more or less normal condition with her but one that boded ill nonetheless.

What's more, George believed that she sometimes saw Jack Rackham.

Rackham still lived. That was one of the amazing things at the camp on Cayo Jorobado. Calico Jack himself must have been the most astounded of all by it. He had thought to die, as George knew from the light in his eyes when George knelt beside him with a knife. He had expected to have his throat cut. It was what he would have done to George if their positions had been reversed. And indeed George had believed that he really *did* die, who in truth only swooned. Friends had climbed the hill a little later intent upon burying

Jack Rackham. They had been astonished, and at first frightened, to find him alive. They had brought him back to camp, and for a little while had tried to keep him hidden; but there could be no secrets in a place like that, and soon the word spread.

When George himself heard it he merely shrugged. He did not go to see Rackham. A visit would be taken as a sign of weakness, something he must avoid. Already it was counted against him, he felt, that he had failed to cut Rackham's throat. In piratical opinion that was a soft spot; no king could afford to be soft.

George never mentioned Rackham, but he worried about the man. Rackham was hardly one to forgive and forget, and he still had friends.

Not kindness, no instinct of motherliness, but only that damnable morbidity of hers took Anne Bonney to her former lover's side, if she went there.

He was pragmatic about it, and felt no qualms of jealousy. He just wanted to stay alive.

When less than a week after the fight the sloop was pronounced ready, and was launched, there was a tremendous celebration on Jorobado. The agreement was that there should be no drinking at sea—an agreement George was sure would be broken—and so the occasion called for a carouse the last night ashore. All that day, indeed, the pirates had been swilling, so that by nightfall there was little gayety, most of the men being stupified, scarcely able to move.

This did not disconcert George Rounsivel. In his experience, so far, a drunken pirate was less of a menace than one with a hangover. They were touchy-tempered at best, but when in their cups, though they talked big, they tended to be fuzzy, amiable. They did not look upon liquor as a release from the daily grind but rather associated it with taverns ashore, with song and whores and laughter. When they could drink they drank as much as possible, for they knew that there would be weeks on end, and even months, when a swig of rum would be hard to come by.

George found them dull when they were tipsy. All the same, he had his duties. No monarch, howsoever petty, can afford to consider only his own feelings. So George, having first locked Anne in the cabin of the *John and Elizabeth,* circulated, slapping backs, waving mugs, sipping, laughing. In this way he came upon Calico Jack.

It was a clear night, and this was near the foot of the west trail, the place from which George had started to sprint that fateful morning five days ago. Rackham was alone in his bitterness, and had not heard George, who shuddered at what he saw.

The man who had been chief for so short a time lay on his back. His eyes were open and he stared up at the stars. Though his lips still were puffed and bruised, as were his cheekbones and the bones above his eyes, the mouth, even so, showed a slit of cruelty, of murderous resolve. No, Jack Rackham would not forget. And he would never cease to fight.

George could not see the cut made by the blow that had felled Rackham, for bandages covered it; but the glare of those eyes, the set of that mashed mouth, were enough. Rackham didn't move a muscle and did not even blink as he lay there What was he thinking?

George tiptoed away.

CHAPTER X

THE *John and Elizabeth* had a deep waist, and very little freeboard even when she rode empty. The waist however was not long, as the forward deck was. It was on the forward deck that most of the men spent most of their time, many even sleeping there in good weather, for the forecastle was hardly fragrant.

The afterdeck was small and almost square. It was raised unexpectedly high, giving the *John and Elizabeth* something of the appearance of an old-fashioned carrack. The swing of the tiller covered a good part of this deck.

Below it were two tiny cabins with a corridor between them so narrow that two thin men had to squeeze to pass. On the left was a two-bunk cabin, which George had taken over. On the right was a one-bunk cabin, where Tom Walker slept and which was visited also, from time to time, by the sailing-master, Ezra Garde, for the charts were kept there. These were the only persons who were permitted to go into the after cabins at all, except by special permission of the skipper

As for Anne, she might go into the waist or up on the afterdeck, but she was not to go to the forward deck. Nor was Rackham—George passed this word quietly—ever to be assigned to the helm.

It would be easier to keep track of Anne here. Nevertheless George was unquiet. Anything could happen in close quarters like that: there were more than forty men in a space twenty would have crowded.

Aboard of the brig *Barkus,* on the run down from the mouth of the Deleware, George had kept his eyes open and had asked many a question, making note of the answers After all, he had already crossed the Atlantic twice, and he had used that time to advantage. He had not the slightest wish to become a seaman—God forbid—but he learned that it was easier for the passenger when he knew the queer lingo that sailors used among themselves.

The first day out on his first voyage he had learned that if you speak of the right-hand side of a ship instead of the starboard side you make a dire mistake and every right-thinking seaman thereafter will despise you. George thought it rather silly to let names mean so much, but he also believed that when in Rome it is well to do as the Romans do; he had mastered the whole grotesque vocabulary. This knowledge, idly acquired, stood him in good stead aboard of the *John and Elizabeth*. Though he was not expected to touch one, if he had ever referred to a sheet, or a halyard, as a "rope"—though manifestly each *was* a rope—he would have lost all their respect and in consequence the leadership.

Yet sailors on the whole, he had thought, were neat men, even prim. Properly officered, they made things fast, tucked in loose ends, folded, tightened, scrubbed, put away. "Shipshape" was a word often on their lips and "smart" was another. The pirates were not like this. For all intents and purposes they had no officers, and they were the most slovenly lot of men George Rounsivel ever had met. Nothing was taut. Nothing was in its place. They loafed, spitting on the dirty deck. As they had done in camp, they ate when and in whatever manner it pleased them, frequently bickering about who should use the stove. The only way in which they were alert was as lookouts. Somebody was always aloft, a glass at his eye. In addition, the men who lolled on deck would rise every now and then to saunter clear around the vessel, squinting at the horizon. It was not greed alone that prompted this vigilance, not just the pistol that had been offered as a reward to the man who first sighted a sail later taken. It was boredom. They had nothing else to do.

George Rounsivel understood, and even sympathized. It had been with trepidation, and only because he could not think of any way to avoid it, that he undertook to lead a band of sea robbers. He didn't yet know what he would do if they overtook a British ship and he was called upon to fire at his own flag or be struck down from behind. But at least he had pictured life on a pirate vessel as *exciting*. It wasn't. That first week, at least, it was almost unbearably dull.

Telling as his judgment was in every minor case, accepted like a pontifical edict, he had but a single vote in council when the band's policy was made. Charles Vane had fallen in large part because of the machinations of Calico Jack Rackham, but a lack of boldness had been the immediate excuse, the springboard. These men were poor. They wanted booty, which meant that they wanted action.

George had presided at the council on the beach, and in time his will had prevailed—but just barely.

It chilled his heart when he learned how many of them were in favor of an immediate descent upon Fort Nassau. He had not expected this. Their reasons were logical enough: not so much the sack of the town, where there was precious little left *to* sack, but the capture of the fort before it could be strengthened and used against them, the establishment of a base—and incidentally the most savage punishment possible for the man who had dared to crimp their dominance in these parts, Woodes Rogers the governor, and all of his family as well. Though George alone had seen them, those eight bodies dangling from the gallows on the beach just outside of Fort Nassau had made a deep impression upon the outcasts. An eye for an eye was their law. It was a matter of pride to them, even a matter of honor, to crush the governor—and to expose his corpse in a public place.

Appalled, George had immediately contended that they were much too weak even to think of attacking New Providence. They must first treble their strength.

The pirates replied that if they didn't get there first Vane would. The presence in New Providence of Vane's confidant and spy, Monk Evans, as reported by George himself, was proof of that. Monk had undoubtedly been doing the same thing George was doing—looking over the fortifications and testing the temper of the populace with the possibility of a descent by sea in his mind.

If indeed that had been the case, George replied, then Evans must have reported that an attack at this time would be impractical. *He* knew, George said. *He* had seen the condition of the fort, and not just from the outside. They should stay away, at least for a little while.

At this point they wavered, and George had thrust in an alternate plan, striving to deflect them from thoughts of Fort Nassau. Why not, he suggested, run up to the Carolina coast? The pickings there were reported to be good. The trading vessels would not be convoyed by warships, as virtually all the British merchantmen in these waters were, or as heavily gunned and manned as the Spanish and French vessels. Moreover—and this was important—the loot could be disposed of, the crown officials in those parts being notoriously eager to turn a dishonest penny. Finally, George had added, both Stede Bonnet and Edward Teach were known to be operating along that coast of narrow inlets and shallow coves, ideal for the concealment of pirate vessels. Perhaps they could take up with one or both of those celebrated operators, and *then*, a much larger force, descend upon Nassau.

This advice prevailed at last, but there were sullen ones, and George had been obliged to compromise to the extent of agreeing to make a long southward loop down toward Cuba first, from thence proceeding directly up the Florida Straits, ready to pounce upon anything that showed itself —and that was weak enough. This involved beating a considerable distance against the trades, tacking four or five miles for every mile forward, and furling all canvas at sundown excepting only a spritsail for way, because of the tiny treacherous keys not easily heard in the dark.

Nor did they see anything in the daylight hours. It was slow work, and wearisome. After a week of it the men were getting twitchy. Bottles were beginning to appear, surreptitiously at first, then in a more open manner. George pretended that he didn't see them.

George took up navigation, giving Ezra Garde something to do, and busied himself with charts and figures, with astrolabe and cross-staff and compass.

Lying alone in his cabin—there was hardly room to stand —he tried to justify his position to himself, falling back upon law. Though he came from one of the great ports of the world, it happened that he knew little about maritime law. Piracy of course was one of those crimes that could only be classed as *mala in se*, evil of itself. But, was it piracy to attack and loot a ship from a nation with which your own nation was virtually at war? A Dutch vessel, an English vessel, an American colonial coaster—those should be left alone, of course. Nor would George Rounsivel tolerate murder even among the crew of a Frencher or Spaniard. It was true too that the pirates carried no letters of marque and reprisal. But people in those parts sometimes made up their laws as they went along, as George already had seen. It might be that in time he would be able to work out a justification, satisfactory at least to his own conscience, for attacking Spanish and French ships. One thing at least was certain: if Great Britain was at war with one by this time she was at war with both, since their thrones held them together, regardless of their peoples. When George left Philadelphia, more than two months ago, it had been considered a sure thing. Everybody said that the very next ship would bring news of war. Had it? Would George be morally right in *assuming* that it had? It would take some time to figure this out. He hoped he'd be allowed that time.

He heard something beneath him, and looked over the edge of his bunk to see that Anne had slipped into the lower bunk. Entoiled in his legal speculation, George had not heard her enter. It was a very hot afternoon, and she was lying there with nothing to cover her nakedness save a strip of linen across her middle. A week ago, even a few days ago, before the bruises had faded from her back and shoulders, she would not have let George see her thus. It was not that she was personally modest—she was, and with good cause, proud of her body—but the sight of those blue marks shamed her. Then, she would only undress for George in the dark. It was different now.

Her head haloed by that flat soft honey-colored hair, she saw him looking down at her. She did not smile, but she did not wear her customary sulky pout. Her eyes, a darker blue than usual, were open very wide.

The *John and Elizabeth* barely moved, speaking very faintly under the forefoot, her wake awash like satin. The timbers emitted small querulous squeals. A spray of sunlight, reflected from the water, leapt through a porthole and swung back and forth across the cabin ceiling.

"Anne—" he started softly.

"Yes?"

She twitched the piece of linen, so that it slid off, leaving her utterly exposed.

"No, no," he said. "It's too hot for that now anyway. But I've meant to ask you, before this—how did you ever happen to get here?"

She kept looking at him.

"Do you really want to know?" she asked at last.

"Yes," he said, "I really want to know."

She closed her eyes, almost as though she welcomed the announcement. She raised her arms, the movement causing those small round breasts to rise a little, and she clasped her hands behind her head.

"All right, I'll tell you."

CHAPTER XI

"THEY TELL me my name was Ryan. Anyway that was my father's name. Anyway he was supposed to be my father. I never knew my mother, making it sort of the other way around for me—I mean, from the way it usually is with a bastard."

Absent-mindedly she slipped the knife out from under her pillow and took a hone from the rack at her side, and soon to the swash of the wake and the squeak of timbers was added a steady wet slap as she put an even keener edge on what already had been razor-sharp. She was never without the knife, the same bright one she had flashed in George Rounsivel's face ten minutes after he met her in the glade on Hunchback Key. Her habit of keeping it under the pillow irritated George, especially during their more intimate moments. "Some night I'm going to nut myself on that thing," he'd grumble.

She tut-tutted this. "If you are gelded, my dear," she assured him, "it won't be by accident."

Now, propped on one elbow, he looked down at her.

"So you're—illegitimate?"

"Why, yes." She seemed surprised. "I came from Cork," she added, as though that explained everything.

In Philadelphia, where the Quaker influence was strong, babies born out of wedlock, though surely not unknown, were not taken for granted. In London, George remembered, the better class of persons seldom mentioned this matter. Seemingly it was not so in Cork.

"My mother, whoever she was, must have been the one that gave me my temper. Father was a quiet man. He was a physician, and he drank a great deal of gin but didn't show it much—I mean, he never fell down. Sometimes when he'd be

110

called in the middle of the night, and I'd help him pack his bag, I used to feel sorry for the person he was going to work on. He never let me go along on those occasions. Said that sort of thing wasn't for young ladies. He always called me a young lady."

She was speaking in a low dreamy voice, almost as though to herself. She held the knife up to what light there was, and squinted thoughtfully at it, and then she went on honing it, more slowly now.

"He doesn't sound like a father of mine, maybe? But I'm sure he was. The reason I'm so sure is that he's very near the only man I ever knew who had the chance but never tried to get my skirt and petticoats up. Don't you think that practically proves it?"

"Well, I suppose so."

"I had an easy time. Father made money. He didn't beat me. Everybody seemed to like him. I always had plenty to eat, and good clothes. I even had a maid. In fact, that was the trouble—the maid."

"Oh?"

"She was English, and I don't like English women. So many English people have Irish maids that I was pleased to be Irish and have an English maid. But she was really there because of Father. I wasn't supposed to know that, but I was fourteen years old and it would have been hard to keep anything from me. She was supposed to sleep on a pallet in the same room with me, but as soon as she'd think I was asleep she'd sneak out to Father's room. I used to go after her, and I'd listen at the door. Naturally I hated her."

"Naturally."

"She wasn't even pretty. I hated her hands. And her ankles. And most of all the way she talked. I used to drop things and make her pick them up. I used to kick her under the table. Father knew this, but he was afraid to scold me. He was always afraid of me. Most men are. And so was she, the fool. She had a bum you could've served tea on. I never have been able to see what my father saw in her."

Anne replaced the hone, and very carefully sheathed the knife. All naked, she stretched.

"They both thought I'd get over it—get over that dislike of her, I mean. They must have both been flummoxed when I went after her with a pair of scissors. But I wasn't. It'd been a long time coming. The wonder was I didn't kill her. I certainly meant to.

"Father was out on a case that afternoon. We were sewing, in the upstairs parlor, Nellie and me—that was her nasty name: Nellie—and something she said made me wild. I can't even remember what it was, now. Something about my father. She was always smirking about Father, always hinting that they might have a big secret to tell me some day. If he'd ever thought of marrying that bitch I'd have gone after *him* too."

She spoke without passion, and without looking directly at George.

"Anyway, I snatched up the scissors and went for her. You never saw anybody so gawped. She all but stayed right there and let me slash her. She only started to run away barely in time. She tried to go downstairs, but I blocked her off. She was twice as big as me, but she was afraid of me. I . . . I must have looked fierce.

"I caught her in the upstairs hall. She went all down in a heap, trying to cover her head with her arms, and I slashed and slashed at her. And every time she felt those scissors tear into her skin she'd let out a scream. She didn't wriggle, just screamed.

"The neighbors were hammering at the door, but they couldn't get in, and I was going to stab her, but my father came back. As soon as I saw him I stopped what I was doing. But I wouldn't say I was sorry. The only thing I was sorry about was that I hadn't killed her. I might almost as well have. She couldn't walk. She could hardly move. Father nursed her for four days, keeping her in a dark room, but I wouldn't go near her myself. She never said anything. But on the afternoon of the fourth day, bandages and all, she somehow got downstairs and out into the street, leaving the door open. We didn't dare go after her. We knew she'd make for the sheriff."

His stomach wambling, George had lain back in his bunk, and he stared at the ceiling.

"My father never put a hand on me. Maybe he was afraid to. But we got out of the house that very night, and aboard a ship. Almost anybody could get passage for America if they were willing to sign an indenture for seven years, but a physician didn't have to sign anything. The sheriff's men never even came looking for us, the ship's captain kept it so quiet. And two days later we sailed. We went to the Carolinas."

George, who was looking over the edge of the bunk again now, nodded knowingly. Physicians, like clergymen, always were welcomed in the colonies, and on a no-questions-asked basis.

Anne was looking earnestly at him with those dark blue eyes. Her own story, the very telling of it, the memory, seemed to have stirred her. She shifted her buttocks a little. She pointed to a place.

"Why don't you come down?" she suggested.

He swallowed.

"Not just now. Go on."

"Well, I never liked Charles Town. Too quiet. Father did well enough. But I wanted to get married, and he wanted me to stay home, and when I finally married Bonney he was furious. It was the only time I'd ever seen him that way.

"Bonney was a sailor, and he wasn't much. He was not as bad as Father said, but I could have done better if I'd waited. But anyway I didn't wait. And when I saw Jack Rackham I wished I had."

"You met Rackham in Charles Town?"

"Yes. He was with Vane. They used to operate off the Carolinas, before they came down here. Well, Bonney was away on a voyage, and I . . . oh, I just let Jack do whatever he wanted with me. I was old enough then. I was sixteen.

"But Bonney was no man, not like Jack Rackham. When he came back—Bonney, I mean—Jack had sailed away. Well, I talked him into taking me down to New Providence, where I knew Jack would be. Father'd heard that we were married, and he wouldn't support me any more anyway."

"Did Bonney know about Rackham?"

"Not till we got down there. Then I told him. And Jack told him too. Jack offered to fight it out with him anywhere he wanted, with any weapons. But Bonney was afraid. Jack had gone off the account when that new governor came along with the pardon proclamation, and he'd taken the oath of allegiance. But there were still certain things against him, some goods he hadn't declared. And Bonney knew it. So we thought the best thing to do was get out of there. So we went to Vane, on Jorobado. And you know the rest."

His joints hurting, George crawled out of the upper bunk. The cabin had been hot; now it was fetid as well. He thought that if he didn't get to the deck he would vomit.

But Anne seized his hand.

"Come on. You know you feel like it."

He stiffened, not looking at her. But he could smell her flesh, and soon he felt her hands slither up his sides, and she started to unbutton his shirt. She pressed against him.

"Lock the door, dear," she whispered.

Sweat stood out all over him and the blood pounded wildly at his temples.

But now there was another pounding, outside. Some pirate

who in his excitement had forgotten the taboo fisted the cabin door even as George reached for the latch.

"*A sail, Captain! A sail!*"

CHAPTER XII

SHE CARRIED no canvas, which is the reason the lookout had not spotted her until they were very near. This vessel, rocking a little in the lazy seas, was small, a squat apple-cheeked boat, probably flat-bottomed, certainly slow. Because she showed no sails—indeed, as they saw when they got closer, no standing rigging of any sort—it was difficult to classify her. There were three spars on her mainmast. She carried no foremast, and the mizzen, a small one, was in the extreme stern and seemed about to topple out of the ship. She might have been what the Dutch called a gallot, a sturdy if unexciting trader generally used for coastal work.

Aboard of the *John and Elizabeth* the false gunwales had been run up forward, and the crew gathered there, arms being passed out. But, as there was clearly to be no chase, and no sign of life showed in the other vessel, it seemed stupid to crouch in hiding, and one by one the pirates rose, intently studying their prey.

"I don't like it."

"Couldn't get me to go aboard of her."

"Plague, you think?"

"Might be."

George made known that he himself would visit the derelict, if such she was. He strapped on a cutlass. He loaded two large pistols and thrust them behind his belt. He had the Moses boat put overside.

"If she really is a derelict she belongs to us," he told Tom Walker, who was to be left in charge.

"She does anyway. But do we want her?"

"You've got the big fellow shotted?"

"I have. And laid. In this sea the helmsman can easily hold us on, and if there's any hanky-panky I could blow that tub out of the water in five minutes."

"Better wait till I leave it first."

He sat in the sternsheets, paying little attention to the two rowers, who were constantly looking ahead, over their shoulders, not liking to have their backs turned to a ghost— if that's what it was.

George had his own doubts. Perhaps a full boarding party would have been better, in the longboat. There was a possibility that the crew of the gallot, having seen the *John and Elizabeth* before the pirates saw them, and having guessed the nature of their business, had hidden themselves below in deadly fear. It was unlikely, but it was conceivable. They might have armed themselves below in preparation for one wild rush.

George could read the name on the counter now, *Schatje*, which looked Dutch, confirming his first impression, but still there was no stir. No smoke rose from the galley. The tiller swung back and forth, untended. That tiller and a section of Jacob's ladder hanging conveniently over the side George approached.

He reached the vessel from windward, and it was not until he had climbed to the deck that his nose told him the terrible story.

A plague ship? Say rather a charnel house!

He staggered, gasping, as though he'd been struck in the chest, the stench was so strong, so abrupt.

"Are you all right, cap'n?" one of the men in the Moses called.

"I'm all right," he replied, shaking his head. "I'm just dreading what I've got to find. You stay there."

He started with the forecastle, which had been stripped of

every bit of bedding, the pegs cleaned of clothes. There was not even a personal knickknack, an ignored, dropped trifle.

The galley was just abaft the forecastle hatch, but it was found only by stains on the deck, for the very bricks of the stove had been removed, and the sandbox dismantled.

There was only one hold, one cargo hatchway. The hatch itself was missing; perhaps it had been broken up for firewood. George leaned over the opening, a large one, and in the sunlight he could see virtually all of the hold, which was empty. There was an acrid smell of bilge, which for the first time George Rounsivel found actually welcome as offsetting, at least for a moment, that other horrid stink that lay like a miasma upon the vessel. He could hear the bilge too as it swished idly back and forth with the slight motion of the gallot, but he heard no scurrying of rats, a sound that might have been expected to greet his appearance. "Is anyone down there?" he called, knowing that nobody was. Then for some time he listened to the eerie echoes of his voice as they were batted back and forth, until at last the swish of the bilge took over again.

He sighed. He rose from his knees, and started for the cabin.

Sooner or later he had to come to the cabin. It was small, square, a deck house that obviously had served as the officers' quarters.

There were two small square windows cut into this deck house, both facing forward, and a door, facing aft. All three were closed, and firmly locked.

The forward part and all the starboard side had been blackened, and below them was a litter of charred chunks of wood and bits of rag. It was clear that this fire had been no accident. Why the attempt to burn the gallot had failed George Rounsivel could not know, but he might guess that it was because of one of those sudden drenching tropical showers so common at that time of the year.

The windows were curtained on the inside. He looked around for something heavy enough to use for smashing the lock of the door, and at last was reduced to drawing the charge from one of his pistols and hammering with its heavy butt.

The men in the Moses, jumpy, yet unwilling to climb a-board the gallot, heard him and instantly called a query.

"I'm all right," he growled. "You stand by."

It was strenuous work, and he was wet with sweat when at last the lock snapped and the door flew open—and he wished that it hadn't.

He knew now why there were no rats in the hold.

Usually your bold rat is a hungry rat, the hungrier it is the bolder. These, blinking balefully up at him from the hideous mess, had been gorged. Their eyes were glassy, their snoots beslobbered with blood. They did not scamper away, only lurched and lumbered off, for they were fat with carrion, gassy, greasy, stupefied.

The scene they left, the feast they quit, once, not long ago, must have been three men—or at least three human beings. They had probably been white, though there was precious little skin left anywhere. Even the color of their hair was difficult to determine. Nor could George do more than guess at the manner of their death. The ankles of each, mere bone now, were tied, the wrists of each as well. The men probably had been kneeling in a row. The ceiling of the cabin was high, for such a structure, and there would have been room to swing a cutlass—or an axe. The men must have been naked, for there was not a scrap of clothing in sight. The pirates were an economical lot, who let nothing go to waste.

Who, then, had these men been? The officers, presumably, the captain and mates of the *Schatje,* cut down in cold blood when they refused to join the pirates or when their own seamen, hating them, deserting to the attacking force, had taken vengeance on them. It didn't matter now. The thing had been done, and not long ago.

The rats were watching George Rounsivel. He saw now that many of them had not sought out their holes after all, but crouched, waiting, in corners. One even returned to the morsel he'd left in the middle of the floor—a long section of the human intestine—and this he dragged to a corner, moving backward all the while, keeping a careful eye on George, and there he began again to eat it.

"All right, I'll go," George snarled.

Made savage by disgust, he yanked out his loaded pistol and fired it squarely at that rat.

The noise was terrific and smoke so filled the cabin that he couldn't even see whether he'd hit the thing. Nor did he care. He backed out, kicking the door shut behind him.

This time the two seamen in the Moses did more than call, they came tumbling.

"It's all right," George said. "I just blasted a rat."

"Scared the wits half out of us, cap'n."

"I know. I'm sorry. It was a stupid thing to do. Anyway, let's get back. There's nothing here to interest us—not a thing."

He reported only informally. The word, he knew, would be passed around, and since there wasn't any loot there was no call for an accounting. The pirates generally nodded their heads, saying with certainty that it sounded like Charles Vane. Their former king, then, must be operating in this vicinity, not far from New Providence.

"It's him all right," Walker said. "He must've enlisted the whole crew. How many would you say?"

"Fifteen to eighteen, from the looks of the forecastle."

"They might've joined up with the proviso that Vane do in their officers. Likely enough it was that way. It usually is. I wouldn't be here myself if certain officers had even once, even for a little while, treated me like a man. I guess not many of us would."

"Look," George said, pointing, "you've got the big one loaded, and you said a while ago that you could knock that gallot right out of the water inside of five minutes, is that right?"

"That's right."

"Well, do it then. Go ahead and do it."

"Aye, aye, sir."

CHAPTER XIII

Spritsail Inlet looked like a good place to fish—but to fish only for fish. But Ezra Garde, the sailing-master, who had picked out and entered this all-but-indistinguishable slit in the dreariness that was the coast between Pamlico and Cape Fear, swore that he had often seen it clogged with pirate craft, while its beaches, blank today, swarmed with merchants and sounded to the clamor of selling.

The only noise now was a faint peevish clittering of palmetto fronds, the only motion theirs and that of the catspaws that sometimes skittered across the surface of the bay. No birds flew overhead. No smoke rose. If man had indeed peopled this place in days gone by, he'd left scant souvenir. No rock was in evidence, no hump or hill, nor any tall tree. A narrow spit strewn with myrtle, scarcely more than a sand bar, was all that divided them from the open sea, but there was in the air no sniff of brine, for the wind was off the land and held only the musty rotten stench of swamps.

To members of the crew, three times as many as would have been needed to man a vessel such as the *John and Elizabeth,* this was no time for rechecking, repainting, retarring—or repose. It wasn't a vacation, but just another day.

They gossiped listlessly. They smoked their pipes and cooked their food. A few fished. One doggedly worked an accordion, singing the while in a cracked baritone.

Since nothing might be expected from right or left, from north or south, and surely not from a wilderness that stretched wearily, the men kept their accustomed vigil only on the east side—the side toward the sea. That spit did nothing to block the view, being low. Even without going aloft, even without a glass, they could have seen anything larger than a rowboat making along this part of the coast.

George Rounsivel, however, like Ezra Garde, like Tom Walker, looked in the other direction, and sighed.

Patience was not a virtue rife among these scavangers of the sea. The voyage, so far, almost three weeks out of Jorobado, was going badly. In all that time they had not even known a chase, a thrill. Their only encounter had been with the *Schatje*, already stripped, and useless to them as a craft because she was so slow. Never another sail had they sighted. This, to be sure, was not the fault of the officers; but the officers would be blamed.

Stay-at-homes, in the security of their chairs, before their fires, were given, George knew, to gloating of this or that pirate hoard, imagining rich treasures. Such colorful rascals (the stay-at-homes fondly supposed) tossed diamonds like dice, gambling for drinks of rare wine by the light of candles that were affixed to massive branches of gold, the loot, no doubt, from some cathedral. The truth was different. Along the coast of the Carolinas, as everywhere too among the Antilles, the plunder was hardly so bright. The pirates in fact would take anything they could get, as witness the three poor devils of that gallot, who had been stripped of their very suits, their very underwear, before they were slaughtered.

Homeward-bound cargoes might consist of cocoa beans, coffee, molasses, mahogany, brazilletto, and other products of field and forest. Ships from England were likely to be loaded with small metal objects, such as nails, of which there were never enough in the American colonies, or else with clothing. Camlet, doeskin and drugget—these were great prizes. They didn't go bad; they could be sold almost anywhere; and the possibility of later identification was so slight as to be meaningless. Thus the pirates, actually preferred, say, eighteen or twenty cases of shoes to the finest chased chalice that ever decorated an altar. The shoes were easier to get rid of.

The accumulated booty in the hold of the *John and Elizabeth,* all of it seized before George Rounsivel had joined the band, was a mixed lot—and unexciting. There were some staves, in not very good condition. There was a great deal of salted fish, which was beginning to stink: probably it would all have to be thrown overboard. There were twelve tierces of "clayed"—that is, semi-refined—sugar. Best of all there were sixty casks of claret, which might fetch as much as five or six eight-pieces each—if they didn't go sour, or if the men did not broach them.

It was not the grabbing of these articles but the spending of the money they were sold for that gave piquancy to the routine of the corsair in West Indian waters The pirates lived for the time when they might swarm ashore at a protected port, their pockets jingling, sluts trailing them, tradesmen groveling as they passed. There had been a time, within living memory too, when those sprees had made up maybe a tenth of a pirate's professional life, if he was lucky. Today it would appear that they made up rather less than a fiftieth. First, the boodle was harder to sell. Second, the towns in which pirates could carouse were few and very far between. Port Royal had been burned to the ground The Spaniards were watching Campeche and Trinidad as a cat watches a mouse-hole. Samana was doubtful today, and unsafe. Ash, Tortudos, and Petit Guaves, hot and unpleasant islands at best, and scantily stocked with women, would not be easy to hold against a surprise attack, and offered no notable hinterland. One of the reasons George had been able to persuade a majority of the Jorobado gang to make for the Carolina coast was that he believed, or had heard, that after they had sold their goods to the merchants who would be represented at Spritsail they would be permitted to roister, all unmolested, in Charles Town.

The first part of this promise, it would seem, had been rash. The second part of course depended upon the first. Cash was good in the grogshops, but not contraband. Once again this was as a result of no error on the part of George Rounsivel; but he would nevertheless be held accountable, and the men behind him were muttering among themselves.

"*There's somebody!*"

"Yes, I saw him," said George. "But just for an instant. He looked small. Almost like a boy."

"He could at least tell us something."

"Unless he runs away."

George looked around. They were at anchor just inside of the spit, no more than a couple of hundred yards from the beach where he and Garde and Walker all had spotted that man skulking among the myrtle. The deck, though crowded, was hardly a scene of animation. Anne Bonney hadn't even taken the trouble to come topside when the hook was let go. Some, disgusted, slept. Others kept watch to eastward. The accordionist pluckily pursued a ditty they all knew too well.

"*My name was William Kidd, when I sailed, when I sailed.*
My name was William Kidd when I sailed.
My name was William Kidd,
God's laws I did forbid.
And so wickedly I did, when I sailed."

"There's for sure nobody *else* there," Walker said. "Nobody hiding."

"That's my conclusion too," George said. "I'll go ashore. But I'll leave you two here. Put the smallboat over, Tom. And pick me a pair of hands for the oars."

"Any preference?"

"Yes. I want Jack Rackham to be one of 'em."

Anyone watching George Rounsivel as he was rowed ashore —seeing the way he sat, the jut of his jaw, the quiet confidence in his eyes, the firmness of the hands clasped each on a kneecap—would have cried: "There's a man who knows what he is doing!"

Anyone would have been wrong.

The truth was that George had no idea what he was going to do next. He was sure of one thing only: that if he means to keep his crown, not to mention the head beneath it, a king must never seem to waver. So he sat serene, his chin high.

His primary purpose in urging a visit to the Carolinas was to get these desperados away from New Providence, get them at least to *think* about something else. Rejoined to Vane surely, and perhaps even by themselves, they could have taken New Providence. They had owned it once; why should they not own it again? Built up, properly fortified, it could be their capital, their base, their stronghold, best of all an open market for their loot. The possession of such a port would have been of incalculable advantage to the whole business of freebooting. It would draw pirates and piratical merchants from all over the world.

George had little loyalty for the town, which he had scarcely seen, and never really lived in, where he'd lain in durance. It could be razed to the last beam, burned to the last scrap of canvas, without a tear from him. But he did feel a certain obligation to the governor, with whom he had a contract, which, though verbal, and it could be contended made under duress, nevertheless *was* a contract. Woodes Rogers had undertaken a tremendous task, and any man should feel sympathy for such an official. Even more did George Rounsivel think of the Angel of Fort Nassau, the governor's dark-haired neice, Delicia. She would not become the property of the king alone, if New Providence was stormed and sacked. She would be passed around.

Was she still there? By this time surely the governor would have returned from his trip to the outer islands, and would have heard of the chase after George, and of George's disappearance. Thomas Robinson was not a reticent man. He might soft-pedal the account of his own activities in Government House that night, but it was sure he would report that Rounsivel had broken in. Would the governor guess why? Would he reason that George might have been in town to try to warn him? Would he sense the nearness of the pirate force, and foresee an early attack? The walls of Fort Nassau still were in no condition to withstand even a short siege. Whilst they were being strengthened and rebuilt, would the governor send his womenfolk away? George prayed that he had.

There was a secondary motive, one he didn't always acknowledge. Tugging at his consciousness from time to time was the realization that he might be able to escape in the Carolinas. There would of course be shore parties, for wood and water if for nothing else, and as skipper he might lead any of these. Through no slip of his own he found himself in an insufferable position. Anywhere among the islands he was doomed. Sooner or later either the law would catch up to him or the pirates would learn that he was a spy. Really, in the long run, every man's hand was against him. He was an outcast.

But they didn't know this in Philadelphia. There were no cities or even settlements along the coast of North Carolina, but a fugitive from a pirate ship assumedly would be able to find his way inland to some plantation, and eventually, with cash, north. George had the cash. The purse of Spanish eight-real pieces, each worth about four shillings, still was more than half full. They were as acceptable as English minted money, and at least as common, in any of the American colonies.

Why shouldn't he flee? He was under no true obligation. He had been most heinously imposed upon. In Philadelphia, where he had friends and position, the pirates would never get him. Woodes Rogers could have hanged him in New Providence, granted; but Rogers could not hang him in Philadelphia.

As for his employers, those moneymen at whose behest he had set forth on this strange voyage, couldn't he report to them in all fairness, that he was convinced that the Bahama Islands, whatever their possibilities, at present had not reached a state of civilization sufficient to justify financial investment from outside.

And then he would be right back where he had started from.

Yet he didn't like it, and for all his seeming serenity as he was rowed ashore his mind seethed with contradictions and doubt.

More immediately there was the approaching beach. He studied it.

Though he was certain that he had seen a man flit from one patch of palmetto to another, there was no sign of this now. When the boat grated upon a sandy shore it might have been touching an island never before viewed by mankind.

"Pull it well up."

In addition to Jack Rackham he had under him one Si Simonson, a quiet young man, efficient, and seemingly unafraid. What Simonson's personal opinion of the king was nobody but himself knew, but it was established at least that the man was no follower of Rackham; doubtless Tom

Walker had picked him for that reason. He carried a cudgel. Rackham had a short cutlass and of course his knife.

Rackham was not defiant. Though he didn't grovel, no touch of the old arrogance remained. His face had cleared, yet habitually he kept it averted, as his eyes were downcast. George was not fooled by this. The man bided his time. He waited for that misstep. There would only be one.

George had an increasing conviction that they were being watched. Still he studied the shore. Scrub-pine, palmetto and myrtle, offered plenty of places for concealment. He was, frankly afraid to plunge into that undergrowth. He was afraid to turn his back upon any part of it.

"You on this side," he said to Rackham, "and you," to Si Simonson, "on my left. Stay about ten feet away. Don't beat the bushes. Just walk. And look."

Was this a will-of-the-wisp they pursued? Several times they stopped, thinking that they'd heard something; but in a moment they would continue. The ground yielded no clue. Yet they were certain that a man was there—somewhere—near at hand.

That was the terrible part of it, that uncertainty. The Spaniards have a phrase for the way these three walked: *la barba sobre el hombro*, the beard on the shoulder. They looked where they were going, but they looked too, and almost as much, back over the way they had come. They couldn't have said why. They all felt the same.

In about twenty minutes—they had moved very slowly— they came upon evidence that some human being recently *had* been here, after all. It gave them no comfort.

It was a camp, if a rude one. There was a lean-to made of thatch, protecting nothing. There were stones assembled to form a crude fireplace, and the inside surfaces of these were warm.

But—who would dwell in this desolate spot? There seemed no reason for the existence of such a camp, mean though it was. Here was no hill, no ford. The camp did not command any manner of pass, road, trail. There was not even a spring.

Puzzled, they stood staring down at the meagre remains of a fire.

"Maybe we'd better—"

Out of a corner of one eye George Rounsivel caught a movement in the bush. He whirled around.

"There he is!"

He started to run.

He was fast, but the other was faster. A shadow, a wraith —and then there was nothing, not even a leaf or broken twig to show where the thing had been.

Threshing through the brush, sobbing with rage, George could hear Rackham and Si Simonson on either side, doing the same. It was humiliating that one man—for they were sure that there was only one—could throw them into such a fright. It was shameful.

Suddenly, as though at a signal, though none had been called, they stopped, all three. They heard nothing. Yet the fellow could not be far away.

"Why don't you come out and say 'hello'?" George called.

They were ranged in a line, all facing the same direction, holding their breath.

"We won't hurt you," George called. "All we want is water."

The voice, when it came, was unexpectedly loud and deep. It came too from an unexpected direction—behind them. They spun around.

"Ain't that Calico Jack Rackham, the one on the right? Yes," as the about-face was executed, "I see it is. So I reckon you're all right. But a man can't be too careful in these parts."

What emerged could in truth have been a ghost or shade. He was small, a wasp, the only thing big about him being his voice. His hair was very long and so matted with dirt that its original color might have been hard to make out; the same could be said of his beard. His eyes were hollows of madness sunk deep into his head as though they'd been pushed there with a stick. Legs and feet were bare, like the head. The only garment this extraordinary creature seemed to wear was a long sad-colored linsey-woolsey shirt, many sizes too large for him, showing in fact more like a monk's robe, an appearance heightened by the piece of rope knotted about his waist. For one so small and spry, and who lately had proved himself so fleet, he walked with an incredibly clumsy gait, feet spread wide, rolling his shoulders.

He stopped; and though he did not move he seemed poised like a suspicious bird, ready to dart away at any moment.

"Don't ye remember me, Jack?" he thundered. "Caleb Hands. We was brethren under Cap'n England two years agone."

"*Hands!* Scald my spit, man, of course I know you! Where've ye been all this time?"

"Working with Edward Teach, till they sabered him."

"Teach is dead? Blackbeard himself?"

"Aye. Couple of Navy vessels came down from Virginny and bottled him at Ocracoke. Then they boarded him. Most of the men quit, right there on deck, once Teach was dead. But three of us got off, and we tried to make it along the coast, meaning to get to Charles Town. But the others fell away. I was the only one to reach this far, which I took it to be as good a place as any to sit and wait for somebody to come along that might be—well, friendly, so to speak."

"Teach was run through, you say?"

"Aye. By a young lieutenant named Maynard. Skewered him five-six times. Teach didn't even know he was dead, he was so drunk. I saw the fight, just before I went over the taffrail."

"And the others?"

"Hanged 'em, I guess. Took 'em back to Virginny anyway."

Hands was watching George Rounsivel and Si Simonson sideways, and now he appealed, deferentially, apologetically, to Rackham.

"Your, uh, your mates here, Jack . . . are they . . . well . . ."

"As stout a pair of pirates as you'll find anywhere in the Little Indies," Rackham promptly replied.

George winced at the word "pirates," and so, oddly, did Caleb Hands. Hands looked embarrassed as he shook hands with Simonson and with George.

"I used to, uh, go looking for some goods that might be assigned to me sometimes, as Jack'll tell ye. But this is no time for the coastal brethren—not here in the Carolinas anyway."

"Stede Bonnet?" asked George.

"He went before Teach. They got him last September down the coast a short piece. I tell you there's no room for a rover in these parts any more. The people are very unfriendly."

"Major Bonnet himself, eh?" said Rackham. "They didn't hang *him?*"

"Him and thirty-two others. Out on the mud flats at a place they call White Point. They buried 'em below the high-water mark. Right in Charles Town *itself*, mind ye!"

"Aye. Things have certainly changed."

"It was when I heard about that that I decided not to go on. I thought I'd take my chances waiting here and just eating fish."

"I can see your point," Rackham muttered.

"Moody came down from Boston not long ago. But he took one look into that harbor, and he sailed away. Dick Worley came down from New York, he went in, and they banged him. He got himself killed in that fight, which made him luckier'n his men. Twenty-four of them they took, a round two dozen, and they hanged every last one. Out at White Point again. More corpses for that mud. It must stink something fierce there at low tide."

The little man harrumphed woefully, and spat.

"That's why maybe I seemed a bit skittish, back a little while ago there. No telling *who* might be coming along, these days. It's been right lonesome here sometimes, but it's better'n kicking air."

"I can see your point," Rackham said again.

Hands was a fussy little fellow, very prim in some of his ways. Quite formally he asked George if the *John and Elizabeth* might be thought to need help "on the account."

George replied that he had no doubt of it, though of course it was a matter for the council to decide. He himself did not fear an addition to the Jack Rackham forces just now. Also, Hands amused him. The little man's voice, like the roar of a lion coming out of a mouse's mouth, was wonderful to hear, his elaborate avoidance of the word "pirate" wonderful to consider. Hands would say "roving" or "cruising" or even, once, "coursing"—a word George had never heard in that connection—but he would never say "pirate" or "piracy." He would speak of "handling goods on the account," or "transferring cargos at sea," but he'd not speak of stealing.

Hands was extremely serious, and strove to be business-like. He asked George about the number of the crew, their quarters, their experience. He even asked to have the articles of comradeship recited to him, something that George, who knew them from memory, having written them, easily did. George did not add that he himself never had sworn to those articles, the ceremony having taken place while he was away from Cayo Jorobado. This had slipped the notice of everybody else; but *he* remembered it.

Solemnly, nodding, Caleb Hands approved the articles.

He consented to go to the sloop. But first, at George's request, he would show them the spring.

In fact there were two springs. One was conveniently near the beach, but its water, probably as a result of this proximity, proved brackish. The other was several miles inland, and they never would have found it in that pathless land had not the infallible Hands guided them. They marked it in their minds, and on the way back to the beach George was busy with plans for landing and filling the casks.

" 'Tis a trim vessel you have out there, Captain, from what I saw of her," Caleb Hands ventured. "Ideal size, I'd think, for . . . well, for patrolling the seas."

"Yes, she's good for that," George said. "Take a look at her lines astern, when we get there. Ah, here we are now!"

He pushed through the last mass of palmetto, and waved grandly toward the bay.

"You see what I mean?" he said.

"What?" said Caleb Hands.

George, who had gestured, now looked along his own arm.

Spritsail Inlet was absolutely empty. There wasn't a trace of the *John and Elizabeth*.

"Hm-m," said George, and took snuff.

As he repocketed the box, flicking a speck from his stock, he might have posed as a model of imperturbability, a man without a care in this world. Instead he reeled.

The numbness of the shock had faded before he finished his brushing, and a succession of fiery emotions tore his breast.

Exultation was first. He was free! He didn't have to desert the ship; the ship had deserted him.

On the heels of this came stabbing swift emptiness, a feeling of lost hope, desolation. He had hated the *John and Elizabeth;* yet in its way, if only for a little while, that sloop had been home. And now it was gone—with all the supplies.

At last he knew puzzlement, and, tumbling over this, swamping it, indignation and anger.

Where in Hell did they think they were going? He, George Rounsivel, might not know much about navigation, but by God he did know something about law, and by piratical law or ordinary maritime law or just everywhere-accepted usage, as it were common law, the captain of a vessel dictated that vessel's movements, none of which could be made without his assent.

Granted that in an emergency an acting captain should use his own best judgment—how could an emergency have risen here?

Anchorages, George had been told at the most awkward times could prove tricky. Mud might shift; the erosion of sandbars, especially near the mouth of a harbor, sometimes resulted in a change of current habits.

Yet Spritsail was renowned as a haven. All mariners averred that its bottom was reliable. It was indeed for this reason rather than its location that the pirates preferred it. Also, Ezra Garde, who had been in and out of Spritsail half a dozen times, with glee had pronounced the place to be, *geographically*, the same as ever.

Nor was there any threat of a squall. The sky, one huge bruise, though low was not menacing. The wind was damp and disagreeable, but it stood unwaveringly off the land.

There was nothing wrong with the *John and Elizabeth's* cable. George himself had examined it that very morning.

"What d'ye suppose happened to those fools?" he drawled.

He sat on the overturned Moses-boat, and stretched his legs.

If he had ever feared that this disappearance meant a rising of the pro-Rackham element—but he hadn't—Calico Jack's behavior now reassured him. The former quarter-master, the short-time king, was in no way flustered. He too, and naturally, made himself comfortable, as did Si

Simonson, kicking off his boots, punching a pillow out of his coat, and stretching himself upon the sand. As for the hard-bitten small Hands, he went, humming, about the business of finding firewood, driftwood, as readily and unconcernedly as though sloops in this God forsaken inlet evaporated every afternoon.

"Sighted a topsail and went after it," Simonson said in casual answer to George's casual remark.

"Of course," said George.

Yes! He should have known it! Pirates used sneak tactics, pounce tactics. They leapt, hit, ran. A chase in the open might be spoiled by the coming of night and a shift of course, or by the appearance of a warship, or even a spell of nasty weather. The experienced, practical freebooter preferred to work offshore, operating out of coves, small bays, creeks, inlets like Spritsail. It was for this reason that skippers, save when they neared their destination, or when they were not sure of their bearings, kept away from shore. When coasters did come close, to check their reckoning, it was likely to be at or near some outthrust landmark—Hatteras, Lookout, Fear—which was why those points were well patrolled. But it could happen here as well. And seemingly it had.

That Tom Walker would give instant chase was to be expected. The men would have consented to nothing less. No doubt Tom had seen that there wasn't time to send a party ashore to seek out the skipper. In addition to the Moses, *John and Elizabeth* carried only a longboat, which it could have taken twenty minutes to launch, even in this weather, and which might be needed in the capture.

If the pirates, gazing across that myrtle-blanketed spit of land, could see the top-hamper of a vessel that was outside, then those aboard the oncoming vessel could easily spot the sloop. Tom had done right.

Caleb Hands caught a mullet and a couple of blues with

as little effort and in scarcely more time than it would have taken him to scoop up three handfuls of sand; and soon they had a fire going. George ate absently, striving to show bored, forcing himself to keep his gaze from the entrance of the inlet. Not so Hands. Though he was the smallest of the four, or perhaps for that reason, Hands was determined to be the first to see the return of the sloop, and while still munching a fish-head he climbed to the top of a scrub-pine, from whence, after a couple of hours, came his shout.

"Here they are! With a prize!"

George's mind was in a whirl. His show of nonchalance had become a strain. On the one hand, he was glad that they had broken what seemed a spell of bad luck, so that his own standing as skipper might be maintained at least a mite longer. He was glad too that he had not been obliged to be present when this happened. On the other hand, he hoped that there had been no slaughter.

"Big one?" he asked after a while, daintily wiping his hands.

"No-o-o, she don't look big. Smaller'n the sloop even. They got her right alongside and I guess they're shifting cargo. But we'll know pretty soon anyway. Here comes the longboat into the bay."

This was in charge of Walker's mate, Eb Nast, who, like the rowers, was in a state of jubilation. They all talked at once.

The prize itself, it came out, was insignificant—a pink out of Kingston, bound, probably illegitimately, for Boston, carrying a low grade of molasses and not much of it. Nevertheless, trifling though she was in herself, she had broken the streak of luck. What's more, she had put in at New Providence for more than a week, and several members of her crew, who had already agreed to sign on the *John and Elizabeth,* had had a look at the ramparts of Fort Nassau and had talked at length with some of the gunners.

"They swear we could smash that place in an afternoon, cap'n sir!"

"Do they?" George was icy. "Doubtless they had a better look than I did."

"Oh, they must have! They say—"

"We'll discuss this later," said George.

His manner was a cold douche on the ardor of the hands, and soon he shifted his ground, becoming milder, more conciliatory. He asked how many of the pink's crew had agreed to go on the account, and was told five. He asked if they had any other reason to think that the Fort Nassau walls would prove weak, and Eb Nast eagerly replied—yes, the prisoner.

"*Prisoner!* We don't want any damned sniveling *prisoners!*"

"This one is different, cap'n sir. You see it's— Well, here we are."

George scrambled up the ladder, cheered by men who had watched the long-boat approach, and immediately and angrily accosted Tom Walker.

"What the Devil's this about a *prisoner?*"

"Why yes, cap'n. Here—"

Coming across the waist was Delicia Rogers.

CHAPTER XIV

THE DECK might have been pneumatic, the way she walked. Her chin was high, her eyes bright with scorn. Not for her the cringing of a captive, the wide-eyed horror of a woman left alone among monsters. In a brown camlet gown over a yellow silk petticoat, she swished saucily. Her breast was bare, frilled along the top of the bodice, and the only ornament she wore, saving her rings, was a large emerald hung at the throat by a thin gold chain.

The sight of George did not unsettle her. *She's heard my name here, she remembered it!* was his thought. He made a leg, bowing low to cover his fluster.

She raised a quizzing-glass.

"Ah, yes, we have met before. You're the ruffian who broke into my uncle's house by the garden window and stole that very sword you're holding now. La, 'tis a small world!"

There was a snigger, and the men edged in. George wished he had some place to put the sword, that large Spanish cavalry saber. He could hardly swing it authoritatively here. There wasn't room.

"Madame's memory is remarkable," he said.

So, he might have added, was Madame's voice—at least it was remarkably unlike the one he remembered. In New Providence this girl had been earnest, crisp, nobody's fool, neat but never officious, and at all times quiet. Now, as though by a trick worked with light, she had been transformed. Not only her voice but also her accent, and her whole demeanor, had changed.

George thought that he knew the reason; as he studied her under lowered lids he became certain of this.

She was afraid. She was all but convulsed with fear as she faced him. Under the rouge, hastily put on, her cheeks had been drained of color. Whenever she didn't bite it her lower lip wobbled. Yet she had decided, probably in the instant before capture, that bravado was her only resource. She must frown them down, never letting her uncertainty show Once she wavered she was lost.

It took courage, that attitude. It took valor of a high order. George felt like cheering.

Instead he bowed again, whispering to her as his face was averted.

"Do they know who you are?"

"Of course," she whispered back. "Some of them have

seen me scores of times, at the fort, at Government House."

He gave a grim nod. He had expected that answer. The exuberance of the men told its own tale. Now there was not a doubt in their minds that soon they would take New Providence back; for didn't they have the governor's niece as hostage?

On the way back to the *John and Elizabeth*, seated beside her in the sternsheets, he asked her under his breath, out of a corner of his mouth, how she, a woman alone, had been passenger aboard of a vessel that sailed such dangerous waters.

Her reply was as low, and hurried.

"My aunt was to have been with me, and two armed servants. My uncle wished to get us off the islands because he'd heard that the pirates might storm Nassau. But my aunt became ill at the last minute, after I'd gone aboard, and the skipper wouldn't wait for her—or for the servants. He was panicky. He'd heard too that the pirates were about to pounce."

Then, in a louder, more imperious voice:

"Captain—if they call you that—permit me to point out that I am no kid to be nabbed in the streets."

"True," he conceded.

On deck of the sloop courageously, if pathetically, she smoothed her petticoat.

"Then let's put an end to this farce. Your scoundrels have tripped that vessel I was aboard of. But the proposal that I myself should be your prisoner is—why, la, sir, 'tis preposterous!"

George Rounsivel looked around. He was willing to fight, but to fight against such crushing odds would be to defeat his own purpose. The men from the pink, excepting the quintet that had elected to join the *John and Elizabeth* crew, were a cowed pack, without arms. His own rascals were too excited even to consider any rational argument.

The eyes he saw were avid, hot. The mouths worked. Even stolid Tom Walker, George believed, would not stand by him if he proposed so outrageous a breach of piratical law as the release of Delicia Rogers.

"I fear that I don't agree," he blandly replied. "We rovers of the sea, ma'am, pick up such treasures as we can. Ofttimes we don't put a price on 'em till later, after the peril's past."

"Peril! Faith, man, there was no combat at all! They swarmed aboard of us like cockroaches!"

She stamped an unseen foot.

"Captain, let's have no more of this nonsense. I demand that you return me to my own vessel at once."

"Ma'am, I will see that you are accommodated here as comfortably as lies within our power."

"Skipper," somebody falsettoed, "why couldn't she bunk in the forecastle?"

There was a great laugh at this, and Delicia colored, anger for a moment swamping her fear.

George however was solemn. He stepped around her, facing all the men in the waist and on the foredeck. He held up the saber.

"Listen! Lady Luck was with us today for sure!"

"And she wasn't the only lady either!"

"That's right, she wasn't. But you know these women. They stick together. They compare notes. And what's more, this one behind me happens to be the niece of Governor Rogers."

He paused as though he had just made an announcement that should startle them; but nobody stirred.

"For that reason, if for no other," George went on, "she should be handled with gloves."

"Her uncle didn't handle John Augur that way! Or Jennings! Or young Dennis Macarty!"

"Need you tell *me* that? Wasn't *I* there?"

There was a mutter of approbation. George's escape was like a legend in the gang, the members of which were proud of it.

"But this woman didn't hang us. No, she tried to comfort us. I ought to know. She brought us fruit. She brought us flowers."

"That helped a hell of a lot when they kicked away that platform!"

"She's entitled to our respect," George pursued. "What's more, she's *goods!* Aye, goods and chattels! You know that. Now listen: If we don't deliver those goods in prime condition d'ye think any bargain we might have made will be respected by the party of the second part? If she'd been banged about, if she'd been dishonored, wouldn't we lose the best card in our hand?"

He did not wait for an answer but turned to the after-deck ladder. With his saber he pointed to a line traced on the deck in tar.

"More than ever this rule holds: Nobody goes aft of that line for any reason whatever excepting officers and the helmsman. Is that clear?"

There were nods, not all of them amiable. But nobody said anything.

George crooked his right arm to Delicia Rogers.

"If you will do me the honor—"

"Is that customary among pirates too?"

"It might be as well," he whispered, "not to use that word."

She understood, and inclined a grave head, and put her hand on George's arm.

In the corridor, necessarily, they were close, almost pressed against one another, and he could feel her trembling.

"You were wonderful," he whispered. "Keep it up. I'll get you out—somehow."

He threw open his cabin door.

Actually, and amazingly, he had forgotten Anne Bonney. She was lying in the lower bunk, hers, largely naked, while she buffed her nails. There was a bottle of rum at her side. Between her painted lips protruded a small thin brown spiral of tobacco leaf, a thing the Spaniards called a *cigaro,* and the smoke from this filled the air.

"Come in, sister," she demanded. "I don't suppose one more bitch is likely to crowd this place."

CHAPTER XV

THE DAYS that followed were dreary. An onlooker, had there been one, might have seen the *John and Elizabeth* as jaunty, her sails set, a trim craft scudding across that cerulean sea with pertness and joy. It was not so, as a closer look would have shown. Fear gripped the sloop. Suspicion stalked it.

The pirates were a volatile lot, who habitually went to extremes, and perhaps it was to have been expected that a mood of doubtfulness would descend upon them as a reaction from the over-exuberance that followed the seizure of the pink. But there could be no question that Caleb Hands, who had helped to bring it about, greatly quickened that mood. For all his grotesque attire, Hands, a tiny man, just at first was inconspicuous; when he protested the release of the pink nobody paid attention. Hands would have burned the thing, with or without those members of its crew who were reluctant to go on the account. The taking-over of goods at sea, he had pointed out, was as much a hanging offense as murder; so why leave any evidence? Scuttled, the pink might stay afloat for a long time, or else she might only half-sink, to be found later. Fired, the way the wind was, inevitably she'd be blown out to sea—and oblivion.

From this talk the others turned away. The last bit of

looting had been done. It was dusk, and a flaming vessel would be a beacon-light for many miles. It would have to be watched against the possibility of rain: they had not forgotten the Dutch gallot Vane had failed to finish. As for prisoners, always excepting the Angel, whose value was unique, there simply was no room for them. Already the *John and Elizabeth* was overmanned, short of water and fuel, low on grub, tight for space. No, take the last chunk of metal from the Jamaicans, leave them a few crumbs of biscuit, half a keg of water, some sail-scraps, and to hell with them! This actually was done, without any formal vote, even without an order from the captain, who in any event was too much occupied with the women in the after-cabin to care. When last seen, as night eagerly closed in, the pink from Jamaica was limping south along the coast—the direction of Charles Town.

"And that's right where she'll go," Hands bitterly predicted. "And she'll make it, just barely. And next morning they'll come swarming out of there like hornets out of a hive, those armed cutters. And they'll start scouring the coast for us."

They scoffed at this, for a little while, for they had been used to thinking of the Carolinas as friendly country. But Hands was emphatic. And when they heard what Jack Rackham said about him, and heard too that little Caleb Hands had witnessed the death of Blackbeard, being one of three men who had escaped alive from that battle at Ocracoke, probably presently the only survivor, they listened with more respect.

"I tell you, you don't know the way folks in these parts look at us rovers of the seas now! It's all different from what it was! They forget how much money the Brethren of the Coast used to spend in their shops. Now they keep saying we've got to be hanged because we spoil their trade. Everything's trade! And I know this—I know *I* sure don't want to be in this part of the Atlantic Ocean when the folks in Charles Town hear about that pink!"

It was a spirit that spread swiftly; and the council held on the foredeck that very night, a few hours after the departure of the pink, voted not to remain in the neighborhood, even for wood and water, as originally planned, not to run up the coast toward Philadelphia nor yet down toward the Florida Strait and, eventually, New Providence, but rather to drive right out to sea on a course due east.

George Rounsivel did not convene this council, and though he more or less presided over it, and though he was many times called "cap'n, sir," an extraordinary courtesy on the part of men who had come to hate the very sound of that word "sir," still he had but a single vote and could not have effected the decision. But far from being in opposition to the tactic George was delighted, forseeing as he did that it would take them out of the lane of unescorted merchant vessels flying the English flag, something he dreaded to meet.

Now if a Spanish or French vessel was encountered—that would be different. For the pink had brought from New Providence more than Delicia Rogers, some low-grade molasses, and a handful of recruits: it had also brought news that war at last was declared. True, the *John and Elizabeth* remained an outlaw ship, certainly not possessed of a letter of marque. But "privateering" was an elastic word; if a prize was big enough, and its military value important enough, much might be forgiven, at least unofficially.

A peril, as he heard it from Ezra Garde, who had opposed the out-to-sea movement, was that they might find themselves in the Horse Latitudes, a belt of alternate squall and dead-calm that strips the northern edge of the trades. But nobody, excepting Garde and George himself, his pupil, took navigation seriously. They could proceed by guess and by God, and they might get there—tomorrow.

So the sloop drove, gay to see, glum to inhabit. Her

decks were slovenly, her standing rigging slack. There was no discipline, hardly any watches. It was necessary to ration both water and wood, and the water shortage was used as an excuse to broach more than one of the wine casks, so that drunkenness increased every day. The weather was chill and rainy. The helmsman always had to be watched: uninterested, he could not be made to steer small. Ezra Garde confessed, though only privately to his skipper, that he no longer had any clear idea of where they were.

Then, the third morning, when the crew would at last have been willing to consent to a southerly course, they stumbled upon a convoy making northeast, and the warship escorting these vessels promptly gave chase. In ordinary circumstances this would be no more than a warning, a notice to run away. A Royal Navy unit could hardly hope to overtake a pirate. The skipper of this one—a sloop, and heavily armed, as they saw by means of the glass—evidently thought well of his charge's speed, or was bored with his mercantile company, or both. At any rate, he kept after them all day, never drawing close but never shaken off either. For this reason, to get every ounce of speed out of the *John and Elizabeth*, with all canvas cracked on, they flew right before the wind. When darkness at last permitted them to make about on a more southerly course, they were a very long way from where they had been ten hours earlier.

By noon of the next day not only were they hopelessly lost—they were becalmed.

The air had become warmer, but it was wet. The sails hung limp. The very gunwales were beaded with moisture. There was never any sunlight, and the horizon was near at hand. Some pirates might have passed the time in sleeping on deck, but the squalls hardly permitted this. The squalls came with no warning in a yellowish-gray sky, pouncing out of the nowhere upon this pitifully small sloop, which for a few minutes would bob and spin like an eggshell while rain lashed it with all the insensate rage of a maniac wielding a whip. This would cease as abruptly as it had started, and the wind would fall away, the heat would return, while steam rose from every exposed surface, the sails, the spars, the very deck-boards reeking, so that it was difficult to breathe. This might happen six times a day.

Tempers were short in that suffocating atmosphere. Uncooked food—the firewood had given out entirely—did not satisfy the men, who were drinking too much claret. There were frequent fights. The five from Jamaica, those out of the pink, loudly and often regretted that they had quit a comfortable berth for such a life as this. Even Caleb Hands couldn't catch any fish. And the sun was not there to shoot, nor was there ever a star at night.

Bad as conditions might have been on deck and in the forecastle, conditions in the officers' cabin were worse.

George had ordered Tom Walker out of the single-bunk room, occupying this himself. The quartermaster, a mountain of patience, made no complaint; but Ezra Garde squawked plaintively when his charts were ejected and he himself commanded not to use the after-cabin again on any pretext.

George, then, slept in the single cabin, when he permitted himself to sleep at all; the two women slept in the other, across the corridor. Because both doors were left ajar, for purposes of ventilation, George often could hear Anne Bonney's voice, though he couldn't distinguish the words. Delicia never answered.

Anne had not proved as receptive as first she'd seemed. She did not like Delicia, whose quiet disdain, not even cold, not even haughty, roiled her. They were natural enemies, those two, who would have hated one another no matter what the circumstances. Delicia took it out in silence, Anne in a steady low venomous line of talk, largely obscene, always insulting, from which Delicia could escape only by fleeing to the deck, though Anne sometimes followed her even there.

There was no delicacy about Anne Bonney, who with fine cunning used her coarseness to hurt Delicia, like turning a knife in a wound. Time and again in Delicia's presence she would call out to George, reminding him of their relations, demanding to know why he never came to her bunk any more.

"What's wrong—the heat sapping you? Or ain't I good enough, now you've got a governor's relation to make eyes at? *She* won't mind. She can look the other way."

"Shut your mouth," George would wearily call.

"Or we could send her up on deck and tell her not to come back without knocking? Or to the forecastle—the boys there'd take on almost anything, the way they feel now. I've seen them looking at me—and for that matter, at her too."

"Shut your mouth."

He too had seen those looks, and they made him tremble. This couldn't go on much longer. Somebody would run mad.

"I don't like it," he told Delicia."

"I don't either. Of course I pretend to ignore them. But I'm not, really. It . . . it's almost as though they were putting their hands on me, under my petticoat."

She never reproached George, even, as now, in the privacy of the women's cabin. Yet, though impersonal, studiously nonintimate, she could be plain-spoken. Hers was a practical nature.

"You know, of course, that I'll protect your honor with everything I have, including my life?"

There couldn't have been anything less Galahadish. He said it dispassionately, seriously, as though he were discussing a law case. And she received it so, inclining her head in acknowledgement.

"Yes, I realize that. I don't know why a man like you should. But—I'm sure you will."

He spread his hands.

"But there's *only* my life! And if that's gone—what else? No, we've got to keep the peace, somehow. I could call out the whole pack of 'em when I see them looking at you that way. But that would be—the end."

"Yes."

"Where's Anne? I don't want her to be talking to any of those men forward. She has a genius for stirring up trouble."

Delicia shrugged. She didn't like to talk about Anne Bonney, or even think about her.

"Whatever we're going to do, we'd better do it soon," George said. "Something'll crack if we don't."

He rose.

"I'd better go see. You wait here."

Anne was not on the afterdeck. She was not in the waist. George went forward.

Men were watching him. Conversations died.

She was not on the forward deck. She could only be down in the forecastle itself.

Sailors were notoriously touchy about the forecastle, their own quarters, their haven. George had heard that on many Royal Navy vessels, probably on most of them, it would be, literally, as much as an officer's life was worth for him to descend unannounced into the forecastle.

He had no reason to think that the *John and Elizabeth* pirates were as resentful as all that, but he had hitherto made it a point never even to go near the forecastle hatch, which except in times of rain was left open. Now, however, he went there directly.

He didn't call out. That would have been cowardly. Instead he climbed down.

This was something like descending into hell. The air was

hot, wet. The place was very dark. It stank so that it made his eyes sting.

He stood at the foot of the ladder, waiting for his eyes to grow accustomed to the gloom. A row of bunks stretched on either side, but immediately he could make out no figures. Yet he could hear the men catch up their breath at sight of him. And there was another sound he heard too, a slight slithering metallic sound. Had somebody drawn a knife?

"All right, Anne," he said at last. "Come on. You know you're not supposed to be down here."

She was sulky, but she obeyed. He heard her stir, cat-like, and then she sidled past him to the ladder. Nobody else moved. Nobody said anything.

She started up the ladder.

"Trouble with you," she muttered, "you don't want any-body else to have any fun. I came here because I thought you'd like to screw that black-haired tart in peace. But no, you have to—"

"Keep going," said George Rounsivel.

After she had reached the deck he turned to the ladder and mounted. That was a terrible thing to do, turn his back to those unseen figures of the forecastle. Death or quick mutilation might have been immediate. But he heard never a sound.

The helmsman—the tiller was untended, having no motion —sat on the taffrail smoking a pipe. Further along the taff-rail, glaring out over a flat oily sea, where the wake would have been if *John and Elizabeth* had had any way, was Anne Bonney.

George gave a general nod, and went below.

"I have been thinking it over," he told Delicia, "and I've decided what we have got to do, you and I."

"What?"

"We've got to get married—right now."

They were all but breathing into each other's faces.

Her violet eyes widened, and they were lovely; her mouth trembled. She whirled away from George, and threw herself face-down upon the lower bunk. Her shoulders jerked as she sobbed with no sound.

It was a measure of her distress that she'd cast herself into Anne Bonney's bunk. She hated that bunk.

George looked down at her for a long while, then quietly went away. He knew little about it, but his instinct told him that when a woman wept she should be left alone.

Thomas Walker, master gunner, was coming across the waist. He had heard of George's visit to the forecastle, and sensed that something was afoot, that his services might be needed. His step steady, his dark face seamed, he was dependability, he was integrity, a man who had lived according to his lights as he could see them. If his duty was by the side of his skipper, then he would be by his skipper's side. Blue eyes interrogative, he regarded George, who ever so slightly shook his head; and then Tom fell away like a cast-off tender.

Anne Bonney still glowered over the taffrail at a listless sea. This was a spot she favored, for in any sort of wind her body would be well outlined, and the men on the forward deck would be given something to hitch their imaginations upon. But this afternoon Anne looked drab, a spoiled slack woman. She was twenty. She looked thirty-five.

The helmsman puffed on, gazing at nothing.

George walked three times around the deck, then went below again.

Delicia had recovered. More, she'd fussed among the bottles and jugs on her dressing table, among the rosewater and perfume, and now as she sat waiting for him on the only stool the room afforded there was over her face no sign of a tear-stain.

"I'm sorry," she said simply. "But it happens nobody ever

proposed marriage to me before. This means something to a woman, the first time. And then—it was you."

"A lawyer and an outcast," he agreed. "An escaped prisoner."

"You may be too harsh on yourself, sir. I don't know. I only know that I think my uncle trusted you, and I love my uncle. But this is no time to go into that."

"It isn't. And I must be harsh on you too, for this is no time for gallantry either. Ma'am, you misread me. I was clumsy, the way I phrased it. I haven't proposed matrimony."

Now she did look up; fear edged her eyes.

"Sir, you mean—"

"No, I don't plan to rape you. Quite the contrary. Didn't I a little while ago say I'd give my life to protect your honor?"

"You did." She managed a small smile as she regained confidence. "You who protest that you mean no gallantry!"

"'Twas sober, ma'am. And so is this."

"And so is—*what?*"

"My suggestion that we appear to be married." He flipped a thumb. "Those cutthroats might break all ten of the commandments every day, but I believe they respect certain civilized institutions. As my wife you would be free of lecherous hands, even lecherous looks. And I don't mean simply out of fear of me, though I count on that as well."

"I see . . . and it is kind of you to think of it, captain. But—then wouldn't they expect us to sleep together?"

"Not with Anne here. She'd do everything she could to prevent it, and she's a resourceful young woman. They know that."

Now Delicia looked at her hands in her lap. When she spoke it was wryly, from a corner of her mouth.

"I—I almost wish you had been sincere, captain. This embarrasses me."

"It embarrasses *me!*"

"The thought is ingenious. And for sure you're better acquainted with these ruffians than ever I could be. But—is it conceivable that they're so stupid they'd believe us to be husband and wife who met again by chance and didn't take the trouble to announce our relationship until we had been at sea for almost a week?"

"Mistress Rogers, I have mismanaged my words. No, I didn't mean that. What I meant," while he reached past her and lifted a Book of Common Prayer from the dressing table, "was that we should be wed right here and now, up on deck, in full sight of them all. *That* they'd credit."

"Oh . . . you mean a mock marriage?"

"Yes. But they wouldn't know that. They are aware in a general way that the captain of a ship at sea is authorized to perform the ceremony in certain circumstances, but they wouldn't know those circumstances. And I will explain, learnedly and at length, that English common law assumes a contract *per verba de presenti* or *per verba de futuro cum copula* to constitute a complete marriage in itself."

"I never went to school, I don't know what that means."

"Nor will they. But they'll reason that if it's in Latin it must be sound."

"But *you're* the captain of this ship! You can't marry *yourself!*"

"I can deputize Tom Walker. This wouldn't be regular, but again *they* won't know that."

"It seems to me, sir, that you are playing upon the ignorance of these men. And that's not kind."

"It seems to me, ma'am, that you are I are not in any position to look for kindness. Also, I'll concoct a glittering paper."

He related that it had been his knowledge of the law and his ability to spout thunderous legal phrases that got him into this trouble in the first place. He told her about the articles of companionship so laboriously framed on Jorobado.

He pointed to the pirates' reverence of documents, of long words.

"In this case the marriage contract will be written right before their faces. If nothing else did it, that alone should convince 'em."

She took the prayer book from his hands.

"Captain," she said at last, "I don't question your honesty. But the conditions are unusual. You might have heard that I inherited a competence from my father, who was killed by the Spaniards? He got his lay of the enterprise all the same; my uncle saw to that. I am worth something over twelve thousand pounds. Did you know that?"

"No. And it wouldn't have made any difference if I had."

"Again, let me stress that I don't call to question your honor. But I must guard what I have. And isn't it possible that your family might later have a claim on my modest fortune? What I'm getting at, captain, is this: Are you absolutely sure that what you propose wouldn't have any legal standing?"

"Absolutely," he replied. "Nothing that happens on this vessel could have any meaning in law. These men are *Hostis humani generis*, enemies of the human race, by their own declaration. That removes them from law—any law—anywhere. The sloop itself doesn't have legal status. Nobody here owns it or has any sort of authorization to sail it. It has no home port, no registration, no clearance. As for the marriage contract itself, I'll give it to you to burn after it's had its effect on the men. And remember, anyway, that I am an escaped felon. Nothing I sign could have any legality. Even if the contract was *cum copula.*"

"What's that mean?"

"Never mind, now."

"But—I'd have to sign as well?"

"You could say afterward that you'd acted under duress. Your life had been threatened. Or your virtue. Or both.

And mind you, ma'am, that would be no more than the truth."

"Yes . . ."

Thomas Walker, quartermaster, acting captain, had a forefinger as stubby as the butt of a hippopotamus. It budged with labor across the page, elaborately indicating each word.

The book itself, a tiny thing of ivory vellum with a goldleaf cross and goldleaf title, in those huge hands looked like a beautiful small bird limned on a tangle of twigs. When it shook—for Tom was nervous—it seemed to be struggling to get away.

Tom could read, but just barely. The words came out lumps of lead.

"Dearly beloved, we are gathered together . . . to join this man and this woman in holy Matrimony; which is an honorable estate, instituted of God in the time of man's innocence, signifying unto us the mystical union that is betwixt Christ and his Church . . ."

The men stood tense, heads bare.

George slipped a hand into one of Delicia's hands.

"I require and charge you both, as ye will answer at the dreadful day of judgement . . . that if either of you know any impedient, why ye may not be lawfully joined together. . . ."

A breeze, halting at first, rustled the marriage contract that lay on the capstan beside them. The spritsail flapped. The maincourse flopped hollowly, and there was a rattle of reefpoints. For the first time in five days *John and Elizabeth* spoke at the bows.

It was an awakening, the termination of the trance. They were away from the doldrums! George squeezed Delicia's hand.

"Those whom God hath joined let no man put asunder. I pronounce you man and wife. I guess that's all. Amen."

There was a crash of cheering, and wine was brought out, also a cask of French brandy somebody until this time had kept hidden. "Kiss her, cap'n! Go on, kiss her!" The canvas had bellied out, stiff. The sloop was rolling.

George put his hands on Delicia's shoulders, and he smiled fondly down into that small intent face.

"We ought to do it—what they're yelling. I mean, for the sake of appearances."

"Would it . . . would it be so painful?"

So they kissed, and the applause was such that for some moments nobody heard Peter Knight, the "boy" of the crew, who had gone forward and who came scampering aft now, flapping his arms, gawky as a stork.

"A sail! A Spaniard! It's a sail!"

CHAPTER XVI

THE LAD WAS RIGHT. Muddle-headed about many things, a dolt, he did know his ships. He had called correctly when he proclaimed this one Spanish, as pirate after pirate soon averred. George, not so skilled in such matters, could get no man to explain why he was sure of the nationality, but he didn't hesitate to make all preparation for attack as he ordered a change of course.

Certainly the newcomer was large—a three-decker, a galleon—but the wild hope that she might be a treasure carrier was early whiffed away. Not since the time of Drake in the Atlantic, Woodes Rogers in the Pacific, had the Spaniards permitted ships laden with bullion to travel alone. This one was slow, lumbering awkwardly across the sea like some wounded animal. Had it become lost? Was it seeking its escort? Yet this was not the time for shipping treasure, the season of the so-called Plate Fleet.

All the same, they went for it immediately. The sloop, happy in the new breeze, fairly leapt through the water. There was something exhilarating, a David-and-Goliath glint, about the scene.

"I wish you wouldn't do it," a voice behind him said.

His "bride" was there, gazing somberly at the vessel they neared.

"She's Spanish, yes," Delicia went on. "But you might think of me. What happens to me if you're killed?"

He nodded as though to acknowledge a fair question, though like her, like everybody aboard of *John and Elizabth*, he was intently watching the galleon.

Running right before the wind, she might have been hard for even the pirate sloop to catch. But none of the topsails were in place, nor was there a jib, and clearly she was crank. She wallowed awkwardly on no fixed course. The likeness to a wounded animal was poetically sound. Had this galleon been crippled in some freak storm? Was her rigging wrecked, and had her tiller been damaged, or the whip-staff, or even the rudder itself?

Or perhaps—an explosion?

She swarmed with hurrying figures, though there were no shouts of defiance when the *John and Elizabeth* drew near, no brandishing of steel, as might have been expected. A gun-port was opened, then another, then a dozen at once, and guns were run out.

The yellow flag of Leon was hauled to the forepeak. That should have been a proud defiant gesture, but somehow it wasn't; somehow it hinted of weakness.

Thoughtful, George Rounsivel watched.

There was a touch of hysteria, he sensed, in the way those Spaniards were scampering back and forth.

"If I'm killed I shall be a hero," he answered quietly, "and they will respect my 'widow'—at least for a little while.

But if I don't lead them to a prize they'll mutiny. Then anything might happen."

"But you can't capture *that?*"

"I wonder. We couldn't hold her, if we did. But why does she look frightened?"

"She doesn't look frightened to me."

"She does to me. Excuse me, ma'am."

He conferred a moment with Ezra Garde, then with Tom Walker, and returned to Delicia's side. He was loading his pistols.

"You'd better go below. I'm sorry I had to choose so bold a thrust at a time like this, but as I see it boldness is our best chance."

"This isn't boldness, sir. This is suicide."

"I don't think so, quite."

By this time they had actually overtaken and passed the galleon and were making about to starboard, not more than four or five cablelengths away, so that if the wind held they should approach her a bit forward of the larboard beam, falling off all the while. It must have looked to those aboard the Spanish ship as though the pirates meant to ram, though this was unthinkable, truly, considering the difference in the size of these vessels. In fact it was part of George's plan, if fired upon, to drive straight ahead until he was so close to the galleon that her cannons could not be depressed to hit so small a sloop, then to veer sharply starboard, passing close to the galleon, right under her counter. The *John and Elizabeth* in the hands of a good sailing-master could make almost directly into the wind's eye, at least in moderate weather like this, and when they ran away they wouldn't present much of a target.

George waved.

"Those guns are mounted for broadside firing, naturally. With carriages like that they can't be *aimed,* excepting as the ship itself is. They can only be *laid.* Still, three or four of them could rake us from stem to stern for a few minutes as we drive in. If that happens everybody on this deck might be killed. That's why I asked you to go below."

"If everybody on deck is killed, how would I survive below anyway?"

"There's logic in that. Well, watch out for splinters. Excuse me. Peter! Break out the rogers!"

The *John and Elizabeth* did not stock an extensive collection of signals. She had no national oriflamme, having no nationality. She had no fleet flag, not being a part of any fleet. She did not even have a distress flag. Who would go to the aid of outcasts?

Indeed, the only flags the *John and Elizabeth* carried were what the pirates called—nobody knew why—rogers, or sometimes jolly-rogers. There were two of these, both large. One was bright red, the other black.

Their messages were understood in these waters. The red flag said: "We are closing. If you make any resistance you will all be killed." The black flag said: "You have had your chance. Now die."

The black flag, was the flag of death.

"Raise the red one," George commanded.

Anne Bonney minced up to him. She pretended not to see Delicia. She made a mock salute, but for all the levity her eyes were shining bright and her mouth had a lascivious twist.

"Cap'n sir, permission to join the boarding party?"

"No. Stay here. Or below. And keep out of the way of that tiller. We might have to put about almighty fast."

Aboard of the galleon, movement had largely ceased, the antlike scurry had subsided.

Aboard of *John and Elizabeth* there never had been any outward show of excitement, no running around. The false gunnels had been raised the moment an alarm was given, and the men, armed to the teeth, some of them bearing knotted lines to which grappling hooks were tied, crouched behind these. Aside from George, the helmsman, and the two women on the afterdeck, young Peter Knight in the waist preparing to hoist the red ensign, and Tom Walker, a linstock in his hand, by the side of the big brass twelve-pounder forward, the Spaniards must have seen this as a ghost boat.

The cannon was the same that George once had been tied to. It was loaded now, but not shotted, being plugged only with wadding, for it was to be used as a warning, not as a weapon.

"Are we close enough?" George called.

"Count twenty," called Tom Walker.

"Count it yourself. And then let fly."

A graveyard silence, save for the speaking at the bows and the silken swish of the wake, held the world. Everything seemed petrified. Caught up in their fate, they were driving forward, or were *driven* forward inexorably, the mouths of twenty cannons gawping at them.

George checked his pistols and took a better grip on the saber he held.

Without moving his head, he looked right. Delicia Rogers was a statue, staring straight ahead, fascinated by that enormous wall of oak and all those grim round metal rings that leered from out of it. She was frightened; but she had told herself, he read, that she would not flinch, she would not close her eyes even when the fighting started.

George looked left. Anne Bonney was tense, her head out-thrust, her mouth working; she tingled with the thought of blood and death to come. Her right hand, like a separate thing a thing over which her mind had no control, was pawing at the top of her bodice.

"You keep that knife to yourself," George said harshly. "And remember what I told you about staying away from the tiller."

The twelve-pounder crashed, a deafening sound that

seemed to jolt the sloop in its tracks. Smoke rolled back over those who stood on the afterdeck.

The red roger was raised.

The false gunnels were torn down, and the men behind them rose, yelling and yammering, making the air hideous as they waved knives, cutlasses, cudgels.

The two vessels got closer . . . and closer . . .

There was a borborygmus grunt, as though some fat man had turned over in his sleep, and a blob of smoke stood out at the mouth of one of the cannons, to be instantly whipped sternward. About halfway between galleon and sloop a geyser rose, and stood a moment, shimmering, and suddenly collapsed.

The yellow flag of Leon came tumbling down.

The Spaniard had struck.

The captain, his head in his arms, wept convulsively. A huge man in sky-blue silk, silver lace, red heels, and a hat with an eight-inch plume, he should have represented gaiety rather than grief; yet the grief was real. The captain was having a run of bad luck.

His bottom needed scraping; yet he'd been given no time to have this done, the galleon being called up to complete a convoy. News of war had reached Panama, and *all* Spanish ships, not simply the treasure galleons, were ordered to cross in convoy. He was undermanned, having scarcely three hundred sailors, many of them sick. His cargo, largely bulk salt, was cheap, vulgar, and hard to handle. Worst of all were his passengers, about whom he was given no choice. Don Fernando de Floridablanca, was both bumptious and well-connected. He had with him a small army of relations and servants, and believed that his position entitled him to call upon the captain for anything that any of these persons might happen to desire.

Six days out, and while they were hove-to at night, another vessel had fouled the rudder of the *Nostra Signiora de Victoria* (she had been Portuguese originally: the name was never changed), and next morning when by flag the captain had sought permission to put into St. Jago, Cuba, he was curtly told to continue his course, repairing as he went. This he had done, making much progress, when two days later in the Florida Straights he had looked around one dawn to find himself alone, having lost the lights of the others. He had decided to take advantage of this and put back for Cuba after all—when a British frigate appeared from the south; and the *Nostra Signiora* of necessity fled.

The chase, lasting all day, had been touch-and-go. When darkness came to reprieve the Spaniard the frigate was almost within gunshot. His jury-rudder well in hand now, under cover of night the galleon captain had headed straight out to sea, despairing of ever making Cuba or of rejoining the convoy, but hoping in this way to shake off the Englishman.

Then came the storm, a day and night of it, tossing him all but on his beam-ends, smashing three of his hatches, flooding his cargo, carrying away much of his rigging, and ruining once more his rudder.

And after the storm—a sail astern!

Assuming with a great sigh that it was the frigate—had he not heard of the persistence of those English?—and knowing that further flight was impossible, he had prepared to resist. It would have been a token resistance.

But now he learned that more than his cargo had been spoiled by sea water. The whole magazine had been flooded. He didn't have a dry crumb of gunpowder aboard of that whole great ship.

Worse still was in store, the worst of all. The craft that was catching up to them was not the frigate but a miserable pirate. And Don Fernando, apprised of the situation, had insisted that they strike. The single shot they had fired—

they'd not even been sure that it would explode—was no more than a ceremony pop meant to save the honor of Spain.

And so the captain sobbed, while George Rounsivel let coins cascade between his fingers, and, paying no heed to them, surveyed this gorgeous, this truly splendid cabin. George never before had been aboard of a ship this size.

He who wept had not told George this story directly, for he could speak no English. A disdainful young officer in scarlet, a toothpick with an unbelievably long name, had interpreted. Gestures too had done a great deal, for the captain was an expressive man. And George's knowledge of Latin had helped.

These three were the only ones in the cabin. There might easily have been thirty more.

"Um-m . . ." said George, still looking around. "And this, you say, is the ship's money complete?"

"Every piece of it, *señor!*"

It was a large chest, oak bound with brass, and full to the top with coins. There were thousands of these; George, letting them dribble between his fingers, felt the fascination of cash, hard cold clicking cash. They testified not only to the immense wealth of the Spanish Indies, but also to the varied nature of the trade there, despite government restrictions, for the coins were of many national enstampments. Some were silver—shillings, testers, ecus, pistolets, eight-real pieces—but the great majority were gold—Louis d'ors, guineas, moidores, maravedis, doubloons, especially doubloons.

"Of course you are lying," George murmured.

"*Señor!*"

A sword whirred out.

"Tut and tut. Put up, my friend. You wouldn't fight me. In the first place, I'm not properly armed." He glanced at the cavalry saber he held, a good enough wand of authority but hardly a weapon with which to meet any hidalgo. "In the second place, you, a Spanish gentleman, surely would not condescent to cross swords with a common thief? In the third place, you know you really *are* lying, after all. And in the fourth place, If you was to take one step in my direction I'd whistle and this cabin would be full of my men. So . . . put up."

The toothpick sheathed, his brow a thundercloud.

The captain had lifted his head and was watching them. He muttered something to the interpreter, who shrugged and made a curt bow.

"His excellency *el capitán* regrets to see that you are not sworded as befits one of your station, and he asks if you would be so kind as to accept a gift of his own blade."

He's afraid of losing more than that, was George's thought. Yet George, delighted, accepted with an alacrity that was probably ill-mannered. It had been some time since he owned a real sword.

The thing was a treasure in itself. A true rapier, whippy, razor-edged, longer than a court sword but as light, it came from Toledo. The name of the maker meant nothing to George, but the heft of the weapon told him what he was getting. The blade was one that could only have come out of Spain.

Even as he strapped it on, even as he mumbled *"Muchas gracias,"* which was most of the Spanish he knew, he was wondering what had prompted the gift. They were eager to be rid of him: that was certain.

When he had boasted that with a whistle he could have filled this cabin, it was no more than the truth. The *Nostra Signiora* might have been short-handed but yet she carried five or six times as many men as the *John and Elizabeth*. Even if some were sick and all were dog-tired after the battle with the storm, and lacked gunpowder, they nevertheless could be a formidable force if ever they got together, if their rage was aroused. It was for this reason that George had given the command that the pirates stay on deck, not going below for any reason whatever, even to pursue a man with gold earrings. It would be too easy to get lost down there, too easy for a small party or a single prowler to be waylaid and slaughtered without any sound that would rise to the rest. This was an order it would not be easy to enforce. The pirates were a greedy lot. It was their natural wish to snatch things, to strip and secret them. But—one pirate striving to wrench one ring from the finger of one Spanish sailor might be enough to bring about a battle.

It had taken four Spaniards to haul this money chest to the middle of the captain's cabin; it would take twice as many, or more, to lower it from the waist of the galleon to the foredeck of the rollicking *John and Elizabeth,* fastened alongside like a tender. At all costs George must keep his forces together and have that operation well guarded.

As he made for the deck he was conscious of the fact that he wore one sword at his side whilst he carried another, clumsier one in his hand. The difference between them, moreover, was marked. He felt oddly lopsided, like a man who walks with a polished jackboot on one foot, a hole-studded, run-over shoe on the other.

He waggled the saber apologetically.

"Tell the *capitán* that I would leave this behind, after his gracious gift, but that it has a sentimental value for a friend of mine, to whom I wish to return it."

He slipped out the key, and from the open doorway turned to look at them. The captain's face showed somewhat glassy, still streaked with tear-lines, but there was a glow of unforgiving hatred behind the self-pity. The toothpick with the long name, the interpreter, made not the slightest attempt to hide his own rage.

It would not be well if the tables were turned here. These men wouldn't show mercy. By international law, such as that was, the captain of a ship at sea was not only permitted but even expected to hang without trial any pirate taken.

"I'll return soon, gentlemen," murmured George. He stepped out on the deck, locking the door behind him.

Hopefully he looked astern. This would be a meet time for the cry "A sail!" So much of his life these days seemed bounded by that call! But the horizon was unspotted.

He glanced at the foretop. There was a lookout posted, and he seemed alert, for he kept turning slowly, to scan all of the sea; but he gave no shout.

The pirates were not idle. They did not stand in one group to be scowled at. It had been George's first order that they search the open-deck area for water casks, for fresh food, and wood. Even as George came out of the captain's cabin a squad under the direction of Tom Walker was lowering a live sheep from galleon to sloop, where several such already were milling about, uncertain of themselves, where too there were piles of firewood and several crates of chickens.

There were only three persons left aboard of the *John and Elizabeth,* the boy Peter and the two women. Now George ordered half a dozen more there.

First, however, he had them haul out the money chest, and he gave them all a glimpse of its contents. He stood aside, glorying in the gasps, while the pirates one by one plunged their arms up to the elbow in gold and silver.

When after that he explained to them the need for an extremely careful handling of the money chest they were disposed to listen and to agree, taking their minds, for a little while at least, away from thoughts of more mundane plunder.

They were all good rope workers. Within minutes they had made a large firm hempen hammock. Lines through the handles of the chest would not have been enough. So they made a net for it, and wrapped it into this. They attached lines to each corner of this net, knotting the lines so that they could be the more surely lowered. Then, and not until then, with six men waiting for it below, while others held the two vessels close together with boat hooks and grappling hooks, they slipped the chest over the side.

About half of the pirates were thus engaged, but George saw to it that the other half did not go prowling. He formed them into a guard, and caused them to stand in a semicircle around the workers, facing out, each cutlass drawn, every pistol cocked. There would ótherwise be a chance of a sudden rush from out of some hold or companionway.

He did more. He formed Si Simonson and two others into a sort of flying squad, giving Si the key to the captain's cabin, and every time George saw a Spaniard, officer or man, who looked like a possible upriser, he pointed that man out to Si and his companions, who promptly clapped him into the captain's cabin.

Not until the job was all but finished did George slip away from the others and go aft to study the horizon. And his lips went into a small tight grin. He glanced aloft; but the lookout was too intent upon the lowering of the coin chest to have seen the vessel that approached. George regarded it again. It was coming fast.

"The bulldogs," he muttered.

When the chest was safely down in the sloop's hold, the pirates would have run every-which-way. Even George could not have restrained them much longer. But he held up both arms, as he thundered for attention.

"You see that dot astern of us? That's an English frigate. She's chased this galleon for three days, and she's not likely to give up now and go after us—unless we're still here when she arrives. You understand?"

He pointed down to the *John and Elizabeth*, a cockleshell, it seemed, alongside of this Spanish leviathan.

"We've got plenty. The rest of you can run around looking

for more, but I'll advise you to hang together and never turn your backs on anybody. And remember this: we sail in half an hour, and anybody who isn't aboard of us then stays *here*. I mean that! I am going down to my cabin now and turn over my glass. It takes exactly half an hour, and when the last grain of sand has run through we cast off, no matter how many are left and no matter who they are. All right? Dismissed!"

He did turn his hourglass over, though he didn't stand and watch it There was no need for this. The pirates operated boisterously but with commendable speed. Before the last grain could have fallen, the decks of the *John and Elizabeth* were crowded with men who laughed and shouted as the two vessels drifted apart, and sometimes waved derisively at the onrushing frigate. Those decks were crowded too with an agglomeration of trinkets and furniture, tapestries and tooled leather, rings, bracelets, swords, muskets, chains, rosaries—not to mention the chickens that cheeped, and the baaing sheep, and the water casks and firewood.

Ezra Garde saluted.

"The course, cap'n sir?"

"Make for New Providence," said George. "Wherever that is."

"Aye, wherever that is."

The loot was stacked in piles and pyramids, so many of them, and so haphazardly strewn about, that it would seem as though order would never be restored there. But already Tom Walker, in his capacity of quartermaster, the man who must supervise the sharing-out, was moving among them, labeling, making notes, restacking, and asking questions. . . .

George Rounsivel, unnoted at the moment, found one article that had escaped attention. This was a piece of paper that had been swept off the capstan, crumpled and forgotten, in the scupper. He picked it up.

It was the "marriage contract." Looking around, to make

sure that he was not being watched, he dropped it over the side. But there was a lump in his throat. He wished so much that the thing had been real!

CHAPTER XVII

IT WAS HARD TO SLEEP, the nights were so hot. In daylight hours the sun shone furiously, so that the very tar in the deck seams bubbled, while to pick up a marlinspike was like taking hold of the wrong end of a poker, and the breeze, when there was any breeze at all, was languid, soupy, soporific. But the nights were hell.

George Rounsivel was learning, as many another had, that marriage can complicate a man's life.

The third day after the sack of the Spaniard, in the middle of the afternoon, he was lying, slimy with sweat, on his bunk. He was there only in order to get out of the blasting sun, as at night, hoping to catch some air, he would lie, like the others, on deck. He did not aspire to any real sleep; he would but doze groggily from time to time, feeling more fuzzy-headed after each nap.

The only sound that came to him, in addition to an occasional sad squeal of timbers, was the steady wet slap-slap of Anne Bonney's knife on the honing-stone across the corridor. There was something fiendish about the way she kept sharpening that already perfectly sharp weapon; but then, there was something fiendish about Anne anyway.

The sound, though it irritated George, at least assured him that she was in her cabin. More and more often these days she was risking brief visits to the forecastle, where George had no doubt she harangued the Rackham forces. Well, he didn't think she would get far. He believed that for the hour at least his leadership was not to be shaken.

It had been a near thing. That galleon had come along none too soon. The great good luck of its being crippled was counted in George's favor, as though he personally had arranged it.

These pirates were a superstitious pack, always prepared to follow anybody who seemed at the time to be blessed by the gods. Even more important to his prestige was the immediacy with which he had ordered an attack. It called for high courage to drive against three tiers of guns; and some of the pirates themselves, George had since learned, had muttered that this might be carrying rashness too far. Calico Jack, beyond all doubt, had been telling them that their new king was a coward. That charge would suit Rackham's book, for had it not worked wonders when brought against Charles Vane? Now Jack Rackham must feel dashed. How Anne Bonney felt George didn't know, and didn't care; but he wished she'd stop honing that damned knife over there.

So just now his position was firm enough, if anything could be considered firm on this listless vessel as it loafed across a scorching sea.

Though the pirates did not know it, their king's first consideration when he had ordered an attack on the galleon was of Delicia Rogers. It was still only the thought of her, so near him here, that could stir his senses. If ever they did reach land, he was determined somehow to smuggle her ashore. He would have to do this alone, for there was nobody he dared, as yet, to take into his confidence. Thomas Walker? He had thought of it. But he must proceed carefully.

One thing he did have, a thing that was sure to be useful, and this was money. His share-and-a-half of the coins in the chest made his purse much heavier.

The division of the spoil, an operation in which all the others took a fanatical interest, and which George found somehow sickening, had occupied most of the waking time these past three days. Though Walker was in charge of this, George as skipper was often appealed to. The cash was easy enough. That was simply a matter of counting, then dividing. But when candlesticks were involved, and necklaces, and bolts of linen, then squabbles were inevitable. George, as must as he could, stayed aloof. Peter Knight the innocent, the one who had sighted the vessel that became a prize, before the division had been awarded a brace of pistols. As the first man to board that prize, George himself was entitled to a similar pair of pistols, but he had pistols already and elected to keep his Spanish sword instead. As for the miscellaneous loot, he simply waived all claim to it. They could divide it among themselves, he decreed. This greatly helped his popularity.

As a pirate king, then, he was doing well. He should have been exultant. He wasn't. He was miserable.

"Stop sharpening that knife," he cried suddenly, snappishly, startling even himself.

The slap-slap ceased. He heard Anne get up, heard her slouch out through the deck door. With a sigh he rose, supposing that he'd better go after her before she stirred up trouble.

"Master Rounsivel—"

"Yes?"

"Please come in."

He entered that cabin quietly, almost reverently. It was hung with clothes, strewn with small feminine articles, and smelled of rosewater, perfume, cigaro smoke, and hot human flesh. Delicia was lying in the upper bunk, the one that had been George's. She had her face turned to the wall, but she lifted a feeble hand to acknowledge his entrance.

"Are you ill?" he asked anxiously.

"Not physically, no. But I don't know how much longer I can stand this."

He sat down, palming his knees.

"Ma'am, I would admire nothing better than to lead you away. But we are surrounded by water, as you may have noticed. The longboat is too much for us to handle, you and I, and the Moses is too small to carry more than a few days water and food."

"I know. And you have been very kind. I shouldn't whimper. But there's one thing—"

"Ma'am, name it."

"Couldn't I get away from this beastly woman? She talks all the time. She seems to talk to herself, but it's all meant for me. She's nasty-mouthed without any letup, even in the middle of the night. It isn't the words. I was brought up in a seafaring neighborhood, and I suppose I know all the very words. But it's her manner. And the details she goes into about . . . well, you and her . . ."

There was some silence.

"I'm sorry, ma'am," he muttered at last, "but I don't see what I can do."

"Couldn't I be moved to that cabin across the way, the one you have now, and you come back here? Then I would at least be alone. I know it's a lot to ask, but—"

"Ma'am, you have forgotten one thing. We are supposed to be married, you and I. Any change of bed would be known forward, and right away. How do you suppose they would think about a man who a few days after his marriage put his wife out and slept with another woman?"

"Are you afraid of your own reputation, then?"

"No, I'm afraid of yours. Or rather, ours, which yours just now depends upon. If we are ever to slip away, as I hope, it will only be because nobody, not even Anne Bonney herself, had suspected us. You must remember that."

She turned, propping herself on an elbow. She had been weeping, but now she managed a smile. She even put out a hand for him to kiss.

"I am sorry, captain. I was weak for a little while. It won't happen again."

George went out on deck. Anne, who doubtless had known that she would be followed, was chatting with the helmsman. Tom Walker was in the waist, a harassed man, still from time to time mumbling figures, adding sums in his head. George scanned the horizon, and sighed, and went to the quartermaster.

"You think Garde will ever get us there?"

"He might."

"By God, it would be good to be on land again!" George cried.

Walker looked at him sideways. The huge man, the one-time blacksmith, who never smiled, from time to time could show some emotion; and George liked to believe that Walker was fond of him. But now Tom shook his head.

"*You* won't be going ashore, cap'n."

"And why not? 'Tis all the clack—we'll have a council about it—but the way the talk runs is we may put in at New Providence and demand that the fort be turned over to us by reason of the hostage we hold. Do you approve of that, Tom? Using a woman like that?"

Tom spat thoughtfully over the side. He answered at last that he would do whatever the council decreed.

"Of course. And so will I. But just supposing that's the way it goes? Why do you say that *I* wouldn't go ashore? Who is better equipped to make terms with the law than I am, the chief?"

"Her husband?" Tom said softly.

"Oh."

"You hadn't thought of that, eh?"

"Well, the truth is, I hadn't, no."

"I'm sure the men trust you, cap'n sir. Leastways as much as they ever trust anybody. But after all—"

"Yes, I see."

He went back to his cabin, and threw himself on his bunk, fairly panting from the heat. Anne Bonney returned, and soon she started to sharpen that knife again. And a sail whoomed out and back, the reefpoints pattering. And a timber creaked . . .

Four days later they sighted land, and to George's amazement it proved to be New Providence.

CHAPTER XVIII

THE LIGHT from the fires were angry, a strident red. It made the bay a blanket of rubies, and pressed upon the hillside a net of inexorable crimson. Though the air that frilled the surface of the bay could scarcely be called even a breeze, on the beach it was different. There the fires swung and swayed, their flames erratically rocking, while the sparks that streamed out of them were a riotous rollicking crowd, now here, now over there. Perhaps the reason for this was the movement of the pirates, who never were still but lurched or danced about the fires, with the frenzy of men obsessed, demons.

In truth there was something infernal about that scene. The shadows of the revelers were black, and they were monstrous. They soared and swooped, flapping their arms, making fantastical motions. The sparks sped skyward, wavering, wobbling, as though they were terrified, as well they might be. It was macabre

So bright was the surface that to George it seemed almost unbelievable that he would not be spotted. But—after all, who cared to scan the bay on a night like this? At most somebody might now and then have tossed a glance toward the *John and Elizabeth,* not two hundred yards from the place of the party. And George, anticipating this, had swum a roundabout course. His head, if seen, might have been taken for a floating coconut, the butt of a log, even a bottle.

Because of this circuitous approach, and also because he swam slowly, never getting his arms above the surface lest he splash, it took him four times as long to reach the sloop as ordinarily it might have done. This was all right. There were four separate fires, four separate groups, on the beach. Even the king would not be immediately missed. For some time it would be supposed by each group that he was with one of the other groups.

Meanwhile, the more drunk the pirates got the slower would be their reaction when at last the truth did dawn upon them.

John and Elizabeth was anchored only by the bow, and by great good fortune she had swung around in such a manner that the starboard side, the side the Moses was on, was away from the shore. George swam to that side.

The women were the only persons aboard of *John and Elizabeth*. It would hardly be advisable to have them on the scene of the brawl. On the other hand, if anything should go wrong on the sloop—if she started to drag her anchor, for instance—they could not be expected to make themselves heard at that distance above the cacophony of the shore; so the Moses-boat had been left to them, launched in advance.

The smaller tender was tied to the base of a Jacob's ladder, and the oars were in it.

George climbed carefully. On the deck he was like a cat. He waited until his breeches, the only article of clothing he wore, had ceased to drip.

He regarded the shore. The figures—they must have been madmen—jigged and darted against the light of the fires. The water gleamed like blood.

Though George had studied the sloop from the beach, and was sure that no detail aboard of her could be made out, he could not escape the conviction that he was bathed in light. When he did move it was very slowly.

At last he went to the door of the after-cabin. This night, blessedly, was comfortable. The women, if they wished, could sleep. Did they? He was certain that one at least lay awake, listening for the signal.

Without having entered the companionway, he scratched lightly on the door. Then he backed to the other side of the waist, where in the shadow of the bulkhead he waited.

As a gesture of goodwill—or so he said—he had left his weapons behind him when they all went to the beach to celebrate in advance the attack they'd soon make on Fort Nassau. It would have been churlish, especially in view of the fact that he himself had proposed this party, to carry that which they regarded as the symbol of his power. Generally, indeed, the pirates were leaving their weapons behind them tonight. After all, they could not be surprised. Cayo Jorobado was their own.

Their landfall of the previous day had not in truth been New Providence, as they first supposed, but at least it was one of the Bahamas. It was Watling's Island, the same that had been Christopher Columbus's first landfall two hundred and twenty-seven years before. Watling's was not presently inhabited, nor had they sighted any sail, so they could assume that they hadn't been seen. From there it would be easy to find their way to New Providence, to Nassau. They could simply feel their way from key to key.

Jorobado was not far off, hardly more than a few miles out of their way, and it was George who suggested that they put up for a few days, to examine the condition of the place, to ascertain if any of the other Brethren of the Coast had lately been there, to make a final refitting, and of course to get drunk. His real purpose had been merely to gain time.

The others, cheering, had agreed. There had not been a single vote against it.

Nor had there been any vote in opposition to an assault

on Fort Nassau. This wasn't even put before the council. It was taken for granted. George himself had been too canny to speak.

When Delicia Rogers appeared from the after-cabin companionway his heart quopped softly. The Angel, truly! She was so beautiful!

She was carrying something in her arms. That was how he had first seen her—carrying something. Then it had been flowers and fruit for the condemned men. Now it was the cavalry saber that belonged to her uncle, the rapier from the galleon, and certain personal articles of her own, not many. Over her shoulders she wore a taffeta traveling cape. It was dun-colored, which was good. Nor was there anything else about her that would have snared a glance—no lace, no jewelry, nothing that would shine or rustle.

She did not carry his pistols. He had told her not to. The pistols were large, they were heavy, and when they worked they were most deplorably loud. The swords would serve. And he had his knife.

She didn't pause on the threshold but came straight to George. She dropped him a mock curtsey and handed him the steel. He grinned at her, nodding approval. Neither said a word. Immensely proud of her for her coolness, wishing he could kiss her, George staidly slipped a hand under her arm and led her to the head of the Jacob's ladder.

This was at the waist, and the *John and Elizabeth* was a low craft, so as Delicia stood in the boat and reached up he easily handed her the goods she had brought. The rapier he had strapped on, and the saber, against the chance of a noisy slip, he held between his teeth. It was an old pirate practice when boarding—to hold a sword between one's teeth. George however was not going *at* an enemy but *away from* one. But he was not ashamed. He didn't have to be.

In the boat he turned from the painter, meaning to set

up the oars first. Delicia was motionless in the sternsheets, upright, even rigid. Yet he knew he could trust her. The courage of that girl! He gave her a friendly nod as he worked out the oars. Then he gasped.

There were no tholepins.

He looked at Delicia. This was the shadowed side of the sloop and there was no moon, but he believed that she was too taut, too near panic, to miss the tholes, without which he couldn't row. He was sure that those pins had been there when the Moses was launched.

He leaned very close to her. His voice might have been a wisp of smoke.

"You're *sure* she's asleep?"

Looking right at him—their eyes were only a few inches apart—Delicia nodded.

George considered.

A tholepin after all was nothing but a small cylinder of wood. It could be improvised—jury-rigged, as the seamen would say. He had his knife. Once they were safely away, out of the bay, in the open waters—provided there had been no alarm—he could take the time to hack a couple of chunks out of the thwarts and whittle these into tholes good enough for a trip to New Providence. It was not what he would have wished, but it was better than going back aboard the sloop. Meanwhile, with an oar each, they could paddle. Everything depended upon speed and silence

He handed her an oar. She looked bewildered, but she took it. He took the other oar, and turned to make loose the painter.

It was then that he saw Anne Bonney. She had a slim head, and though he couldn't see her face he knew that she had never looked better. She had assurance now. She didn't squirm or pout. Even here there was enough of the light from the fires to outline the whole upper part of her body above the gunnels, and outline too the pistol she held.

It was one of George's pistols.

She gave a small, almost a loving giggle. She cocked the gun.

At that instant, like a fiend emerging from the depths, Jack Rackham appeared by her side. He held the other pistol.

"Were you going somewhere?" he asked.

Upright, holding an oar, George regarded the pistols. He knew them well, Brass-barreled, with ivory ball-butts, they were very large, very heavy, and could carry a tremendous charge of powder and a ball the size of the end of your thumb. They had been given to him on his accession to the throne, and as much as the Spanish saber were part of the apparatus of his sovereignty. It was ironical that they should be turned against him.

The muzzles, looking as big as cannons, were no more than six feet from his face. He could not have reached them with his hands. He might have reached them with his rapier— but to draw meant death.

George never left those pistols loaded. When loaded they were dangerous things even to touch. They might go off at any instant—or might not go off at all, even when fired.

Since they were held a little above the level of his eyes George could not see whether there was powder in the pans. Yet he had no doubt that they were loaded. Anne Bonney would have seen to that.

At this distance, if even one of them worked it would all but rip his head off.

The water between boat and sloop clucked pleasantly. From the shore came a burst of song.

George nodded knowingly. He felt no fear for the need to concentrate upon their present problem left him no time for nerves. He kept his poise. If he didn't know what he was about to do next, at least he *looked* as if he did. He was not unfamiliar with such situations. In a courtroom, fazed, habitually he would stand motionless, a very picture of promise, while his mind whirled with possibilities and his will was beset by doubts he wouldn't show. Until he had made his decision as to which way to jump, he could always present the appearance of a man whose next step would be so sure, so crushingly right, an answer to all questions, that out of respect for those who watched him he purposely paused, giving them a chance to prepare themselves for pulverization.

Though they may deny it, and indignantly, there is at least a touch of the actor in every barrister who's worth his salt.

At last, after fully half a minute, George gravely inclined his head. He was careful not to let any other part of himself move.

"My felicitations," he murmumred. "You have brought it off extremely well."

Rackham too was wet, and like George he was bare down to the waist. Droplets of water on his shoulders and along the top of his forearms glittered red in the light of the faraway fires behind him, and his hair was a sopped, close-fitting toque.

But the pistols were dry.

Rackham opened his mouth, and George spoke swiftly, purposing to keep the man off his verbal balance.

"There is one thing you forgot. The lady and I are married. What could be more natural than for a new husband to swim out to his wife?"

Anne said harshly: "I'm here."

"Asleep. And nobody on deck. What an opportunity! Romance can cover a multitude of sins—if they're small enough "

He did not dare turn his head to look at Delicia, just as

he didn't dare to move his hands, in both of which he held the oar awkwardly, like a man about to cast a fishnet.

Rackham's face was not hard to read. Despite the shadow, despite lingering bruises, and cuts even yet not healed, the face told of ambition. Rackham's pride had been stabbed, and he wasn't likely to forget it. He might hate George Rounsivel. He might in a queer perverted way love Anne Bonney. But most of his thoughts were concerned with his own position, his power. He had been upon that throne for so short a time! He would get back.

"If I am not here," George started, meaning that if he were permitted to escape, "the council would elect you again."

"Yes," said Calico Jack. "And that's just why I am going to kill you."

He cocked the pistol.

George carefully cleared his throat, for he wished to be sure that he could speak.

"That won't do you any good," he said at last.

"It won't do *you* any good either," Rackham pointed out.

George forced his lips to spread into a small grin of acknowledgement. He gave the tiniest possible bow, as though before superior intelligence.

"Yet if you'll consider that—"

Ducking his head, he swung the oar. It caught Rackham off guard, knocking the pistol out of his hand so that it plopped into the bay. Anne had a split-second longer, and she used it to step back out of reach of the oar, pulling the trigger as she did so.

There was a blue-purple flare above the pan, and a hiss, but there was no explosion.

Anne did not lose her presence of mind. She fell to one knee, behind the gunnel where George couldn't reach her with that oar, and she recocked the gun and began to bank it in such a way as to force more powder out of the touch-hole and into the pan. Rackham, his own pistol gone, knelt by her side.

George pushed against the side of the sloop with the oar, meaning to get clearance for the Moses. He had forgotten the painter, and his movement, when the boat was yanked back, all but pitched him over the side.

He whipped out the knife and cut them free. He started to paddle. He could hear Delicia doing the same.

After half-a-dozen strong strokes they could exhale, though they didn't pause in their paddling. The pistol Anne Bonney held couldn't throw a bullet more than fifty or sixty feet.

Yet if they didn't fear a ball they did fear a shot. Even the din of those on the beach would be punctured by such a sound. And the longboat would be launched. Delicia and George alone, clumsily paddling, could not hope to keep ahead of the longboat.

But there was no shot.

When they had slipped through the pass and turned the nose of the Moses toward New Providence, beyond the horizon, they relaxed a little.

They drifted, panting.

"So he thought better of it." George mused. "I wonder why."

"I think," whispered Delicia, "that we haven't heard the last of that man."

"My dear," said George, "I think you're right."

He turned, and put a hand on her knee.

"You were wonderful," he said.

Her oar lay across the thwarts, and she was fussing with something in her lap, a small bundle of personal belongings Her hands trembled.

"Thank you," she said as calmly as she could.

The tholepins could wait. Distance first. He picked up his

oar, noting as he did so that his own hands were not as steady as they had been a few minutes ago.

"With luck," he predicted, "we'll make it before the sun gets high."

CHAPTER XIX

THE FINGERTIPS were most marvelously discreet. This might have been a woman. It was instead a small girlish man named Aki, the governor's own body-servant, picked up in God knew what remote Pacific island. He was dainty but thorough. Nor was he garrulous, as masseurs, wigmakers, tailors, and such so often were; this was as well, since nobody but his own master could make anything out of what Aki supposed to be English.

The oil he smeared on George's shoulders and neck and back smelled like coconuts, though not as sweet. He used plenty of it.

They had not made New Providence before the sun got high, or even before noon, and despite an earlier lesson George had embarked upon that perilous voyage without covering for either head or torso. Delicia, using an inner petticoat she had drawn forth without embarrassment or giggle, using also needle-and-thread and a pair of sewing scissors she produced from nowhere, had manufactured for him a couple of garments calculated to cover the exposed spots. But these were not fully effective, and he seethed in many places, when at last they stepped ashore.

Delicia herself had survived much better. What with her cape and a linen peaked cap she fished from out of its folds, she had kept her skin unscorched. Her eyes had been bright, and her manner light And this morning she remained that way, a bird for movement, as George could see when by moving his head a trifle he looked down upon the courtyard of Fort Nassau.

She was crossing that court. She wore a pert small lace cap, and her hoop-petticoat swung saucily on either side. She carried something in her arms, a familiar position; she was again taking something to somebody.

Forgetting Aki, the only other person in the governor's tower chamber, George scowled when he saw Thomas Robinson step out from under an archway and salute her with a bow. She responded with a conventional curtsey, a bob, abrupt.

George could not hear what they said, and wouldn't have cared, but it was clear that Robinson, who no doubt already had congratulated her on her escape, now did nothing more than offer, somewhat elaborately, to relieve her of her burden. She refused. Unchagrined, he fell into step beside her.

That was the least she could do, as the niece of the governor, when she met in so public a place the captain of the guard. All the same, George scowled. He watched them until they had passed from sight.

There was a step, and George rolled his head the other way in time to see Woodes Rogers enter the room.

His Excellency looked much as he had, in this same chamber, how long ago—two months? ten years? Tall, broad of shoulder, a majestic unfaltering figure, when he walked, he limped, and when he spoke it was in a thin, preternaturally high voice.

"You may go, Aki. If you're through? Yes."

He threw himself into an X-chair, and placed a paper on the desk.

"Rounsivel, your report's magnificent!"

George flushed. He had been troubled about that report. He would have preferred more preparation· he didn't like to dash a thing off. A good part of the previous afternoon had been spent in giving an informal oral report, in having his back treated, and in trying on new clothes in his cell— he was technically a prisoner, under sentence of death. Not until dusk, when he had called for candles, did he call also for paper, ink, plume.

He had written the treatise more than once in his mind; but white paper that seems to stretch endlessly, a wetted pen held above it—these have the trick of making plans look absurd.

"You must understand, sir, that that's only . . . well, it's just a first draft. I'd like to polish it a bit."

"It's superb!"

"You would send then to ask a pardon for me?"

"I have already done so. Your treatment of my niece in itself would have prompted it. But this—" He down-knuckled the paper— "This is piracy's death warrant."

"Thank you, sir."

It was a world-famous author who spoke, and George Rounsivel would have been something less than human if he didn't feel delighted. In truth, though he would have wished to touch up the wording, he himself was pleased with the *content* of his report. He had thought about it many times, though until last night he had not made any manner of outline or notes, as he would have liked to do, for he was aware that a few of the Jorobado gang, and notably Jack Rackham, could read.

The report was divided into two parts.

The first part was matter-of-fact and immediate, specific. It recommended consultation with the governors of North Carolina, South Carolina, and Jamaica, about way and means of keeping the Florida Strait safe from sea robbers. It urged stronger restraining methods and much sterner punishments for any who were found to have dealt with pirates, whether harboring them, helping them, supplying them, or, worst of all, buying their loot. It told of piratical habits and in particular the piratical frame of mind, the reverence for writing, the dependence upon chiefs or kings, and offered suggestions as to how this could be taken advantage of. It pointed out that the Bahamas were a maritime colony, and proposed that the governor issue a decree creating a sea militia, the members of which would do their required military service in vessels constructed and maintained for this purpose. Such vessels might be modeled after the Spanish *guardacostas*. They need not be armed, but they should be low, narrow, shallow of draft, and extremely fast—that is, like the pirates' vessels. Among other duties, these militiamen should question the seamen of vessels from New York and Bermuda who could often be found raking salt in the southern islands.

That was a dreary and not notably profitable trade—they carried the salt all the way to the Newfoundland coast where fishermen always needed it for preserving their catch. The salt raker, approached by a pirate, seldom was above getting for supplies or even for cash, goods he knew had been bought with blood. However, the salt raker was not naturally a criminal. He wasn't fierce. He could be frightened. If he was warned, loudly, that any deal with a proven pirate would make him liable to hang, he'd stop it.

The most powerful enemy of piracy in this part of the world, the report went on, was not recognized as such, perhaps because it was also an enemy of the merchant and the Royal Navy. This was the teredo, that persistent, insistent, dioecious, ship's worm. George had estimated that freebooters spent a third of their time scraping their bottoms. The teredo slowed them, in a matter of months; they couldn't risk being slow. A suitable careening site, the report stated, must offer both wood and water, and a high lookout point, a cove or creek that was protected from squalls, a gently sloping beach. There could not be too many such places in the Bahamas for listing, and each of them should be visited periodically by the *guardacostas*. This would make impossible in the future a base such as Jorobado, unknown to the authorities at Fort Nassau, barely over the horizon. It would force the sea robbers to resort to the awkward inefficient method of careening at sea known as "boot-topping," whereby in calm weather and far from land all the guns of a sloop are run to one side, so that she is tipped far over, almost on her beam-ends; and the exposed side is then scraped, after which, if the seas allow, the process is reversed. Pirates dreaded boot-topping, as well they might. Caught in that position they would be helpless.

It was the second part of the report that George himself fancied. Though of fewer words, this was longer-reaching, for in effect it asked the question: *What makes a pirate?* He had sundry answers, none of them cheery.

"I'm having copies made, and I'll see that they're passed around where they will do the most good." The governor gave a thin thorny smile. "R.N. captains ain't going to like that last paragraph."

"Yet it's the truth! Man after man I talked to, if he wasn't a deserter from the Navy he was a deserter from a merchant ship because he feared that the Navy would press him; then he'd be flogged every time he sneezed. And caned, and put into bilboes, and keelhauled. He'd be starved half to death, so that he could hardly drag himself around —and cursed and kicked because he didn't move fast enough. He'd never see his pay, and he'd never be permitted to go ashore." George spread calloused hands. "Well, your excellency can catch their point of view? If a man's to be treated like a dog he might as well pick his own kennel."

"Don't some of them think it's a lark?"

"Some, yes. Just at first. They soon learn it isn't, but then it's too late. It's easier to get *into* piracy, your excellency, than it is to get *out* again. They're always afraid of being exposed. They're afraid their old comrades'll find them out. Deserting from a pirate gang, governor, is as bad as deserting from the Navy. They don't go in for forgiveness, those men. If they ever lay hands on *me*, for instance . . . well, there's no need to go into that now."

"*You* certainly found it easier to get into than get out of, didn't you?"

"Aye. And about that, governor—"

"Yes?"

"Now that we've terminated our contract, as I take it, I want to ask you one thing: If I had refused to break out of this place two months ago *would* you have hanged me?"

Woodes Rogers had eyes the color of violets, but they could be slatey. They were mild and understanding now, reminding George of Delicia's eyes.

"No," he said simply. "But I believed that I would, at the time. I had to make myself believe it, so that I could be convincing to you. There was a great deal at stake, Rounsivel. I was desperate. I cheated you, in effect. I lied to you. But . . . I was desperate."

"I see."

"And now, even besides what you have done for my niece—and I'll never be able to thank you for that—even besides that, I am eternally in your debt, sir. You have done a masterful piece of work."

There were two windows in this tower room, one facing the bay, one the courtyard. It was through the window on the bay side that George Rounsivel had first seen the tropics. Through the other, a little while ago, he had last seen Delicia Rogers. He went to that other now.

She was recrossing the court, Thomas Robinson at her side. Robinson minced, pointing his toes in the fashionable London manner. He wore more ribbons and bows than she, who was always a plain dresser, yet his affectations and la-di-das did nothing to make her show masculine.

A hand slid over George's shoulder.

"She tells me that your literary flair isn't confined to reports, Rounsivel. It seems you wrote a certain paper whilst at sea . . . Whatever happened to it?"

"I threw it overboard."

"Oh? She has a fortune. And you might have had a claim."

"Your excellency is being rude."

"True. Forgive me, Rounsivel."

The governor hobbled to the other window.

"You said that if they got you now they'd kill you?"

"Oh, for sure. And in a very leisurely manner."

"Well, they've lost no time coming."

"*Eh?*"

He went quickly to the other window. The customary harbor craft were in sight, anchored or beached, but nothing was coming in past Hog Island.

"You can't make them out from here, but they're in the offing just beyond the pass. My scouts have brought me word. Two sloops that seem to have met by chance. One's the *John and Elizabeth*, and the other, they think, is the *Revenge*, which was seized last month off Hispaniola by Charles Vane. They're sending in a longboat from the *John and Elizabeth*, with a white flag. There it comes around the island, right now. Want this glass?"

"I don't need it, sir. I know what they're coming for. Me."

"I'm afraid they are."

"Well, if they want me they can take me—at a price. May I have my sword back, sir?"

The sword has always been a symbol of might, of power, authority. Woodes Rogers could have thought only that George was asking for a return of his blade as evidence that his prisoner's status was but nominal. The law was the law, as nobody knew better than George Rounsivel, a convicted felon under sentence of death; but since his return to New Providence the previous afternoon it had been shown in many ways that if he was indeed a prisoner he was a privileged one. Though he had stayed the night in a cell, he was provided with every comfort there, and the door was left open. The taking of his weapons might have been no more than a matter of routine, as their return, at this time, could be considered a mark of confidence in him. In any event, the governor did not hesitate. He handed George his sheath knife, the rapier that had been "given" him by the captain of the *Nostra Signiore,* and the long cavalry saber. The first two George strapped on. The third he handed back.

"This is yours. I, uh, I borrowed it."

If Woodes Rogers could have chuckled he would have chuckled then. But his nature was a decorous one.

"Oh, yes. I heard about that. Robinson's been twitchy to have at you, ever since."

"Pity I can't accommodate him." George glanced out of the window. The longboat was about to be beached, out of range of muskets or even cannon. George could not distinguish any of the faces, but there were almost twenty men. The flag was conspicuous: a man in the bow, upright, held it. "And now, if your excellency will order the gate opened—"

His excellency sprang to his feet.

"Good God, Rounsivel, you don't really mean to go out there!"

Gazing through the window, George frowned a little. He did not look forward with delight to a surrender, but he was made even more uneasy by the prospect of appearing to pose as a hero.

"I don't see anything else for it, sir. If they do what they want with me it may slake their rage. They may not attack. Perhaps I could even help to dissuade them, with lies about the strength of this place. But if they *don't* have me, then they certainly *will* attack. It's the least we can do for . . . for . . . your niece."

"You've already risked your life to save her! D'ye want to

do that every day? It would be nothing less than suicide for you to go out there. And remember, we need fighting men."

"Your excellency's making it very awkward. Will you please order that gate swung open?"

In truth the gate—it was directly below this tower room —might have been open then. At least, a party had issued forth upon the beach down there, a party of three, the middle one, Corporal Pugh, carrying a white flag. They did not hurry; even from behind they looked ready to spin around at the slightest alarm and sprint back to cover. The pirates walked toward them a little, then stopped; the party from the fort also stopped. They began to shout back and forth. It was impossible, in the tower, to make out what they said. Soon, however, the Pugh party, moving faster now, started back for the gate.

"Excuse me, Sir Galahad—"

The governor pushed past him and leaned out of the window.

"Pugh! You corporal down there! What'd they say?"

The soldier executed a trim salute, then cupped his hands informally.

"They say they want George Rounsivel! They must have him!"

"Well, let's not keep them waiting," muttered George.

The governor was looking at him, and seemed about to say something, but changed his mind and limped to the door.

"Stay here a few minutes," he tossed over a shoulder.

It was as good as an order; but a prisoner who has not given his parole can ignore orders. The door was open. George had his rapier. He might have gone down the spiral staircase and sallied forth from the gate—fighting his way out, if need be. But he would be chased; and if he was going to his death he preferred to go at his own pace, not scurrying like a hare.

He did not even turn his head when the governor left,

but still watched the pirates down the beach. They had planted the flag in the sand, and were waiting. But they were alert! With the glass, though he could not make out the faces, he saw that the men were armed, and saw too that each carried at his waist the cloth or leather purse containing coins, his share of the *Nostra Signiore* money. That was like them, never trusting one another.

There was a rush of feet, and he turned to clasp Delicia Rogers in his arms.

She went there naturally, without hesitation; they kissed, while she clung to him with the wild desperation of one who feels herself slipping over the lip of a precipice.

"George, you can't go out there!"

"Your uncle was shrewd to have sent you," he murmured. "Or were you listening at the door?"

"No, he sent me. He told me what you meant to do. That's madness, George! You'd be killed if you went!"

"And *you'd* be killed if I didn't. Dearest, you don't think those men would go away without me? If you do, you don't know them as well as I do."

"I won't let you! It . . . it would be desertion!"

"No it wouldn't. And you know that. What you don't seem to know, my dearest, is that it's more than a gesture. It isn't just for you—it's for myself too. I feel dirty, having mixed with those men. I've got to make myself feel clean again."

"But . . . just when we . .   when we're like this at last—"

"That does make it harder," he whispered.

They kissed.

"I trust I am not intruding?" said Thomas Robinson.

Arms skimbo, feet spread, he stood in the doorway. There was a sour sardonic smile at his mouth, and his eyes swam with venom

George put his beloved carefully aside, placing her behind the desk. If steel was bared that might be the only safe place.

"You are," he said coldly. "What the Devil do you want?"

"You. Please don't scowl. The captain-general sent me, and I am obliged to take his commands. I am to ask if you're sticking to the plan of giving yourself up to those rogues out there. If so, I'm to arrest you."

"I am already under arrest."

Robinson smiled crookedly.

"Not the way I'd do it," he said. "But I see you're sworded? And of course if you'd care to resist—" He glanced at Delicia, moving his eyes as though that very motion hurt them. "If the lady would leave the room . . ."

"No," George said quickly. "I have a rendezvous, and I'll not risk being late."

"I weep to hear you say that."

"I'm sure you do."

"And now, if you'll have the goodness to precede me down the stairs—"

"May I examine those pistols first?"

The request jolted Robinson, whose hands went to the two small silver guns he carried in the scarf flung across his left shoulder. But soon he was smiling again.

"I see. You fear you might be shot in the back whilst trying to escape, eh? You needn't. I'd hardly be such a fool as to go around with these things loaded. Look—"

He took them out, cocked them, snapped them, whacked them against the heel of his hands to prove that no powder could be forced out of the touchhole.

"Very well," said George.

He went to Delicia, and bowed, and kissed her hand. He was formal, but at the same time tender.

"Good-bye, my dearest. I regret like you that we didn't learn sooner. Good-bye."

She said nothing, simply stood there with tears streaming down her cheeks.

The gate still was open, though the Pugh party had

returned. There appeared to be some difficulty in bringing the two leaves together. The soldiers, always clumsy, were inexcusably slow now. Or—did they have their orders?

George stopped. He looked at Robinson, who blandly looked back.

"Why not?" Robinson said in a low voice. "You are something of a veteran at escaping from Fort Nassau. Would another time hurt? I'd raise a hullaballoo, of course, but nobody would shoot after you—not straight anyway."

"Damn it, man, I'm an important prisoner now! You'd be cashiered if you let me get away!"

"And d'ye think I'd mind being cashiered, in the circumstances?"

"No," George said slowly, at last. "No, I don't think you would. All right."

With three strides he was at the gate, and he slipped between its closing halves. He ran a few yards, then slowed to a walk.

There were shouts behind him, the clank of the chain, banging on the gate. A shot was fired, but George never heard the ball.

He kept walking toward the men down the beach.

Then he heard his name called, again and again, from the tower. Delicia was imploring him to come back.

He didn't turn his head. He didn't dare to. He kept walking.

He was not afraid of death in itself. Only a coward can die more than once. George had for so long existed side by side with the realization that he was lucky to be alive that the mere ending of consciousness would come not as a shock but as a confirmation. What he did dread was to be mauled by these ruffians, to be manhandled, hacked, beaten. And it was toward this, he was sure, that he walked. Yet his step was steady. He had ceased to struggle. He had ceased to care. He might have been walking in his sleep.

The sun was very strong, and the sand was light and bright, fiercely reflecting it. The clamor at the gate died, nobody having ventured out after him, for all their brazen fury. Still George did not turn, nor did he look directly at the men he approached.

They must have seen him emerge from the fort, and they were silent, no doubt watching him, probably not sure, because of the glare, of his identity. Not until he was halfway to them did they recognize him, and then they set up a great shout and started to run at him.

Here it comes, he told himself. But he kept his eyes open.

He stopped, and drew, and put himself into guard position, moving with a deliberate, feline, almost scornful grace.

It was not until then that he really looked at the men who were racing toward him.

Their mouths were open, as he had expected, but not to yell in rage, only to cheer. If their arms were raised it was in welcome, not menace. They were overcome with joy at seeing him. They gibbered.

He swallowed, and lowered his point. An instant later he was engulfed by men who slapped his shoulders, slapped his back, pumped his hand, and fairly wept with relief and happiness—not only Tom Walker, not only Si Simonson and Ezra Garde, but all of them.

"Gawd bless ye, cap'n sir!"

"We thought you was dead!"

"Did they harm you here? We'll rip the place to pieces!"

They all talked, babbled rather, at the same time. George never did get a clear picture of what had happened the night he and Delicia left the sloop. Seemingly Rackham, while his doxy was engaged in repriming her pistol, had been smitten with an idea Calculating that he himself would be better off if George was gone, and fearing that George, if brought back, might defy him to his face, splitting the gang, he had not given an alarm. Later, however, he reported that he was sure George and Delicia had escaped in the Moses-boat. He had given no reason for this conviction, nor had Anne Bonney. They were all puzzled and suspicious, and among George's followers the belief grew that Calico Jack had somehow contrived secretly to sell out George, turning him over to the authorities at Fort Nassau—or at least tricking him into going there under false pretenses, knowing that he'd be nabbed. Perhaps Miss Rogers had been a bribe? They couldn't explain it, but neither could Rackham, who waxed evasive. There had been a council. There had almost been a fight, the gang being divided between pro-Rackham and pro-Rounsivel men. In one thing only were they agreed—that they should proceed at once to New Providence.

The meeting with Vane's *Revenge* had been pure chance, but it was no coincidence that Vane was planning to do the same thing they were planning to do, and it wasn't difficult for them both to agree to work together in the assault, burying their differences at least until fort and town had been taken.

It was at this point that George's friends had stepped forward to declare that they weren't willing to take part in any attack on the fort if Captain Rounsivel was in it. They proposed to land near there with a flag, and have a parley, insisting that they at least be permitted to see George, to learn that he was alive. Rackham, no doubt glad to get rid of the dissidents even at the price of a longboat, and secure in the belief that the balance of his force, combined with that of Charles Vane, could take Fort Nassau, had agreed to this.

"He'd've had a tussle on his hands if he'd done anything less," Walker said.

George was sincerely touched. There were tears in his eyes as he thanked them, and he insisted on shaking hands all the way around once more, a sight that must have astonished them in the fort.

"But I will tell you that I left of my own accord. I shouldn't have done that. I should have taken you into my confidence and explained how I felt about Delicia—about my wife."

"How did Jack know this?"

"Guessed it, I guess. He tried to stop us, but we got away anyway."

"He didn't tell us that!"

"It would have made him look foolish."

"But . . . are you all right, cap'n sir? How did they come to let you out like this? Ain't they making to hang you?"

"No," George said thoughtfully. "No, they won't hang me."

"They hanged Cunningham and Augur and—"

"I know, but those men had taken amnesty and then foresworn it."

"Taken what?"

"The King's pardon. The Captain-General isn't a bloodthirsty man. But he hates to be hoodwinked, as Augur and the others tried to do. But *I* didn't. I'll get a pardon. So will you, if you only ask for it properly. Why not? You must be sick of petty pickings. And the Carolina coast's closed now. But they need men here. Seafaring men. Gunners like you, Tom. Navigators like Ezra."

"With our record—"

"Good God, Woodes Rogers has fought with pirates as much as he's ever fought against them. D'ye think he's a man to be finicky about anybody's record, out here? Look at Tom Cockran. Look at Ben Hornigold. Each one's master of his own vessel now, and he was allowed to keep everything he had. You would be too—so long as you haven't taken the King's pardon and then broken your word. You didn't, did you?"

They had not. For one reason or other—absence from the

island at the time, skepticism, fear that though they might go unhanged all their property would be taken—these men never had announced themselves to be on the side of law and order.

"Then that's all right," cried George. "And you've got your money. What can you lose?"

"Our lives. If Vane and Rackham take the fort."

"If you'll fight with us they won't take it."

"Cap'n sir, we trust *you*, sure. But how do we know we can trust this Governor Rogers?"

"I'll give you my life on it."

As they wavered, he went gleefully to work. He appealed to each individually: brought out with no trouble that they were indeed sick of a pirate's life and that the high times were past, the big prizes gone for good. They might have quit piracy ere this, had they trusted anybody on the opposite side. They hadn't even known, as a certainty, that any other existence was open to them. But George told them so. Attorney Rounsivel from Philadelphia told them so.

"What's more, you'll be in the service of the colonial government, and no warship will ever dare to press you."

"But look here: You're so sure you could get us pardons. How? That proclamation said the King's pardon would run out January 5, and here it is almost March."

"Nonsense! Haven't you ever heard of a gubernatorial writ of *nunc pro tunc?*"

"No."

"Neither had I, until just now. I made it up. But the Governor-General doesn't know that, and *he's* the law in this part of the world. They won't know it in London either, but they'll never admit that. And it will hold."

"Oh?"

"Such a writ would be retroactive, of course."

"It would?"

"Surely. In the very nature of it."

"But . . . what *is* it, this nunky-tunk thing?"

"Authority for the governor in his capacity of military commander to extend for not more than sixty days the provisions of the King's pardoning proclamation, provided he has good reasons to do so and believes it to be in the best interests of the colony and the Crown, especially the Crown."

"And the governor don't have any such right, the way things stand now?"

"No. But he doesn't know that. You have no notion how uncertain he is of his own powers. It's his inclination in those circumstances to do what he thinks best and let the legalisms fall where they may. He's no fool, Woodes Rogers! He'll *want* to believe in this beautiful privilege of *nunc pro tunc* that I have invented. And when a man *wants* to believe in anything hard enough you can always *make* him believe it, if only your Latin holds out. Come along. We'll put it up to him. You've got a flag anyway. You have nothing to fear."

Ezra Garde said: "Here comes Vane now. And Rackham'll be right behind him. They're going to start a bombardment."

Across low flat Hog Island they could make out the top hamper of the *Revenge* brig, getting closer. It had been seen elsewhere. Back of the town the hills were straked with refugees who would wait for the blow.

"Come on," said George. "You want to be under cover when the shooting starts, don't you?"

They started for the fort. There was a cough, smoke, and not thirty feet before them a spear of sand rose, scattered, and fell fluttering.

"I thought you said they would welcome us? Is that how?"

George was furious. In his excitement he had not sheathed but had been slapping the flat of the rapier against his thigh as he walked. Now he shook the thing at the fort. He ran there.

"Damn you, Robinson! These men are carrying a flag! You can't shoot at a parley flag!"

The captain of the guard, wherever he was, was given no chance to answer. The governor had appeared at the tower room window, his niece behind him. In that curiously high, effeminate voice the governor called down.

"Who are these men, Rounsivel, and what do they want?"

"They're my friends, and they want to fight for the fort!"

"How do we know they won't turn against us, once they inside?"

"Damn it, didn't I say they were my friends?"

The governor nodded gravely.

"Very well," he called. "Robinson, throw that gate open."

CHAPTER XX

THEIR BATTLEFIELD was the pellucid water of the bay. The pirates with their two vessels dominated but made no try to sack the town, knowing from experience that it wouldn't be worth the trouble. Instead they came to a point opposite the fort, though a good distance away, and anchored there, *John and Elizabeth,* the nearer, being bow-to, while *Revenge* took up a berth behind her and safely out of reach. Thus they could bring to bear only a single gun, but that was the best they had, the long brass twelve-pounder, Tom Walker's joy, to which George once had been tied. *John and Elizabeth,* being slight of beam, offered a tiny target, while none of the fort's pieces could menace the brig beyond it or do much to delay communication between the vessels or between either of them and the shore. So it was that the air over the greater part of Nassau Bay at any given daylight hour was likely to be loud with the whine of cannonballs, which, when they fell short, as many did, would raise geysers of water, or, worse, would ricochet, hissing, spewing spray.

Any artillery man in his right mind, given a choice between land and the deck of a vessel from which to fire a gun repeatedly, with no hesitation would plump for the land. A vessel might rock. If she was free she might be drifting; if she was anchored she might drag her anchor, making it necessary to change calculations and aim. It was easier to build a solid emplacement on even the shiftiest land than on the largest and steadiest of ships. Fire was what the cannoneer most dreaded, and fire was closer than ever when your magazine was below your feet, encased in nothing but wood. On land the powder could be stored some distance away in a stone structure.

At Nassau the situation was otherwise. The bay was a lake. The bottom was firm, and *John and Elizabeth*, with hooks down both fore and aft, was as steady as a rock. The platform Tom Walker had built was monumental, yet, like the rest of the forward part of *John and Elizabeth*, it offered almost nothing to hit, so that at least nine-tenths of the shooting they did from the fort was a waste of powder and iron. Merely hulling the sloop would not suffice. Several holes made within a short time, the last before the first could be plugged, might cause *John and Elizabeth* for a little while to dip at the bows; but they could be quickly repaired. The chances against such a series of hits, Tom glumly calculated, were about a thousand to one. The only thing that would surely knock that brass cannon out would be a direct hit upon its muzzle or its primer, and the chances against *that* were about a million to one—poor military odds.

Powder arrangements were ingenious. The magazine aboard of the sloop was located far astern, where even a lucky shot from the fort could hardly get it, but it was apparent anyway that the pirates did not depend upon this. Instead they brought up powder as needed from the brig *Revenge*, anchored out of range. Their smallboats in making this transfer could pick the best times—immediately after a shot from the fort, during a rain squall, or of course at night.

The pirates' plan was clear and it was exceedingly simple —so simple indeed as to seem almost the work of a genius.

"Is Vane as sharp as that?" George asked Si Simonson.

"He's marvelous sharp. Him and Rackham working together—if they *will* work together—they can think of all sorts of things."

Since it was clear that most of the shots from the fort were wasted, not even serving to intimidate those who worked the smallboats between the vessels, and since though powder was plentiful there was a limited supply of ball, firing from the fort was gradually reduced—a fact the pirates no doubt were quick to note. On the other hand, the brass twelve-pounder was fired with an infuriating regularity—once every four and a half minutes, Tom Walker estimated. This was lightning handling, which the big man could not help but admire. Tom wondered how they kept the barrel cool. Ezra Garde wondered how the foremast stayed upight under so many recoils.

Virtually all of these shots took effect. Even the ones that fell short often skipped across the surface of the water to slam at least into the wooden palisade.

Fort Nassau was roughly rectangular, and its corners were bastions constructed more or less after the Vauban style. On paper this was all very well; but more than paper would be needed to defend the fort. The wall was thick—much thicker at the bottom than at the top—but only about twelve feet high. Its lowness and gentle slope—a truly agile man, carrying no equipment, and given a good start, could almost have *run* up the outside of it—were the result of an absence of hard stone in the Bahamas. None having been obtainable from England, which preferred to ignore these small hot flat islands, the builders of Fort Nassau had perforce used the local stuff which though plentiful was soft, and dry. Whenever a ball plopped into it there rose from the point of impact a whiff of dust. The holes to some extent sealed themselves, the stuff was so crumby, but a large number of them soon weakened a section of wall, which had no core, no spine, to lend it strength.

There was also a wooden palisade, six to seven feet high, made of poles set close together, bound with liana, and sharpened on the top. This was meant but to give pause to sallies. It was not cut for cannons or even muskets. It wasn't towered, nor was there any fosse before it. Along the bay side, because of sand and tide, the palisade was especially vulnerable; it was there that it was being battered. Before the end of the first afternoon the palisade along the beach was little more than a fence of splinters, a line of jagged scarecrows. The balls from the twelve-pounder were ripping right through it, and over the place where the members of the Augur gang had been executed, to slam into the main wall, shuddering this. For a stretch of fully two hundred feet, wherever it wasn't knocked out entirely, the mortar was being loosened. Sometimes a large round section of the outer shell of the wall, shaken loose by shock, would fall away without even having been directly hit.

"It just gets tired," Si Simonson remarked.

Not all of the fighting went on between these two positions. There was some inside of the fort as well.

The defenders at the time George brought the beach party in had numbered a little over two hundred. Somewhat more than half of these were civilians, who either had been employed strengthening the defenses or else had taken refuge in the fort at the first alarm. These ate more than their share of food, drank more than their share of water, and got in the way. They had only one possible use, and they failed in that, being cowardly. Formed into "patching parties," they were supposed to climb outside of the wall on the shore side as soon as the sun had set and before the rise of the moon, and there replace dislodged stones, cram cement into opened seams, and otherwise, whether raised on temporary scaffolds or lowered in boatswains' chairs, do what they could to repair the day's damage. The pirates, however, had anticipated this defense, and the twelve-pounder was not silent all through the dark period but banged and flashed at irregular, unpredictable intervals, sometimes once an hour, sometimes once every ten minues. After the second night of this not even loaded pistols could force a civilian outside.

The permanent defenders, ninety-odd, were almost as bad. Some were militiamen from the town, loafers who either had been empressed into the service or had enlisted because they could not make a living any other way. The rest, the majority, were the worst of all, being those wan sagging droopy superannuated wretches-disguised-as-soldiers who had come over with Woodes Rogers last summer.

In such surroundings the nineteen brethren of the coast George had brought in from the beach were sure to be marked. They wore no sort of uniform and didn't pretend to discipline, but whatever they might *not* have been they *were* fighters. They couldn't keep the scorn from their eyes when they gazed upon the riffraff here collected under the leadership of Captain Robinson. They were an elite corps, and they knew it and acted it. They wouldn't take orders from Robinson or even from the governor himself, but only from George. This amused Woodes Rogers, who knew that he could give his orders through George and be obeyed; but it infuriated Robinson, who passed many caustic comments about "Rounsivel's private army."

The truth is, Thomas Robinson had turned sour. His clothes still were brave, his plume gleamed; but the bounce, the arrogance, were gone, leaving irascibility. Once he had smiled most of the time, though it was a supercilious smile. Now he only scowled.

In part this might have been the climate, to which, like most of the others, he was unaccustomed. In part no doubt it was discouragement in his task of training and leading such miserable somnambulists, over whom, to give him credit, he had worked hard. But the most part of Thomas Robinson's trouble was disappointment about Delicia.

How he felt in his heart was of no immediate importance. Doubtless he liked and admired the governor's niece—indeed it would have been difficult not to—but his first thought was for himself. His vanity had been pricked when the girl made it clear that she preferred George Rounsivel. Perhaps even more telling was the fact that by losing her he was losing his only chance to make a fortune, if a small one, out here.

He was frank about it.

"Damn you, Rounsivel, she would have taken me, if only out of boredom, if you hadn't come along."

George did not smile. He had no more love for Robinson than Robinson had for him, but he realized that since his return to Nassau he and Delicia, despite themselves, had been behaving like moonstruck idiots. There was no privacy at Fort Nassau. There were no grottos in which they could crouch, whispering, not any nooks to which they could retreat; there were no walks they could take down leafy lanes. In consequence, breathlessly excited to find themselves in love, they let off sly smiles seen by everybody, and sighs heard everywhere, or they brushed their hands together in passing, a gesture that never failed to bring a snigger from onlookers.

"No doubt what you say is true," George replied tonelessly.

This was the fourth afternoon of the bombardment. They stood in the bailey or yard on the beach side, where they'd been examining holes in the pavement made by a few balls that sailed clear over the top of the wall. There was nobody else near at hand. Soldiers and civilians alike avoided this part of the yard, where there was always a chance of getting struck by flying chunks of stone when a ball walloped the wall near the top, spraying the air with shards.

"No doubt it is, unless sir, you're disposed to call me a liar?"

"Oh, no," George replied. "Don't you think we'd better have these filled now, without waiting for night? When the attack comes it'll be on this side and we'll need every inch of level space we can get."

Robinson did not even look at the craters.

"I am not a vindictive man," he went on, "and under any other conditions I think I might have permitted you to live."

"Eh?"

"I mean, I would ignore your challenge."

"I am not aware that I have challenged you, sir."

"Ain't you, now? Yet I can remember three separate occasions when you backed away from a fight promising to give me satisfaction later."

"I do not take that to be a challenge."

"I do."

George shrugged, starting to turn away.

"Please yourself. All I can say is that we are in the midst of a battle, which is no time for personal quarrels."

"That," drawled Robinson, "is just the sort of answer I might have expected from you, you illegitimate son of an illegitimate mother."

George whirled, drawing.

"Now, by God, you can't—"

Robinson too had drawn, swift as light, and though he did back before that rush he was smiling again, for the first time in days, his teeth showing white behind his bright red lips. Crouching, his guard high, he slipped his steel over George's hilt. It was as quick as the lick of a snake's tongue. Robinson could have killed, in that split-second. He must have been afraid to go all the way in. Instead his point ripped a slit in George's sleeve.

George drove ahead, Robinson, smiling, sure of himself now, stood his ground.

"Stop!"

The voice should have been one of thunder. It wasn't. It was a plaintive high baa-lamb sound, and coming from anybody else it would have been ridiculous. But it was the only voice these two would have obeyed.

As though moved by one piece of mechanism, they stepped back, each lowering his point.

Woodes Rogers hobbled into the space between them.

"That will do, gentlemen! Put up!"

Like scolded schoolboys they sheathed.

"You will promise me, on your honor, that you will not fight one another within these walls again, no matter what the provocation."

Mumbling, shamefaced—after all, he could have clapped either or both of them into irons—they promised.

"Very well, now come with me. I'll give you something to take that belligerency out on."

He limped for the gate tower, and meekly they followed him. It wasn't until they had reached the foot of the steps that George Rounsivel felt something tickle the palm of his right hand, and raised that hand to see blood.

He looked at it a moment, blinking. A ball thumped the wall near its top, and chunks of stone flew, sprinkling the bailey, whilst languid dust rose. George gulped, amazed. Until this time he had not known that he was wounded. He wiped his hand on the seat of his breeches, and went upstairs.

"Look!"

A bony forefinger indicated the sloop, from which even at that moment a shot was fired, so that smoke all but blotted it from sight. It must have been a full hit, the ball burying itself in the wall, for even as this distance the men in the tower room could feel the floor shiver under their feet.

They did not need to wait for the smoke to be blown away to see what the captain-general meant. The forepeak still was in sight, though it flew a different flag now. The red roger, which flapped there throughout the four days of the bombardment, had been run down, and the other, the black flag of death, had been raised.

"Think of that, my merries, the next time you feel inclined to act like drunken rufflers in a tavern."

So many things had happened inside or barely outside of this window! Now the captain-general stood spread-legged before it, and he hooked his thumbs into the pockets of his waistcoat, and, flamingo-like, jerked his head out toward the bay. He belched thoughtfully.

"They'll come rowing in at night, either with the last cannonshot or else just before the crack of dawn. And they'll scramble over what little's left, and then start to slash about. How long would you say, Robinson?"

"The day after tomorrow, sir. Possibly one day longer."

"Um-m. It's what I had figured. You, Rounsivel?"

"I should say the same, sir."

"And—they have how many men?"

Robinson said quickly: "You'd better ask this pirate, your excellency. He came from there."

"Very well," not looking around. "Rounsivel?"

"There should be twenty-four of the sloop's crew, sir. All men, no boys. All armed."

"The brig?"

"I have only the estimate of my men, who didn't have a real chance to count. But . . . about forty."

"That is, we have almost twice their numbers of armed men. If they storm us, would they take us?"

"Yes," promptly.

"You, Rounsivel?"

"Yes."

What are we going to do?"

It was a rhetorical question, since there could be but one answer. A breach was a matter of hours; when the pirates came raging through, such was their reputation for ferocity, and such too was the terror inspired by that black jolly-roger, the fort would fall with a crash, almost without resistance, and slaughter would follow. Retreat, now or later, was out of the question. There was simply nowhere to go. Individual townsmen could scuttle back into the hills and hide away for a little while, but men with arms, uniformed men, would be ruthlessly pursued. This was a small island, and there was no forest, no jungle.

To attack would be to invite disaster. Surprise, the very nut of such a tactic, was out of the question, for it would be impossible to collect the boats, most of them in or near the town, without being seen. Only small arms could be taken. All of the soldiers were poor boatmen, and most of them could not even swim.

There was only one thing to be done; and Thomas Robinson glibly named it.

"Cut out that gun."

George nodded agreement, and Woodes Rogers too nodded, though he still was staring at the black flag.

"But how?" he said.

Robinson shrugged.

"Take a boat tonight, just a few men. Sneak aboard. Rush the gun and cut it free and roll it on its trucks to the side and over."

"There is one objection to that," George interposed. "That cannon hasn't got any trucks. It's mounted on a solid platform, and it uses ordinary recoil pads, like a land gun. It *is* a land gun, practically. It isn't laid to poke through a porthole."

"It'd unstep the foremast!"

"It probably has. That's a measure of their confidence. They're willing to sacrifice a whole stick, which would cut speed in half, because they are so sure that they won't run away and that they'll have plenty of time later to repair the damage."

"There is another objection to Captain Robinson's plan," Woodes Rogers put in. "That's shoal water over there, only a few fathoms. There are any number of men in town, spongers and pearlers, who could put a line around anything on that bottom. The water's clear as glass. And with tackle, in a few hours they'd have the thing up again."

He turned to George.

"You know the gun itself, you say?"

"I should!"

"Would it be easy to spike?"

George was candid. He confessed that he wasn't even sure what was meant by spiking a gun, but he offered to call Tom Walker.

"Do that, please."

Robinson frowned, for here was another tacit admission of Rounsivel's independent command, another passing-by of the garrison. Yet even Robison was obliged to concede that Tom Walker was superior as a gunner to the Fort Nassau man, a wizened nincompoop named Andrews. For these past four days Tom, out of sheer impatience and disgust, had taken over command of the fort's pitiful battery.

Now, having answered the summons, he stood before them, a moon-faced, immensely serious man.

"Yes sir, it could be spiked. By two men, if they was spry."

"How?"

"Well, you'd take three or four of those lead tompions we have that're made for the muzzle of the ten-pounders, and put 'em in, one after the other. They'd fit, just about. Ram 'em home. Then take the fattiest marlinspike you can find and put it smacketty-dab into the touchhole, which is on top, and pound it in as hard as you can with a maul. Unless of course the thing was loaded. Then you wouldn't put in the tompions first, because if you did and you got a spark from pounding the spike it would blow up everything, including you. But they're not likely to leave it loaded."

"Wouldn't that make a lot of noise?"

"Aye."

"And two men could do it?"

"One alone *could*, but that'd take longer."

"Of the two methods you described, if there was only time for one which would be better?"

"The marlinspike. That gun's old, and the touchhole always was too big. It must've got pitted around the edges. Anyway somebody's worked an iron ring in there, to make the hole smaller, but that too was pretty badly pitted, last I saw it And it would be much worse now, after all that firing. A marlinspike properly banged in would make it twice as big, and that'd be so dangerous that you couldn't get any gunner to come close to it with a linstock. I know *I* wouldn't. Too much chance of getting a flare-back—burn your hair off, put your eyes out."

"Could it be repaired?"

"Not with anything they've got on this island. Matter of fact, I doubt such a spiking could be repaired anywhere this side of Plymouth, sir."

"Thank you, Walker." He turned to the others. "Now, the matter of a boat—"

"The Moses-boat," George said immediately. "It's dark, it's low, and it's got short oars and the quietest thole pins you ever knew It'll only hold three men, but that's all that are needed"

"Good But it will be dangerous, this assignment. It's one for volunteers. Do you have any such, Captain Robinson?"

"Not a damned one. Most of my men, they couldn't step on a cockroach without screaming. Even if you got 'em drunk they wouldn't go out for a thing like this. But I'll go, of course."

"Um-m . . . I'd be reluctant to lose so valuable a man."

"I shall make every effort to return, sir."

"Rounsivel, what about your group?"

"Beg pardon, sir," Tom Walker broke in, touching his hat as a sailor should, "but we've most of us signed articles of companionship together. Shooting back and forth—that's one thing. But to climb right aboard of that sloop and maybe kill a couple of guards—that's something different."

"Your ethics mystify me," Woodes Rogers said.

"I can't answer for the others, but I know how *I* feel, Governor, and I'm pretty sure they would too."

"But *I* haven't signed those articles," George cried.

"That's right, you never did, did you?"

The governor looked at Robinson and he looked at George, and shook his head, but he said nothing.

"Another one never signed," Tom Walker went on, "and that's Peter Knight. He's only a boy and might not be much use in a tussle, but he could hold the boat there, which is all you'd really need him for anyway."

"Would he go, Tom?"

"Cap'n sir, he'd go clear through Hell on his bare feet if you was to lead the way."

Thus it was that soon after sundown two men and a knobby red-haired boy came out through a smashed portion of the palisade on the beach side of Fort Nassau carrying the Moses-boat, which they launched.

George was in high spirits. Though he had suffered in this craft yet somehow he believed that it meant good luck to him, for hadn't he, despite the suffering, won through? Hadn't he got Delicia? He laughed. He nodded back toward the fort.

"Do you realize that this is the first time I've ever left that building unshot at?"

"Shut up," said Thomas Robinson.

The night was dark, the water smooth. The sky was all unstudded by stars, suggesting that there might be a late moon, and the air didn't smell of rain.

Peter rowed without a sound, leaning over the oars with the absorption of a watchmaker. There was no hiss at the bows, no gurgle in the wake.

For the most part George strained his eyes ahead, eager to catch the first sight of *John and Elizabeth*, but when he did turn to glance at his companion in the sternsheets he caught in Robinson's face, even in that dim light, a glint of savagery that perturbed him. Was Robinson planning treachery? Did he take this to be a good time for murder?

The opportunity was made of gold. After such a lion's-mouth operation as this would be, if either returned without the other that occasion could hardly excite anything worse than comment. The governor had not been pleased to see them go off together, and had troubled to remind them of their promise not to fight; but George remembered, as he looked back at the queer-staring Robinson, that the promise, given only a few hours ago, had contained the qualifying phrase "within these walls." They were not presently within any walls at all.

The Moses-boat moved like a ghost. *Revenge* was bright with lights, and resounded to the song and shouts of the pirates, who were having a party there; but it was some time before George could even distinguish the outlines of *John and Elizabeth*, which rode utterly without a gleam. A small vessel, slim, low, she nonetheless loomed large from where he sat.

He checked his equipment, which was scanty enough.

None of them was armed in any conventional sense. Each

wore only dark breeches and a dark tight-fitting waistcoat —no hat, shoes, stockings, not even a shirt lest the white of the sleeves show. Peter carried no weapon of any sort, George and Robinson only a sheath knife each. A rapier would have been too long, a pistol too noisy, a cutlass too heavy. George had in his lap a knotted rope and a grappling hook he hoped he wouldn't need, and in his pockets three heavy leaden tompions. Robinson had two marlinspikes—in case he lost one—and across his knees was an enormous maul. The maul, iron-headed, was so heavy that it would have taken a strong man even to lift it, much less swing it; but Robinson was very strong.

At George's wave they approached the larboard side, where the Jacob's ladder hung. This was contrary to the original plan, which would have taken them to the opposite side on the theory that smallboats from *Revenge* might approach or leave the Jacob's ladder. However, when George saw that no boat was paintered there he signaled for larboard. Even if his throw was perfect, the clunk of the grappling hook might awaken a guard.

He gestured to Peter that after the two had climbed aboard he, Peter, should take the Moses around to the other side of the sloop. Then if a smallboat did come they would not be trapped.

It was reasonable to suppose that most of the pirates were spending most of their time aboard of *Revenge* rather than *John and Elizabeth*. The brig was out of range. It was not subject—regularly in daytime, occasionally at night—to the shock of the twelve-pounder and the constant threat that the foremast would give 'way. Moreover it was a much larger and no doubt more comfortable vessel.

A couple of gunners were all who should be expected to be on the deck of the sloop at this hour. But they might at any time be relieved or checked. This was why George waved the Moses to the other side of the sloop.

Peter was not intelligent, but he could understand that. He nodded.

George fetched a full breath, and climbed to the waist.

It was as dark as a dungeon there, and George congratulated himself that he knew it so well. A misstep might have meant death.

Ordinarily after sunset this waist would be scattered with sleepers, but tonight there were none. George did not trust to his eyes—and indeed there was little enough to be seen —but stood silent for a moment, alert for the sound of a snore, a twitch, any mumble or mutter. All he heard was the blurred faraway drunken cacophony from the brig.

Satisfied, he went to the other side, the starboard side, and fastened the grappling hook to the top of the gunwale, afterward lowering the knotted rope into the water. This would give Peter something to hold, to keep the Moses alongside. It would also provide a quiet way down to the boat if silence, in an escape, should prove more imperative than speed; for though there was not much freeboard at the waist, and any active man could have jumped to the Moses-boat, in such darkness a jumper might land on the thwarts, either himself falling into the sea, or capsizing the boat, or both, with much noise.

Pausing a moment, pensive, he looked aft. The officers' cabin was no more than a clump of shadows; he heard not a sound from it, and saw no light. Was Anne Bonney there? Probably. Rackham would be sure to keep her as much could be from the others. Was Calico Jack himself there? Probably, again. They might even be making love, right at this instant, scarcely more than a few feet from where George Rounsivel stood. Well, he would do everything he could to keep from disturbing them.

As he started for the forward deck he sensed rather than saw Robinson reach the top of the Jacob's, slither over the gunwale, drop to the waist. George did not reach out to guide the man with a hand. He had already described, to the last tiny detail, the waist and forward deck. Robinson could do it alone.

George climbed.

The forward deck, even more than the waist, on an ordinary night would have been cluttered with the figures of men who slept. George could see but one, immediately. Though he did not think so, for he heard no snores, there yet might be others further forward, where, as the gunwales converged, the shadows were thicker.

The one he could see was lying full-length on the gun platform, his head cradled in a pile of oakum. Undoubtedly he was the gunner of the evening, who would fire another shot when he woke—or was jogged. Would somebody come down from forward to shake him? Or would Jack Rackham come up from aft?

George knelt, leaning low, squinting. The man was a tall scrawny wagtail, Ellis Hunt by name. He had been an assistant to Walker, who like George despised him, for he toadied shamelessly to Jack Rackham. He lay on his back, and out of his open mouth from time to time came a thin, throaty whistle. His adam's apple, a large one, trembled.

George slipped out his knife.

It might not be necessary to kill. Perhaps if he held the point at Hunt's throat and then roused him with a gentle shake—

But the man might scream even then, in sheer fright. George sheathed, and worked from a pocket one of the tompions. Heavy as a rock, held in the open hand, this could be slammed against the head just over an ear—

Even then there would be the chance of a groan. It would be safest to make a swift search of the deck first, before Robinson got up here. Crouching, George did this. He found nobody.

There was the faintest of thuds, a catch-up of breath, the

scrape of bare feet. George wheeled; what happened he saw only in silhouette, which however was enough.

Robinson had kicked the prone Ellis Hunt, whether by accident or contemptuously, having assumed that George already had killed the man. Whatever the reason, Hunt, astounded, had sprung to his feet, staggering back, away from Thomas Robinson, whom he might have taken for a specter.

And Robinson swung the maul.

As a stroke it was brilliant. Perhaps too in the long run it was merciful: likely enough Ellis Hunt never knew what hit him. At any rate, Hunt uttered not so much as a squeal. The only sound—and it sickened George—was that of the maul striking the head. This was hollow, a liquid plop, as if somebody had squashed a pumpkin.

George had been running forward, thinking to strike with his tompion, and he was in time to catch Hunt from behind, under the armpits, and lower him to the deck. It made a ghastly corpse. The whole side of the head was a pulp, and blood and brains and wet chunks of scalp bubbled out on George's breast as he let the thing down.

He hauled it underneath the barrel, where it would be out of the way, and scampered around to the far side of the platform. There, as he had expected, he found the gunner's implements laid out—wormer, sponge, linstock, ladle, scraper —also the passing box, three balls, a bag of powder, and the match.

He smelled powder, and his hands told him that the box had not been fully closed, while the top of the bag too was a little open. No doubt powder was scattered about the deck. Any stray breeze could do it. This was arrant carelessness, and never would have happened while Tom Walker was in charge. Perhaps they had been firing the twelve-pounder too often? Perhaps they had been groggy, or drunk?

The match at least was as it should have been. A tiny

tongue of unwobbling light, it rose from the end of a wick
wick fastened to a disk of cork in several inches of whale oil
at the bottom of a tub. Except for a small hole in the middle,
a hole barely large enough to admit a linstock, the top of
the tub was covered, so that the match gave off the faintest
of glow. The tub itself was heavy, of course, against the
possibility that it should be upset.

Robinson already had worked one of the marlinspikes out
of his pocket and was fitting this into the touchhole. However, it was part of the plan that before Robinson started
to hammer the spike George should determine whether or
not the cannon was loaded. For this purpose George seized
the ladle.

True, the twelve-pounder *should not* have been left loaded;
but men who were so careless that they would leave a gunpowder bag uncovered might do almost anything.

The ladle was long, and like the cannon, brass. Five-sixths
of it was nothing but a narrow rod. The rest was the
scoop, which precisely fitted the bore of the cannon and
would hold a measured charge of powder—powder that
could be left in the lower end of the gun by a mere twisting
of the ladle before it was withdrawn.

George did not need to twist, since he would deposit no
powder. He simply slid the thing its full length into the
mouth of the cannon, and his fingers told him when the end
had struck metal.

There was no ball in there, no powder. The gun was
empty.

He withdrew the ladle and started to cram tompions into
the muzzle. They went hard: he had to knock them with
the heels of his hands. He had three, and when he had
stuffed the third one in he seized the ladle again, reversed
it, and started to use it as a ramrod, punching the tompions
still further in.

When he had withdrawn the ladle he didn't drop it to

the deck but carefully placed it there, lest it clang. Then he ran around the larboard side of the gun, stepping for a horrid instant on an outstretched arm of the body that lay underneath, and heaved himself up to a sitting position on one of the trunnions.

This had been prearranged, for they knew that they would not dare to whisper.

Robinson had worked the spike into the touchhole as well as he could, but it sagged there. George seized it. Robinson, who must have been standing on something steady on the other side of the gun, some keg or box, showed a huge black shadow from the hips up. He lifted the maul.

What if he hits me? was George's wild fleeting thought.

Robinson swung with all his strength, and the blow landed flush on the head of the spike. It made a short but loud and carrying sound—the jumble of the *Revenge* revel instantly ceased—but George scarcely noted this for the pain that streaked up his right arm, the string of the blow to the hand that had held the iron spike.

He released the spike. He had to, for he had no feeling in his right hand. The spike slanted and he straightened it with his left hand.

Robinson swung again.

George flinched, winced, but didn't let go. The shock was stunning. With a sob, swaying, not feeling it, he let his left hand fall away. The spike this time stayed in place.

Robinson lifted the maul again. He swung it high.

This time he does mean me! thought George, and shoved with his knees against the gun, pushing his rump over the end of the trunnion, so that he tumbled backward.

He heard that enormous hammer whistle past his head as though it had been a rattan. Meeting no resistance, it must by its very force have been torn out of Robinson's hands, and George as he landed heard it crash to the deck.

A door was flung open, aft.

"Hunt!" It was Jack Rackham's voice. "What the Devil are you doing up there?"

On his back in the scuppers, both hands paralyzed for the moment by pain, George saw Robinson loom like an avenging angel above the twelve-pounder, and in silhouette saw him snick out his knife; and then Robinson sprang.

George had all his wits about him. Though he'd struck the deck hard, on the back of his shoulders, he kept his wind. He would not take out his knife, for he feared he couldn't hold it, and, dropping it, would not be able to find it again; but for the rest he was ready for a fight. He rolled.

Robinson's leap, though fierce, was frenzied, clumsy. He jumped feet first, possibly hoping to land on George and knock the breath out of him. But George was no longer there. Robinson teetered, went to one knee, and had to put his hands on the deck to get his balance.

Meanwhile George had rolled aft, to fetch up beside the gunner's tools near the head of the waist ladder.

Rackham appeared there, or his head did. He was climbing the ladder with one hand while he held a cutlass in the other. George heaved up his legs and kicked Rackham full in the face, and the pirate, who had been about to reach for another rung with his free hand, went over backward like a bowling pin.

George got up. He kicked the powder bag, sending its contents everywhere. He reached for the top of the match tub.

He could feel it! His hands were functioning!

He tore the lid off. He did not try to overturn the tub, his first plan, for he remembered that not only were match tubs made very heavy but sometimes they were nailed to the deck to keep them from sliding. Instead he reached in, scooped up the burning wick, and threw this at the place where he had kicked the powder bag.

There was a bright blue flash, not an explosion but a hollow flat slap as though two padded boards had been clapped together. Instantly little spears of flame started to run this way and that, sometimes catching seams to pursue those, sometimes helterskeltering wildly. There must have been gunpowder everywhere—not much of it in any one place, but widely scattered. These past few days there had been almost no breath of breeze to blow it away, so that it had found lodgement wherever it fell.

George laughed. It felt good to have the feeling back in his hands.

The flames swept past and around him, making remorselessly for the waist, not because there was any movement of air to push or suck them but seemingly because it was in this direction that they found their fuel. Some zigzagged crazily. Some almost died, then sprang high again, twisting back and forth as though trying to make up their minds which way to run. Had the stuff been spilled from leaky bags as it was brought up from the waist, from *Revenge?* Or had it been spilled all the way back from the *John and Elizabeth's* magazine?

Thomas Robinson had recovered his feet, and held his knife before him, point-out. He started for George.

"Good," said George, and drew his own knife, and ran to meet the man.

The stage was set for ferocity and rash attack, for a quick ending; yet after the first encounter, in which each was cut, neither badly, the two, as if by mutual agreement—though they hadn't said a word—fell into a cautious crouch. Sidestepping, edgy as racehorses, they circled one another, moving in general forward, away from the flames.

They closed again, but not all the way, and immediately sprang back. George's blade had cut, only superficially, the outer part of Robinson's left upper arm; Robinson might not even have felt it. Robinson's knife, slashing up, meant for George's throat, had torn away the lower part of the left ear. It didn't hurt, or even tickle, but George could feel blood ooze out of it to meander lazily down his neck and shoulder.

George moved in a little.

Robinson backed—and his buttocks met the top of the gunwale. He was in no kind of corner and could not possibly have felt panic, even a twinge of it. Nobody will ever know what Thomas Robinson *did* feel at that instant of time, except that he was reminded by the pressure of the gunwale against it of the spare marlinspike in his left hip pocket. He reached for this. Perhaps the movement was only one of irritability, or was made because of a nervous notion that the spike on that side somehow endangered his balance. More likely he thought to throw it at George with his left hand.

He got the marlinspike out, and raised it. But he raised his knife, perhaps unwittingly, at the same time.

And George lunged.

He went in very low, thrusting up, indeed as though he had been holding a sword, save that he was much closer than a swordsman would have been. Also, he ducked his head as he went, meaning to get under the other's knife, which could have ripped his face open. So that he did not see where he struck. But he felt it—and it was soft.

Robinson, doubling up, fell upon him. George twisted, and twisted again, but he never ceased to stab. And when at last he rose, panting, he knew that there was no quiver left in the body of Captain Thomas Robinson.

There was a great deal of blood. Not only was George's knife wet and red, but his whole fist was, even his wrist And blood still dribbled doggedly from his ear.

Thirty feet away, near the head of the waist ladder, Calico Jack Rackham was jigging like a marionette swung on strings as he tried to stamp out the flames. There was another of those muffled slaps, as of two boards banged together, and a hundred new flames leapt to life. A second bag?

Rackham, already burned, saw that he could not possibly put out the blaze alone. He was sobbing as he tumbled down the ladder to the waist. The flames, some blue, some red now, leaping higher and higher, pursued him: whether because of the air movement when he ran, or because it was in the waist that they found more to feed on, those flames, bending his way, fairly leapt after him, eager, avid, reaching, like the furies in a Greek tragedy as they yammer at the heels of the doomed.

George could not have got past that place alive. He didn't try. He dropped his knife, put a hand on the gunwale, yelled *"Peter, here!"* and vaulted head-foremost into the sea.

It was so mild that he scarcely knew when he entered it, but he knew a moment later when his head popped free.

John and Elizabeth burned angrily, streaming with sparks. The moon was rising, and by its light George could see a longboat being lowered from *Revenge*. Nearer, gawping, was Peter Knight and the Moses. Peter helped him to scramble aboard.

"Captain Robinson—"

"He's not coming," gasped George. *"Now row like Hell!"*

When the sloop blew up they were not more than two hundred feet away. The very water was jolted, as though by a subterranean blast. They ducked, covering their heads with their arms, and all around them, after a few seconds, they heard things fall with a hiss into the sea, some loudly, some very quietly, as though in apology. None fell into the boat.

The moon had rolled high by the time they reached the shore near Fort Nassau, and George, standing, looked back. There was no sign of the sloop, not even a bit of smoking wreckage. And *Revenge* was leaving. Every inch of canvas raised, the brig was making for the mouth of the bay. The pirates who held her were giving up. They'd had enough of these waters.

CHAPTER XXI

IT WAS ONLY four months later, amazingly, when the governor of His Majesty's Bahaman possessions, having summoned his legal advisor, who also was the captain of the guard, passed over to this personage a paper that had just come from home.

"I thought that this might interest you."

George Rounsivel read it twice, the first time hastily, the second time with scrupulous care, nodding his head in approval.

It was an affirmation of his pardon—that is, it was the pardon itself.

"Well set forth," he declared at last. "Hardly a word I would have changed."

"Whitehall no doubt would be glad to hear that."

"Admirable . . . yes . . ."

Suddenly he threw the document into the air, and whirled on his heel. "Excuse me, sir!" And he rushed downstairs, calling for Delicia.

Woodes Rogers smiled, something he seldom did. He picked up the pardon and put it into the proper drawer Giving them time, he took snuff. He rose and hobbled to the window, from where he looked out on a bay where vessels of all sorts came and went. The fort was firm now, and well cannoned; he no longer feared attack by the Spaniards. The town was spreading, and small plantations too were springing up. Nobody even talked of piracy any longer. In so short a time it had become nothing but an evil memory.

Only the previous day the captain-general had received word from his opposite number in Jamaica that the last hold-out among the so-called brethren of the coast, the once redoubtable Charles Vane, had been captured there—and hanged.

After a while, thoughtful, he went downstairs. He found the two of them near the gate, and was in no wise startled by their announcement.

"Now that I'm legally qualified to at last, sir, I have proposed marriage to your niece. And she's accepted."

Delicia looked lovelier than ever, her cheeks flushed, her eyes bright. She always reminded him—and it always hurt him—of his younger brother, her father. As for Rounsivel, the captain-general reflected, he looked no more silly than any other young man in the circumstances.

"My congratulations," Woodes Rogers murmured. "You know full well that you have my permission, Indeed," he added bluntly, "I would not even have made protest if you'd consummated the previous contract some time ago."

"We will make this one *nunc pro tunc*," George said solemnly. "That is to say 'now for then'."

"I see. And you will be leaving here?"

"Your excellency must forgive us that. We can visit you, we hope, from time to time? But Miss Rogers and I are agreed that we would do better in some quiet, less violent place."

"Philadelphia?"

"Yes, sir. Philadelphia."